SYLVIA MERCEDES

THE VENATRIX CHRONICLES BOOK 5

For Ariel,
The very first "official" fan of The Venatrix Chronicles

THE VENATRIX

Drauval Borough

Skada Mountains

Aalis River

Castra Brecar

Wodechran

Sang River

Tchanor City

Aldreda Borough

The Great Barrier

Dulimurian

The Witchwood

Sang River

KINGDOM
OF
PERRINION

THE VENATRIX

Aalis River

Rivanduru

Caiduru

Höllen

Elsinoe

Dunloch Castle

Milisendis

Cabralet

WODECHRAN
BOROUGH

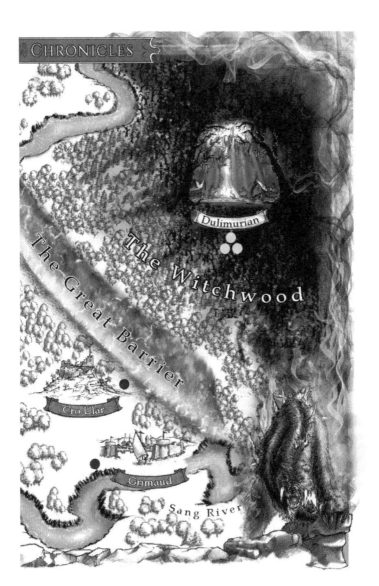

Dulimurian

The Witchwood

The Great Barrier

Cro Ular

Grimaud

Sang River

GLOSSARY OF SHADES

Shades: Disembodied spirit-beings who have escaped from their hellish dimension—the Haunts—and entered the mortal world. They cannot exist in a physical reality without mortal hosts, whom they possess and endow with unnatural powers. If left unchecked, they will gain ascendancy within a host-body and oust the original soul, taking full possession.

The following are the known varieties of shades as catalogued by the Order of Saint Evander:

ANATHEMAS
Abilities pertain to blood and curse-casting.

APPARITIONS
Abilities pertain to mind control and manipulation.

ARCANES
Mysterious entities with abilities not fully understood, but which seem to pertain to energies such as heat, motion, light, magnetism, and electricity.

ELEMENTALS

Abilities pertain to the natural elements of wind, fire, water, earth.

EVANESCERS

Abilities pertain to *evanescing*, or instantaneous distance-travel.

FERALS

Abilities pertain to heightened senses, augmented strength and agility.

LURES

Abilities pertain to enchanting voices and siren calls.

SEERS

Abilities pertain to visions, foretelling, and predictions. May also look into the past.

SHIFTERS

Abilities pertain to temporary transformation of host-bodies.

TRANSMUTERS

Abilities pertain to the transformation and manipulation of material substances.

PROLOGUE

THE GRAND VANDERIAN SHIFTED ON HER HARD SEAT, wishing she'd thought to surreptitiously sneak in a cushion. She could easily have hidden one beneath her bounteous robes. Upraised on a dais to stand slightly above all other seats beneath the great cupola, her tall chair was carved from stone, old stone, its edges rounded by time and use. Like a symbol of the times, it felt ready to crumble away beneath her bony backside.

Forty Venator Domini sat below her: twenty at her

right hand, twenty at her left, men and women from all the great castras across the Five Kingdoms of Gaulia. They had been summoned for a special council, and some had journeyed great distances to assemble here in the Sacred City of Roihm on this occasion. All eyes in the room were now fixed on a single point: the face of the solemn-eyed young woman standing in the center of the council's circle beneath the great dome.

In these hard years, numerous heresies creeping like cancer through its ranks threatened the stability of the Evanderian Order. The Council of Agla must make a move to cement its power once more. But it must be the right move. Did this woman offer the answer the Order so desperately needed? Or was she yet another false hope about to be exposed?

She was a venatrix. From the north. She had journeyed with her castra mistress, one Domina d'Arcand, who even now passionately addressed the council. The young venatrix stood nearby with downcast gaze. She had not yet spoken a word, allowing her domina to speak for her.

The domina finished saying her piece, and while fading echoes of her voice still lingered in recesses of the domed hall, members of the Agla Council exchanged sidelong glances. A few patches of murmuring broke out in their midst.

The Grand Vanderian raised a hand, and the murmuring stopped. She turned to her right and beckoned to du Radomil, the official spokesman of the council. Seeing her gesture, he gathered his vestal robes and stood at once. He was a tall, bony man with a nose like a heron's beak poised to skewer some unsuspecting fish. He now turned that nose on the two women below.

"Domina d'Arcand," he said, "you make your claims with a great deal of confidence. But let me be certain that I and my esteemed brethren have understood you correctly. You are saying that this young woman, your protégée . . . she can wear it. The Crown of Mauval. And . . . survive?"

"She is of the blood du Mauvalis," Domina d'Arcand answered, her voice trembling slightly as she sought to repress her fervor. But she couldn't hide the shimmering excitement in her soul, which reverberated through the ether around her, visible to shadow sight. "She is descended from Emperor Mauval the Great himself. The phasmators of Roihm have inspected her blood and tested her spirit. She is the one. And she is ready. We await only the approval of this council and the Grand Vanderian's authorization."

"If so, why was such authorization refused the last time you brought her here?" du Radomil persisted. "Or am I mistaken? The records show that you brought this same young woman to Agla before and were refused."

Domina d'Arcand lowered her chin respectfully, but the Grand Vanderian felt the sharp shudder in her spirit. "She was deemed unready when we first came to make our case. Too young, too inexperienced. But," she added, with vehemence, "that was thirteen years ago. She has accomplished a great deal since. She has proven her value to the Order time and again."

While the domina spoke, the Grand Vanderian watched the young venatrix's reactions. She did not move, hardly seemed to breathe. But the shade she carried inside her pulsed with power. An Elemental, one of surprising potency that trembled just beneath its binding suppressions.

Du Radomil drew breath to launch into some new

speech, but the Grand Vanderian cut him off with a well-timed cough. "Let the venatrix step forward," she said, beckoning.

At this, the young woman looked up. Then, as though suddenly galvanized, she took three long strides toward the high seat and bowed low. She was, the Grand Vanderain noted with a slight curl of her lip, very beautiful, after a dark, deadly fashion. Taller than average, with long brown hair, half of which she tied back in a knot, leaving the rest to fall in waves across her shoulders. She held herself straight, her old and rather threadbare uniform carefully brushed, its buckles polished to a brilliant shine.

"Your name," du Radomil demanded.

The young woman answered in a clear, deep voice, "Odile, Venatrix di Mauvalis."

"And why have you come before this council, Venatrix di Mauvalis?"

The venatrix did not look at du Radomil. She focused her gaze on the Grand Vanderian, her eyes like arrows to the mark.

"I've come to claim Mauval's Crown," she said.

The whole of that room seemed to draw a single sharp breath. Even the Grand Vanderian pulled back slightly in her hard seat. Such a claim made so boldly raised many hackles.

The Grand Vanderian leaned heavily on the right arm of her chair and narrowed her eyes at the girl. "I've refused you once," she said. "What makes you think I will change my mind?"

The venatrix shifted on her feet, her stance faintly aggressive though her expression remained respectful, even demure. "Grand Vanderian," she said, "thirteen years ago you told me that I had not yet experienced enough of the hardships our Order requires of us. You said that until I had lived, lost, and suffered, I could not know what it truly means to be a venatrix of Evander. That I could not be worthy to wear Mauval's Crown."

She swallowed. For the briefest of moments, a shimmer like tears gleamed in her eyes and a ripple passed through her soul. The moment lapsed, and her expression hardened to stone.

"I have hunted shades across wild countrysides and through city streets. I have rooted out nests of shade-taken and stood by at the pyres of inborn. I have saved souls and damned souls, I have killed and liberated and destroyed. I have lost and gained, I have suffered and learned. I have . . . become."

With every word she spoke, the glow in her soul intensified. Hard like ice, bright like a star, it seemed to pulse out from her until the mere physical body in which she stood was subsumed by her spirit aura. Shadow-light gleamed in every pair of eyes in that room, reflecting the power of her soul, and none could have looked away from her even had they wished to.

"Give me the treasure created by my ancestor," Odile di Mauvalis said, "and I will do all that you ever dreamed and more. By the power contained within that *eitr* band, I will bear the weight that even now crushes your souls. I will show you salvation in place of death."

For a moment she held the whole chamber captivated, as though her voice had cast a spell.

Then one of the council stood abruptly, drawing all eyes his way. It was old Dominus du Velimir of Talmain. He was older than most of those present—so old that many wondered why he had not been dealt the Gentle

Death and sent to his final rest long ago. But he maintained control of his body and control of his shade and retained his seat in this council year after year, decade after decade.

"Grand Vanderian, you cannot entertain this folly." His voice was strong despite his age. "The Crown of Mauval is the most dangerous weapon the world has ever known. All who have attempted to claim its power since the early days of its creation have died. I was there sixty years ago. I was still a young apprentice when Venator du Charulf, carrying the same shade this woman now bears in her body, declared himself a fit vessel for the Crown's power. He was as skilled as she and more experienced. He could shape statues of oblidite and make them dance on his command. So they gave him the Crown—and when, within seconds, it overwhelmed him, he exploded in a blast of pure *oblivis* that slaughtered all within a ten-mile radius! I alone survived, saved by my master, hurtled from danger at the last instant. But I saw the aftermath."

The old man shook his head, gazing round at his fellow councilmen. "No one else remembers. But take my word for it: Mauval's Crown must remain in the vaults. It would be better for the world if it were forgotten."

Domina d'Arcand inclined her head and made a respectful sign in old du Velimir's direction. But she turned to the Grand Vanderian once more, her eyes shining and hard. "I know the history as well as any man or woman in this chamber," she said. "I know the names of all who have tried to wear the Crown since the days of its creation. Mauval the Great, by whose skill and secret craft it was first created, linked it to his own blood and bone so that none but he or one of his heirs could wear it and survive." She swept a hand to indicate Venatrix Odile. "She is of the blood. She can survive. Like Mauval himself, she can unite the power in the Crown to that power which she carries inside her. She can plumb the full depths of those conjoined abilities. Think of it, my sisters, my brothers! Think of what it could mean!"

The domina paused then, letting her words sink in. The Grand Vanderian could almost hear the thoughts churning through the heads of each member of that council. Everyone knew the histories and the legends of Mauval the Great: he who controlled and manipulated the strange element of *oblivis*. According to legend, his powers were so profound that he could plunge shadowy fingers into shade-taken mortals and extract shades without harming mortal bodies or mortal souls.

How many shade-taken had the members of this very council killed among them? How many men and women? How many children? The Grand Vanderian could not remember her own tally . . . save for the children. She remembered each of them with such vivid clarity, it sometimes frightened her. Their little faces haunted her dreams. They hovered just behind her waking eyes.

This was the temptation of Mauval's legacy. This was the temptation of the Crown. To find one who could command the full extent of its power would mean tremendous change within the Order. Most shade-taken would still need to be hunted down and killed to save their souls. But the children . . .

The children could be subdued. And brought here to Roihm, where this stern-faced venatrix would wait for them. She would don the Crown, call up its power, and purge the evil from their souls. Then they could be sent home, whole and living, to their families.

It was said Mauval was even able to separate inborn

spirits from their hosts. All those pyres lit across Gaulia could suddenly be snuffed out. Forever.

The Grand Vanderian took care that none of these thoughts showed in her face, that no one could sense the sudden longing that surged in her heart. Because the rest of Mauval's legacy remained as well. A legacy of tyranny and brutality and slaughter. The legacy of a monster.

But Mauval had not been a member of Saint Evander's Order. He did not have brethren of greater age and wisdom to guide his every move.

The Grand Vanderian studied the young woman standing with bowed shoulders and dropped gaze at the side of her domina. She was tall and strong, still young but with lines of maturity beginning to deepen across her brow and at the corners of her eyes. Whatever her suffering had been in the last thirteen years, it had aged her, hardened her. Transformed her from an ardent child into a deadly huntress.

Could she be the vessel they needed? Could she truly become their salvation?

The Grand Vanderian stood. All eyes in the chamber went to her, from the domini seated to her right and left, to the marksmen hidden in their alcoves above. Even Venatrix Odile looked up sharply, like a rabbit watching the hawk circle in the sky. The Grand Vanderian smiled at this, feeling the potency of her own force as mistress of this mighty assembly.

She stepped down from the high seat and approached the young woman slowly. She drew close enough to see the length of her dark lashes against the pallor of her soft cheeks.

"If I let you touch Mauval's Crown," she said, enunciating each word clearly so that all could hear, "even just to sample its power, it will most likely kill you. Your domina has told you that you will be able to wear it because of your heritage. But your blood has been mixed and mingled since the days of Mauval. No one can say how it will react to the spirit contained within the *eitr*. It may kill you even as it has killed all others before you. Do you understand?"

The venatrix nodded. "I understand, Grand Vanderian," she murmured.

"There is more," the Grand Vanderian continued. "You will have mere seconds to prove your control. We cannot risk a slaughter. If I see even the faintest sign that you are faltering, I will give the order, and the twenty-four marksmen even now surrounding you will shoot you with the Gentle Death. But your death will not be gentle. You will die, Venatrix Odile, violently. And none here will be able to save your soul from the damnation to follow. I would never ask any soul to risk so much." She drew a shuddering breath, the cords of her throat tightening. "What do you say, Odile, Venatrix di Mauvalis?"

The young woman lifted her gaze to meet the Grand Vanderian's. Her eyes were black as a starless sky, and behind the disks of her pupils flickered a shadow darker and deeper still. "It is my honor to give my life for the service of Evander and my Goddess," she said. "At your bidding, Grand Vanderian." She bowed her head respectfully, one fist pressed against her heart.

The Grand Vanderian nodded. She liked this answer. She liked the woman's humility.

"By the three holy names," she declared, raising both arms so that the sleeves of her dark robes fell back to her elbows, "by the GoddessHeart, GoddessHead, and GoddessSoul, I hereby command the Holy Council of

Evander to give answer, yea or nay. Who wills that Mauval's Crown be brought forth, that this girl be given her chance? Say you now—"

The room filled with a chorus of voices speaking in answer, "*Yea.*"

"Who wills that the Crown remain untouched?" the Grand Vanderian continued. "Say you now—"

"Nay."

Only one voice. Old Dominus du Velimir stood gazing round at his brethren, seeing the resolve in their eyes. He did not try to speak, did not try to argue, when it was only his voice against so many.

"Your vote is noted, Dominus du Velimir," du Radomil spoke for his mistress. "The will of the council is made known."

Du Velimir bowed. Without a word, he stepped down from his seat, down to the center of the room, and walked across the open space for the door. No one stopped him. No one called out to him. He passed close by Venatrix Odile, but he did not look her in the eye. He left the council, shutting the door fast behind him.

The Grand Vanderian waited until the last echo of its

closing died away. Then she returned to her seat—that old, crumbling seat—and she gazed down at the woman standing there with her eyes downcast. A shiver of foreboding moved in her heart.

But it wasn't strong enough to stop her. Not now that the vote was cast.

"Let the Crown be brought forth," the Grand Vanderian said.

CHAPTER I

TWO HUNDRED YEARS LATER

AYLETH HISSED SHARPLY THROUGH HER TEETH, sprang back from the window as though stung, and pressed both hands over her heart. But the pain searing through her breast wasn't physical. This pain bypassed the body entirely, aimed directly at the soul.

A blood-ward curse.

"Haunts damn," she growled and drew several long breaths through her nose as the throbbing slowly receded.

Two days now, imprisoned in her own room.

Somehow the indignity of her situation felt worse than if the Venator Dominus had seen fit to throw her in a dungeon. What was she in his eyes, some misbehaving child?

What was she in his eyes . . . at all? Two days of confinement provided ample time to ponder the question, but she had yet to settle on a satisfactory answer. He mistrusted her, yes. Possibly feared her. But . . . why? Had she not fought by his side to protect the prince in the most recent attack? Had she not proven her loyalty by dealing the iron poison to suppress her shade following the battle? What had she done to deserve house arrest?

No one had come to speak to her in the meantime. Not Dominus Fendrel, not Prince Gerard, not . . . anyone. Venatrix Everild opened her door twice daily to slide in a platter of food and change out a chamber pot. Nothing else. No word of what might be taking place beyond these four walls. She had only her guesses, confused as they were, and whatever she could glimpse from her window. Even then, she had to stay two paces back from the glass or risk Fendrel's blood ward slicing at her soul.

Her heart still pounded against her breastbone from the shock of the curse. She let her hands drop, her fingers curling into fists. The *sòm* drug sludged through her veins, making her head spin and her stomach heave if she moved too quickly. She could shrug off such discomforts. However, its influence on her spirit, on the world of her soul, was profound. It placed a wall between her and her shade.

"*Laranta?*" Ayleth whispered inside her own mind. She knew it was useless, but she couldn't help herself. To be separated from her shade was akin to being separated from her own right hand. "*Laranta, can you hear me?*"

Behind that drug barrier, she felt her shade move. She thought she heard the faintest echoing hint of an answering voice, a sharp bark of *Here, Mistress! Here, here!* But that might have been her imagination filling in what she hoped to hear, not reality at all.

For the thousandth time, Ayleth wondered what, exactly, the Venator Dominus thought she might do? Ordinarily, *sòm* was used among Evanderians only in cases of wounds or sickness, when a venatrix lacked a sound enough mind to bind and suppress her own shade. The drug prevented an indwelling shade from ousting the resident mortal soul and taking full possession of the host body.

But . . . Laranta would never hurt her like that. At least, never on purpose.

Laranta *loved* her.

"More heresy," Ayleth whispered as the thought passed through her drug-addled brain. Shades could not feel love. Shades experienced no emotion of their own, at least not as mortals understood emotion. Saint Evander taught that any feelings shades knew were stolen directly from their hosts.

Ayleth bowed her head, squeezing her eyes tightly shut, resisting the urge to collapse back on her rumpled bed. Heresy or no heresy, it didn't matter now. She wasn't sick, and Dominus Fendrel hadn't forced her to take the *sòm* for her own protection. He kept her imprisoned in this room, drugged, and separated from her shade because he . . . what? Thought her a threat to the prince? The very prince whose life she had saved three nights ago? Did Fendrel suspect her of being in league with the Crimson Devils, Ylaire di Jocosa and Inren di Karel?

None of this made any sense!

Opening her eyes, she shifted her position to the left, trying to angle herself to get the clearest view out her window without activating the blood wards. Fendrel had put the wards in place while she was unconscious, using her own blood, she guessed by evidence of the cuts on the index and middle finger of her right hand. Wards couldn't block her vision, however. From a certain angle close to the wall, with her head tilted to one side, she could just glimpse part of the circle drive that looped the courtyard of Dunloch. Even a half step more, and the ward would strike her again, but . . .

Ayleth snatched up the small spindly chair from beside the bed, carried it to the wall, and stepped onto the seat to elevate her vision. The added height improved her view, if only slightly. Now she could glimpse, between outbuildings, the glittering lake and even some of the far shore.

Something shimmered in the air. Ayleth narrowed her eyes and unconsciously tried to use Laranta's powers to augment her vision, like reaching to an empty sheath for a dagger. Huffing with frustration, she shook her head and looked again, limited to her mortal vision. She didn't need shadow sight to identify what her mortal senses *almost* perceived: a spell. A barrier spell surrounding all of Dunloch.

So, it hadn't been lowered since the recent attack.

Movement in the courtyard drew her attention: A mounted figure trotted along the drive, heading away from Dunloch. Someone wearing a red hood.

"Terryn?" Ayleth whispered before she could stop herself.

But no. It couldn't be Terryn. The horse was too dark, not the rich red chestnut of Venator du Balafre's mare. And the figure itself, though tall and broad, was neither tall nor broad enough. Venatrix Everild, Ayleth decided. Everild was leaving Dunloch.

What did it mean? The barrier, the lone rider . . . Did King Guardin and his son remain at Dunloch even after the witches' attack? Had Dominus Fendrel left the barrier spell in place to keep them safe while he waited for reinforcements? And what of Lady Cerine, kidnapped by the Phantomwitch three nights ago? Had no effort been made to recover her? Or was her rescue Everild's purpose as she rode forth now?

No venatrix, however skilled, could face both the Warpwitch and the Phantomwitch on her own.

Ayleth cursed and pounded a fist against the wall. What was Fendrel thinking, keeping her penned in like this? She should be out with Everild on the hunt! Fendrel couldn't go; he needed to stay to ensure the safety of the king and the prince. Terryn couldn't go; he still suffered under the Warpwitch's curse. Until that curse was truly broken, he would be more of a liability than any help. But Ayleth was perfectly hale and whole, ready to fight, ready to hunt, and ready to rescue Lady Cerine.

"Why am I a prisoner?" she whispered, stepping down from the chair to slump into its seat. "What have I done?"

Venatrix Everild rode as near to the Witchwood boundary as she dared. Her horse obeyed her urging as they left the open country of Wodechran Borough and entered the deep shadows of the fringe forest, but the nearer they drew to the darkness of the Witchwood itself, the more frequently the beast tossed its head, shivered, and shied at nothing. At last Everild dismounted, tied her mount to a tree with a sympathetic pat on its cheek, and continued on foot.

She could hardly blame the horse. If she had any choice in the matter, she wouldn't take a single step closer to the Witchwood either. Now that she approached it, now that she smelled the stink of it permeating the air and roiling through the ground beneath her feet, now that she experienced that indefinable shuddering of the soul caused by mere proximity to this vast and hideous curse, she couldn't believe she had ever desired the outpost of Wodechran Borough for herself. The primary duty of Wodechran's venatrix or venator was to maintain the Great Barrier, the enormous and complex song spell established nearly twenty years ago to keep the Witchwood at bay. A noble task, and one for which Everild had trained hard over the years. She knew how to play the spell on her Vocos; she knew how to channel her shade's powers to create and sustain the spell. But . . .

She shivered as she pushed her way deeper through the fringe forest. Prestigious or otherwise, this was no longer a post she coveted. Nevertheless, the Great Barrier must be maintained. With Terryn du Balafre currently suffering under a curse and out of action, and with reinforcements not yet arrived from the castra, it fell to Everild to accomplish the task.

As she neared the barrier, her eyes darted at every shadow, and she felt as jumpy as her horse. Within her body, her shade hummed with power. Before setting out from Dunloch, she had played a complex variation of the Summoning on her double-headed Vocos pipes, calling up the shade's powers while maintaining careful and protective bindings that prevented it from overwhelming her. She felt the hum of the Great Barrier well before she saw it through the thick foliage of the fringe forest. Pushing through a last stand of trees, she looked ahead with shadow sight and beheld the web-like spell stretching from tall trunk to tall trunk in a huge wall, extending for miles in a nearly straight line.

Beyond the spell, the Witchwood waited with poisonous patience.

Everild drew a shuddering breath and squared her shoulders. She had never been so close to the Witchwood before. Stories of its horror suddenly seemed insignificant when compared to the reality before her. By all accounts she'd heard, this evil forest had sprung from a curse cast by Dread Odile herself, just before the Chosen King's sword sliced her head from her shoulders. If this tale was true, the curse was powerful indeed. The golden glow of a midday autumn sun bathed the fringe forest where Everild stood—but beyond the Great Barrier, all was darkness, shadow, the air thick with poison like curls of smoke.

Everild blinked and looked away quickly, focusing her attention on the spell. The song webbing looked sturdy enough, but it was better to be safe than sorry. The last thing Perrinion needed right now was more shade-taken monsters escaping from the Witchwood.

Everild stepped up to the barrier, taking care not to let her gaze drift to the forest beyond. Reaching out with her shade's senses, she touched one of the humming spell threads. It was, as she had guessed, strong. But as she extended her senses to the right, she felt that strength falter. Somewhere nearby, the spell song was fading, in need of reinforcement.

Setting out at a brisk pace, Everild tromped through the fringe forest, the spell web humming on her left. She followed it for two miles before she found the thin place. It was the work of a few moments to unsheath her Vocos pipes and play a reinforcing variation of the song to mend the flaw. She moved on as quickly as possible, all the while beset by the unrelenting, eager, hungry closeness of the Witchwood on the far side of that song.

Suddenly, Everild drew up short.

As though out of nowhere, a little figure stepped from behind a tree, directly into her line of view. A child, she realized at second glance. A girl child, no more than three or four years of age, with long ratty hair of a color indistinguishable beneath the grime. Huge pale eyes blinked out from a dirt-encrusted face.

Behind those eyes shimmered the unmistakable power of a shade.

Moving with care, Everild slid her hand to the quivers of poisoned darts slung across her chest. Child or not, any shade-taken was a threat and must be dealt with. But she couldn't use her poisons without first determining the variety of shade carried within that little host. She sought with her shadow sight.

And blinked in surprise at the ascendant flare of brilliant jade.

A Seer. The girl carried a Seer inside her. Which meant she was an inborn, for Seers only ever manifested in inborn hosts.

Everild let out a slow breath, her hands freezing over her quivers. She couldn't kill this child outright without damning her soul. A violent death by fire was required to save an inborn, a death Everild was not prepared to deal. Perhaps she could subdue the child. Perhaps she could knock her unconscious and carry her back to Dunloch, there to be dealt with according to Evander's law.

The venatrix slipped a dart from her quiver and slowly slotted it into her scorpiona. The girl watched her every move, eyes unblinking. Just as Everild slipped the safety free on the scorpiona's firing mechanism, those wide, innocent eyes flicked up to meet hers, jade-colored light flashing bright.

"I can take you to the princess," she said.

Everild froze again. The voice was human, or mostly human. There was a strange, echoing quality to it, which might mean it was the possessing shade that spoke, using its host body's mouth.

"She's close by," the child continued, tipping her head to one side. "She's hurt."

Everild's thumb tensed over the trigger. Every instinct told her to fire, but something in that voice made her pause. "Who?" she demanded in a growl. "Who do you mean?"

"The princess," the child said again. "In the white gown."

A knot formed on Everild's brow. Her face tightened beneath the bandages wrapped across her broken nose. "Lady Cerine?" she asked, easing her thumb off the trigger but keeping her scorpiona leveled at the child. "Are you telling me you know where to find Lady Cerine?"

"She's . . . hurt," the girl said. "She doesn't move. I'll take you."

Everild drew a long breath. Lady Cerine had been *evanesced* out of Dunloch by the Phantomwitch three nights ago at her own wedding ball. Fendrel doubted the lady was still alive. He assumed that one or the other of the witches had stolen her body and ousted her soul, if they hadn't simply killed her outright following their escape from Dunloch.

Something in the child's words seemed truthful, however, shade or no shade. It might be that Lady Cerine's body lay close at hand, discarded by the witches who had no further use for her. If so, would it not be right to carry her remains back to the grieving prince, back to where the lady might be laid to rest according to the correct ceremonies? Better than leaving her out here in the wild to be savaged by beasts and rot away.

Everild eyed the child, switching from shadow sight to mortal and back again. A Seer shade was hardly dangerous. Though their powers could be useful in their way, Seers had no combat abilities. And in such a host, scarcely beyond toddling infanthood, it could pose no threat. It could cause no harm to follow the little one, see if what she said was true . . . and then take her down quietly with paralysis poison and carry her back for the necessary violent death.

"All right," she said, nodding once. "Take me to the . . . the princess."

Without a word, the child turned and trotted through the fringe forest, uncomfortably near to the barrier-song webbing. Everild made long strides in pursuit, keeping her scorpiona up and ready, just in case.

They had walked no more than three minutes before Everild saw the body lying on the ground ahead of her, overshadowed by tall trees. A body wearing a tattered white ball gown trimmed in gold. Even without the gown, Everild would have recognized the shorn head of Lady Cerine, her hair cut close to the scalp according to the practice of the Siveline Sisterhood. There could be no mistaking the lady.

She lay so still . . .

The child hurried ahead and fell to her knees beside the lady, placing one hand on Cerine's arm. Then she looked up and back at Everild. Tears shimmered in her huge eyes.

"I'm sorry," she said. Then she spoke again, this time her sweet mortal voice mingling with the strange, otherworldly cadences of a shade. "*I'm so sorry.*"

Warning erupted in Everild's senses. A hunter's instincts raged wildly through her veins . . . but too late.

She took a step back, her scorpiona rising, and started to whirl in place.

Something caught her by the throat.

Then came the pain.

CHAPTER 2

TERRYN STOOD OUTSIDE THE DOOR TO THE PRINCE'S study, his hand frozen in an upraised fist, his knuckles hovering above the wood panels. Moments passed, heartbeats pounding in his throat. He couldn't quite bring himself to knock.

Coward.

Grimacing, Terryn lowered his hand and bowed his head, studying his feet. He'd not seen Gerard since three nights ago. Three nights ago, when, under the enthralling power of the Warpwitch, he'd almost killed him. Three nights ago . . . a night he couldn't even remember.

It didn't seem possible, somehow. His whole life had been devoted to the service of the Golden Prince. Fendrel had brought Terryn into the Order of Saint Evander and raised him to take Fendrel's own place one day as Black Hood, right-hand servant to the king. Terryn had always known his twofold purpose in life: to fulfill his vows to the Goddess, and to do so by serving the Goddess's chosen one.

But in the moment of crisis he had turned on Gerard.

Guilt knifed through his conscience, more painful than any physical wound. He didn't feel the curse. Even now, searching down inside himself, Terryn could sense no trace of the Warpwitch's magic. He remembered when Ylaire had first implanted it inside him, long ago, when he was a small child. She had tattooed his face with her sigil, plunging the power of her shade directly into his blood. But when Fendrel found Terryn, he'd carved that sigil off his cheek, bleeding the curse out of him. Or so Terryn had been told.

Had Fendrel lied to him all these years? Or was he

merely mistaken?

Terryn's jaw clenched. He was supposed to be in bed still, resting after his ordeal. Fendrel had assured him that he'd sent for reinforcements from the castra, including the Phasmatrix Domina, who should be able to purge the curse out of Terryn's system once and for all. If not . . .

Well, if not, Terryn knew what his future held. A venator cursed was a venator compromised, unsafe to send into the field. He would be dealt the Gentle Death. His soul would be parted from that of his shade. He would, if the Goddess was merciful, ascend to Her Light and not be dragged to the hell of the Haunts. And that would be the end of it. Of everything.

He could only hope the Phasmatrix would be able to offer something more. That, or . . .

Or he could dare to consider *her* suggestion.

His throat tightened as he tried to swallow, but his mouth was too dry. He pulled himself upright, swiftly pushing that thought to the back of his mind where it could do no harm. He had enough problems to contend with. Adding heresy to the mix would only compound the evils of his situation.

He faced the door again. He must act now, before the castra reinforcements arrived. Before he lost his chance forever. Raising his fist, he rapped thrice on the door, then waited, turning his head slightly to hear a response. None came, so he rapped again, harder, until his knuckles stung.

A sharp voice growled from the room beyond, a voice he barely recognized: "What?"

"It's me, Gerard," Terryn said.

Nothing at first. Three breaths passed before he heard what might be the scrape of a chair, followed by footsteps on the hardwood floor beyond and the clunk of a lock being turned. The door cracked open. Terryn peered through in time to glimpse of the side of Gerard's face as the prince turned and stalked across the office to his desk.

"Close the door behind you," Gerard said, casting the words back over his shoulder.

Terryn obediently pulled the door shut as his gaze took in the room. There could be no clearer indication of the prince's mental state than the condition of his office. Ordinarily this room was grand, well balanced, every piece of furniture arranged just so, every book in its proper place. Even Gerard's broad desk by the window, though habitually piled with work documents, had always been ordered with care and precision for optimal flow of productivity.

Now the room looked as if it belonged to a madman. The gilded chairs by the fireplace were askew, one lying on its side, the other pushed up against the open hearth. Books were pulled down from their shelves and scattered every which way, loose papers strewing the floor like dead leaves, many of them torn as though ripped straight from their bindings. Gerard's desk suffered gouges in its legs and along its surface, as though he'd taken out frustration on it with a knife.

But Gerard himself looked worse by far. He still wore his wedding garments, Terryn noted. Only the jacket had been cast aside on the floor. His embroidered jerkin was unlaced and sagging, his shirt pulled loose from his trousers. His feet were bare and must be ice cold, for no fire alleviated the autumn chill in the walls and floor. Wild tufts of hair framed his pale face and fell over his forehead as he slumped into his desk chair across the room from Terryn. Both arms rested limply across the pile of parchments, broken quills, and spilled ink.

Worst of all were his eyes. Hollow, shadow-ringed, raw, and red, they stared out from his face, the eyes of a broken man. A man who had been failed by those he trusted most.

Terryn nearly lost his courage again, nearly fled the room without speaking a word. But no matter how his heart failed him, he marched across the space between door and desk, drawing himself to full attention before his prince.

"I have come to . . . apologize," he said, his voice rough as he strove to control it.

Gerard leaned back in his chair, one arm falling in his lap, the other still outstretched on the desk. He didn't say anything, merely waited.

"I . . . I allowed Lady Cerine to be taken," Terryn continued. "I turned on you. I would have killed you if not for . . . for . . ."

If not for Ayleth.

Ayleth who had thrown herself at him, wrapping her arms around his body even as spines burst through his clothing, even as his limbs broke and reformed in a hideous new shape brought on by the Warpwitch's curse. These memories flashed like the remnants of a fevered dream through his mind, then vanished. Terryn closed his eyes briefly, trying to clear his head, trying to focus his thoughts on what he needed to say.

"My Prince." He forced his eyes open, forced himself to look into Gerard's haunted face. "I no longer deserve to be your servant. I deserve nothing better than the judgment of the castra, and when that judgment comes, I will face it without a word. But I swear to you, I *swear* it, Gerard"—his voice broke, but he recovered himself at once—"I would do anything to protect you. Anything."

The prince lowered his gaze, relieving Terryn briefly of his strange stare. His eyes drifted across the overfull desk before him, and his mouth twisted suddenly into a harsh, mirthless grin. "Do you make these promises to your Golden Prince, Terryn?"

Terryn blinked once. "I do," he answered.

That grin widened, and Gerard turned his head to one side as though twisting a crick in his neck. "And what if there were no prophesied Golden Prince? What if I were nothing? Nothing at all. What if everything we were told was a lie, and I have no more claim to the throne than you, or . . . or Billin the courier, or the guard at the gate, or the rat-catcher in the basement? What would you say then, Terryn?"

"I . . ." Terryn hesitated, swallowed. Gerard had said something similar a few days before the ill-fated wedding. Why these thoughts plagued him, why he suffered such a crisis of faith, Terryn couldn't guess.

But Terryn's own conviction remained as unshaken as it had ever been. "I will serve you, Gerard, until my dying breath. You are my prince. You are my . . ." He couldn't say it. He'd never dared say it aloud, certainly never dreamed of saying it in Gerard's presence. He knew that Gerard knew, however. Everyone knew, though no one spoke of it.

The words hung in the air, unspoken yet true: *You are my brother.*

Gerard swallowed, that awful grin vanishing from his face. "Thank you," he whispered. For a moment he looked like himself. Pale, haggard, frightened, but again, if only briefly, the noble prince. The promised hope of Perrinion.

Terryn nodded. There was so much he wished to say, but nothing made sense as it piled up on his tongue. Instead, he saluted his prince and turned to go, not waiting to be dismissed.

Gerard's voice stopped him before he reached the door. "Did you know they've arrested Ayleth?"

Terryn's breath caught. For a moment, he couldn't move, couldn't think. Then, as though suddenly reclaiming use of his own body, he whirled to face the prince. "Arrested her?"

Gerard nodded, drawing a deep breath, his brow stern. "She's been held in her room for two days now."

"Why?" The word came out as a deep bark, more aggressive than Terryn intended. "What has she done?"

"I don't know." Gerard shook his head slowly, his eyes not straying from Terryn's face. "My uncle will not tell me, and my father will not see me. I know only that the castra has been sent for."

"But that was for . . ."

Terryn's voice trailed away. He'd assumed Fendrel sent for the castra to deal with his curse and to provide reinforcements against the witches. But no. He remembered now: Fendrel had sent a messenger to Castra Breçar *before* the night of the ball. Well before Terryn's curse was revealed.

And now Ayleth was under arrest.

"Do you know what they've accused her of? Do you know why they're holding her?" Terryn demanded. At Gerard's slow headshake, he strode back across the room, planting his fists on the desktop as he leaned in. "You *know* what she's done for you. You know how she's fought, how she's suffered. She is your devoted venatrix. She nearly died for your sake. She is loyal to Perrinion, loyal to the House du Glaive. She may be . . . unorthodox in some of her practices, but I have never known a more worthy venatrix."

Gerard met Terryn's gaze, his face tense and strained. "You don't have to convince me of Ayleth's worth or loyalty. But this is castra business. If I were king, I might have some say, but my father . . . he listens to Fendrel. And Fendrel is the Black Hood. Fendrel is the Venator Dominus."

Fendrel, who hated Ayleth for some reason Terryn could not fathom. Not just because she stood in the way of Terryn's taking Wodechran Borough and the outpost of Milisendis. Not just because she had, through sheer stubbornness and drive, unhorsed all of Fendrel's neat plans for Terryn, for Gerard, for the future of the kingdom. No, there was something *more* driving Fendrel's hatred. Something deeper, something darker. Something Terryn hardly dared question.

"He'll kill her," Terryn said. "He will, Gerard. He'll kill her to get her out of the way."

"I . . . I have no power with the castra," Gerard said again. "There's nothing I can do."

"You can try." Terryn's fists clenched so tight, his knuckles stood out sharp and white. "Don't hide in this room. Don't let your . . . your sorrow break you."

Gerard said nothing. His stricken face drained of color, and he looked down again at the parchments piled before him.

"I know you loved Cerine," Terryn pressed. "I know I failed you. I know I let her be taken. But please, Gerard, don't let Ayleth suffer for my failure."

For too long the prince made no answer. From the movement of his eyes, he seemed to be reading the parchment before him. It was enough to drive Terryn mad, and he had to forcibly restrain himself from ripping that page out from under Gerard's gaze and tearing it to pieces.

But at last, Gerard said, "I will speak to Fendrel and my father. I swear, Terryn. I won't . . . I won't let them hurt her."

Hollow words. Terryn knew it. Gerard knew it. The Golden Prince could never gainsay the will of the Chosen King . . . or the Black Hood.

There was nothing more to be said or done. Terryn pulled back from the desk, his heart beating painfully against his breastbone. He turned away without a salute, without another word, and marched from the room, shutting the door hard behind him.

CHAPTER 3

THE NORTH TOWER, THE HIGHEST TOWER OF DUNLOCH, boasted a sweeping view of the east and west towers and the island on which the castle stood; the lake, the single bridge, the ominous gate opening into sprawling parklands; and beyond all this, the fields and villages and farmlands of Wodechran Borough. From up here, a man could detect any sign of approaching attack long before it drew near. Or so Fendrel tried to make himself believe.

Though he wanted to direct his gaze anywhere else, he

found himself turning time and again to face east, toward the Witchwood looming on the horizon. Those rolling hills and valleys of poisonous forest, only just held at bay by the song spell he himself had crafted years ago. A spell he could feel weakening.

The newer barrier established around Dunloch Castle shimmered with greater power and intensity. With Everild's help, Fendrel hoped to maintain the spell at full capacity for many weeks, if necessary. And now that Terryn was up and about again, he might also be able to help. The Warpwitch's curse could not penetrate the barrier spell, and Terryn should be trustworthy enough.

Fendrel's face darkened as he circled the tower, staring out across the landscape of Wodechran Borough. Did Terryn still merit his confidence? Only a month ago he would have trusted Terryn even as he trusted his own right arm. But was Terryn still the same man, devoted to the cause of Evander above all else? Or had the pretty face of a young witch-girl turned his head?

His hand clenched unconsciously into a fist, and pain shot up his forearm. Only days ago, Fendrel had driven three spikes into his flesh to suppress his shade with iron poison. His dark Anathema spirit had risen to such power and ascendancy during his battle with the Phantomwitch, he'd felt his own soul weakening its hold on his body. Another minute, and the shade would have taken full possession.

He must be careful. They must all be careful. So much hung in such precarious balance!

"I'll put an end to it," he whispered, a vow caught on the wind and carried away across the rippling waters of Loch du Nóiv. "I'll put an end to it all."

A door creaked, drawing his attention. Fendrel turned to see his brother emerge from the tower stairwell. The frigid wind caught at the king's cloak, blowing it behind him in scarlet billows. Guardin gripped the folds of fabric and drew them closer as he approached Fendrel, his hands shaking.

He looked old. Almost as old as Fendrel felt. The king was still the strong, upright figure of majesty he had always been, still the promise of the Goddess fulfilled. But . . . old.

"Any sign of them?" the king asked as he drew alongside his brother.

Fendrel shook his head. "Any day now. Any hour. It's been six days since I sent the messenger. They will come."

Guardin was silent for some moments. Neither brother looked at the other; both instead looked to the north road, down which they expected their help to arrive.

"We should kill her now," the king said at last. "Before it's too late."

"We've come this far," Fendrel growled. "We're safe enough."

"Safe? How can we be safe? How can anything we've sought to accomplish these last twenty years be safe now that Gerard knows?"

At this, Fendrel waved a dismissive hand. "We had to tell him eventually. You could not pass on your crown without also passing on your secret. It is just as well that he knows the truth."

"And what truth is that, exactly?"

For the space of several cold breaths, Fendrel did not answer. Then he turned to his brother, fixing him with a hard stare. "You are the Chosen King," he said. "You cut

Dread Odile's head from her body. You ended her reign. You have led this nation with strength and brought it from ruin to prosperity. You are the fulfillment of the prophecy, the hero foretold. That is the truth."

"Not the whole truth," Guardin answered. His steely gaze cut into Fendrel's, sharp as any sword. "You know what liars we are, Fendrel. We can lie to each other. And we can lie to the kingdom. We can lie to my son, and the castra, and the shade-taken, and the witches, and the Haunts themselves. But we cannot lie to the Goddess. She knows."

"The Goddess's will is fulfilled," Fendrel said, though his voice caught in his throat. "The Golden Age is come."

"If that is true," Guardin answered, "it is *despite* our deeds."

A red roaring built up in Fendrel's head, a rage such as he had rarely felt, and not in many years. With it, he felt the power of his shade as it strained against the suppressions binding it, fighting against his will. If he didn't maintain control, he would lose it completely, lose his soul. He dug his nails into his palms, and the veins in his forehead bulged with his effort simply to keep from speaking the words he wanted to hurl at his brother.

The door creaked again. Both men started and turned. "Gerard," the king said, speaking as though caught in some guilty act.

The prince appeared in the doorway where his father had stood minutes before. He wore no cloak, just an unfastened jerkin and untucked shirt, but he didn't flinch as the cold wind blasted him. He strode forward to meet his father and uncle, planting himself firmly before them beneath the low, gray sky.

"Why have you imprisoned Ayleth?" he demanded.

Fendrel felt his brother's gaze flick to his face but didn't meet it. "Castra business," he answered shortly.

"She saved my life. She saved your life and all of Dunloch. She is a heroine." Gerard's eyes moved from venator to king and back again. His face was as pale as a winter dawn, his eyes too bright in their hollow sockets and red-rimmed. "So, she is part of this . . . this little web you've woven. I don't know how. I can't fathom a connection. But she's part of it, part of your secret."

"Gerard—" Guardin began, but Fendrel held up a hand, and the king fell silent.

"Does she know?" Gerard demanded, fixing his attention fully on Fendrel. "Did she discover the truth about Dread Odile? Did she threaten to tell the castra? No . . . no, for you wouldn't have summoned the castra here if that were the case."

Fendrel made certain his face was a mask of stone.

Gerard cursed bitterly, using words that did not befit a prince. "If you kill her, you only stray further from the purpose of the Goddess."

"You don't know what you're talking about," Guardin said.

Gerard rounded on his father, his lips pulled back in a snarl. "I know more than you do. I know that we've all built our lives, our fortunes, our destinies, on a foundation of lies. Lies that go back even farther than the lie you two have conspired to maintain. Saint Evander's own teachings are built on nothing more than a false translation. Did you know this, Father? Did you know he lied as well, to further his own agenda, to bring ruin down on the shade-taken he hated? And on that lie you have founded your life, even as you now ask me to found my life on your lie." He shook his head grimly, his face very white. "I tell you, I won't have it."

"And what will you do?" Fendrel's voice was a sliver of darkness breathed between his tight lips. "Do you intend to give up your throne? To abdicate? Will you end the royal line of the du Glaives?"

"I intend to tell the castra the truth," Gerard answered, drawing back his shoulders, his eyes shining with a light akin to madness. "I intend to lead them down to the vault and show them what you keep hidden there. I intend to tell the ministers of Telianor, the whole of Perrinion. Let them decide by whom they will be ruled. Let them decide if they still wish to serve the man who did *not* slay Dread Odile."

Guardin inhaled sharply and took a half-lunging step toward his son. But Fendrel caught his brother by the shirtfront, restraining him. Guardin pushed against that hold, sending bolts of agony shooting from Fendrel's wound. Fendrel didn't budge. After a brief struggle, Guardin subsided.

"What do you think will happen next?" Fendrel asked so softly that his words were almost lost to the wind. "Do you think your faithful ministers will suffer you or your father to live?"

Gerard faltered, but only for a moment. "That decision will be theirs to make."

"And the castra? What do you think they will do when they find out? Do you think they'll hold the secret close and quiet?"

To this Gerard made no answer.

Fendrel took a step nearer, towering over his nephew, the power of his shade swelling inside him with every word. "Word will get out," he said. "Don't think for an instant that Inren and Ylaire represent the last of Odile's supporters. Shade-taken from across the kingdoms will hear and will flock to Perrinion, eager to restore their goddess to her throne, eager to enjoy once more the madness of power she bestowed upon her subjects. And they will find her. Mark my words. Even if we cut her into a hundred pieces and distribute them throughout Gaulia, they will find her."

"But . . . they can't restore her," Gerard said. "You saw to that."

Guardin drew a sharp breath, but Fendrel cut him off before he could speak. "It won't matter. Knowing she lives will be enough. They will venerate their living-dead queen and unite under her banner once more. They'll choose one of their number to lead in her name. Ylaire di Jocosa. Or Inren. Or one of the other Crimson Devils come out from hiding. And they'll never back down. Not again. Divided, they are dangerous. United, they are more terrible by far. And no song spell will stop them this time, no matter how many brave Evanderians sacrifice their lives."

Gerard opened his mouth, his face so stricken with rage and frustration, he no longer looked like himself. No words came. No argument.

Fendrel took another step and grasped the prince tightly by the shoulders. "The translation of the *Seion-Ebathe* has been debated for years. Greater minds than yours have questioned and wrestled with the teachings of the Saint. We live by faith alone, Gerard. We know the will of the Goddess does not always manifest as we imagine or even desire. We know only that She expects Her children to act, not to wait passively for divine intercession. You are struggling in your faith, but listen to me now; listen to one who has faced his doubts and conquered them one after another, like demons to be wrestled to the ground. Listen to me, for my faith is unshakable. I *know* that you are the Golden Prince. I *know* your father was chosen to end the rule of Dread Odile. I *know* your line, the line of the du Glaives, will be great, not only in Perrinion, but throughout all of Gaulia. Under your rule, we will see safety and peace restored. A new day is dawning, a day in which we need not fear the darkness of the Haunts. I *know* this, Gerard. I know it so that you don't have to."

Struggling to swallow, struggling even to breathe, Gerard nonetheless met Fendrel's gaze. "And you would kill Ayleth for your faith?" he asked.

"I would do much worse," Fendrel answered, the conviction of ages lacing each word like poison.

They stood locked in that gaze, neither willing to break, neither willing to back down. Fendrel stood firm. But he couldn't dismiss the surprise he felt at the strength in his nephew's eyes. Gerard was not Guardin, not one to be easily led. His nephew would defy him if he could only find a way.

The clarion call of a trumpet sang through the air.

Relieved despite himself, Fendrel turned from the prince, gazing beyond the spell barrier, out across Loch du Nóiv, to the north road. At last, riders approached the castle. Fendrel narrowed his eyes. Unless he was much mistaken, those were red hoods he saw.

The Phasmatrix Domina was come at last.

CHAPTER 4

AYLETH BLINKED.

She didn't mean to. She intended to keep her eyes firmly open despite the lulling pull of the *sòm*. She refused to succumb, refused to sink into that unrestful numbness. Though the bed called to her, she propped herself up in the spindly chair by the wall, determined to remain upright, to maintain consciousness.

But she blinked. Just once.

And when she opened her eyes again, her small

chamber in Dunloch Castle was gone, and she sat beneath a tall pine tree in the forest of her mind.

A small sigh escaped her lips. She hadn't meant to sleep, but now that she was here, it was a relief to leave behind all the confusion and fear of the waking world. Her forest was comforting, familiar . . . and mostly recovered from the ravages of *oblivis* poison. Traces of ash still floated in the air, but when she breathed, she smelled only fresh growing things and renewal.

Maybe it would be all right to hide here for a while.

Fog crept along the forest floor, drifting around her bare feet. She knew what it was: the *sòm* drug, clouding her mind, keeping Laranta from reaching her. At first, Ayleth tried to ignore it, but the longer she sat beneath that tree, the thicker the fog grew. Finally, she got to her feet and drifted off through the forest, searching for somewhere the fog wasn't so dense, somewhere she could see and think and breathe more easily.

A shadow flickered on the edge of her vision.

Ayleth stopped. Taking care to control every movement, to allow not even the faintest trace of a flinch, she turned. The shadow was gone. But an instant later, another one flickered, again just on the outer edge of her peripheral vision. She turned again, more quickly this time, but too late.

Drawing a long breath, she continued, her bare feet rustling the pine straw, which she couldn't see through the thick coils of *sòm* fog.

A third shadow. A fourth. A fifth.

Her heartbeat quickened—not here in her mentally projected body, but somewhere far off where her physical body slept. It pulsed a rhythm beneath her feet, and Ayleth hastened in time to that rhythm, following the shadows.

They felt familiar. Terribly familiar. And they all led in a single direction. To the deep-cut gorge that slashed through her mind, plunging into darkness far below.

Ayleth halted on the edge of the gorge. The pine trees dared not draw close to its edge, leaving a clear strip between the forest and the brink. Overhead, the canopy of gray clouds seemed closer than ever, thickened by the *sòm*. The gorge was so deep that more clouds drifted below Ayleth's feet. But beneath them, she could sense, if not quite see, the gully waiting far below.

At the edges of her vision, she saw shimmering shadows pour over the edge of the gorge. When she turned to look at them directly, they were gone, yet she felt the pull of them as though they silently urged her to follow. To follow them back to that place of forgotten memories, to the part of her mind Hollis had blocked with powerful spells.

Ayleth curled her hands into fists. She'd almost forgotten the strange secrets she'd uncovered the last time she dared to venture this deep into her mind. Well, no, that wasn't true . . . she'd not forgotten. She'd simply not allowed herself to dwell on dreams. Life was complicated and confusing enough as it was.

But what if the answer to everything waited below?

Somewhere in the physical world, her fingernails drove into her palms so hard, she almost woke herself up. Determined not to let the opportunity pass, she swung out over the edge of the gorge and began to descend beneath the film of *sòm* fog, down into the shadows, to the pile of rubble waiting below. She landed on top of broken stones that shifted and heaved under her feet. Moving with caution, she slipped and slid to the floor of this dark gully in the deeper reaches of her own consciousness.

But there were greater depths still to be plumbed.

The shadows congregated on the edges of her vision, long, lithe, and low. Wolves? Or the shadows of wolves? They moved alongside her, leading her down the gully to that place where a hole like the mouth of a well plunged into the rock.

Ayleth approached the lip of that hole and peered down.

Hollis's spells blocked the opening, interwoven strands of magic and music forming a webbing too strong to be penetrated by any means Ayleth possessed. But if Ayleth remembered correctly, one of those strands had loosened the last time she was here. She knelt, seeking a weakness, searching for opportunity. She had to be careful; another overt attack on the spell might bring a second avalanche crashing down on her soul. But if she could—

Her chin hit the floor hard, jarring her jaw.

Ayleth lay stunned for three gasping breaths before

she scrambled upright, her hands shaking. Her eyes, blinking and dazzled, still believed she saw a hole and gleaming spell threads in front of her. But no . . . no, that was only a dream . . .

"Haunts damn," she growled, slumping back against the wall of her chamber. The spindly chair lay on its side. She must have listed in her sleep and fallen, knocking herself back into the waking world. The room, her prison, remained just as before. The bed was neatly made, though rumpled. In one corner lay the mounds of a crimson ball gown. Sunlight now made a golden line on the floor to the other side of her blood-warded window, indicating that morning had progressed well into afternoon. Another day lost.

Ayleth drew her knees up to her chest. Her mind was still drug-addled, but not as bad as it had been before she dozed off. Soon they would come to dose her again, but for the moment she enjoyed brief clarity. She pressed her face to her knees, half wishing they'd come with their dose again soon. Maybe being drugged was better than being trapped here with only her thoughts for company.

Her thoughts . . . and those strange, shadowy figures

from her dream . . .

A distant sound plucked at her ear. Ayleth lifted her head slowly, turning toward the window. She couldn't open it, but the faint sound again penetrated the glass panes: a heralding horn. Someone had come to Dunloch.

She stood slowly, her brows drawing together, and returned her chair to its place close to the wall. But when she once again climbed up to regain that narrow view of the courtyard, she couldn't see anything new.

Who would dare come to Dunloch at this time? All the guests from the prince's wedding had fled, allowed through a narrow gap in the barrier spell before it was closed fast behind them. Had someone sent word to Telianor, requesting soldiers? But no, that was impossible—messengers could not travel the distance in two days, and certainly no one could respond so quickly. Whoever was coming had been sent for well before the attack on Hallow's Night.

Her head spun. Dark spots burst on the edges of her vision. Knowing she would topple to the floor in another moment, Ayleth climbed down from the chair and sagged heavily into its seat. She would simply have to wait and see who had arrived and for what purpose. If anyone bothered to let her know.

At the sound of the heralding trumpets, Terryn pulled his hood up over his head and hastened out to the castle's front courtyard. He doubted Fendrel would send for him, so he didn't wait.

A single bridge connected the island to the shore. At the end of the bridge loomed a fortified gate, a worthy point of defense against mortal opponents. Shade-taken would be more difficult to stop. But as Terryn strode swiftly across the bridge to the gate, he felt, even from across the water, the power of the barrier spell surrounding Dunloch. Nothing could get through this barrier so long as it was periodically reinforced by someone who knew the complexities of the spell.

The guards at the gate greeted Terryn with solemn salutes, recognizing him by the color of his hood. Their captain stepped forward, saying, "Members of your Order have arrived. We can open the gates, but we cannot let them through."

Terryn nodded. The un-taken guards lacked the means to open the barrier spell even to friends. Terryn could do it; he had constructed this barrier himself only days ago, and he knew its intricacies. But he wouldn't dare let anyone through without Fendrel's express command, not even a party from the castra.

Instead, he stepped up to the gate's spy slot and peered out to the road beyond. A company of fifteen on horseback met his vision. All bore the red hoods of Evander's Order, except for the woman in the center. Her hood was white, and Terryn recognized her at once without even seeing her face—Esabel, Phasmatrix di Conradin.

His heart turned to a block of ice in his breast.

"Terryn. You were not summoned here."

At the sound of his former master's voice, Terryn instantly assumed a mask of stony calm, an expression he'd learned from Fendrel himself and perfected over the years. He turned and met the Venator Dominus with a salute, saying only, "I heard the herald trumpet. I came to offer my assistance in the opening of the barrier."

Fendrel approached through the gathered guardsmen,

his eyes bright beneath the shadow of his black hood. He held his Vocos pipes in one hand, already opened into their double-headed position. Though Terryn's shade was deeply suppressed, he sensed the vibration of Fendrel's Anathema shade in the depths of the dominus's dark pupils. Those shade-brightened eyes studied Terryn carefully, looking beyond his outer, mortal form down into his soul. Searching for some trace of the Warpwitch's curse, no doubt. But as long as the Warpwitch remained on the far side of this barrier, she could not manipulate Terryn according to her will.

Fendrel blinked, and the shadow-light in his eyes momentarily dimmed. "Very well," he said. "Stand with me."

Terryn drew in beside his former master and slid his own Vocos pipes from their sheath on his belt. At a barked order from the Venator Dominus, the guards sprang forward to open the gates, which groaned as they swung on their massive hinges. Beyond gleamed the barrier, a webbing of song spell. Threads of music strung together, shimmering in the spirit realm beyond mortal sight.

Raising his Vocos to his lips, Terryn played a quick trill of the Song of Searching. He closed his eyes, letting his conscious awareness pass from this world into the realm of his mind, where all was stark and barren, a world of stone. Hard, harsh stone spread endlessly from horizon to horizon save for one strange, lumpen mass just before his view. This was shaped like an enormous lizard covered over in long-hardened magma.

His mortal body still playing the Vocos pipes, Terryn's spirit-self walked swiftly across the cracked and broken ground to the tortured shape. He needed to access his shade's power, but this must be done with precision. Only days ago, the Warpwitch's curse had brought his shade roaring to such extremes of power inside him that it had nearly broken his mortal body into a thousand pieces. Since then, he had worked hard to get the shade back under layer upon layer of suppression, making certain it had no opportunity to break free. Those bindings manifested in his mind as this hardened stone covering; but beneath it, he felt heat. Heat like the brilliance of a fallen sun.

And in the simmering of that heat, a voice manifested

in a small, subtle whisper: *What is my name?*

In the realm of his mind, Terryn shivered. But his mortal body did not falter in the song he played. He had heard this voice too many times to let it affect him now, particularly not with Fendrel watching him at his work. He shifted the song into a new melody—the Song of Harvesting. The melody wrapped around his soul as he strode up to the stone shape and, extending one hand, reached in beneath the hardened exterior to scoop out a handful of magic.

The being trapped in stone hissed. Once more, the otherworldly voice cried, *Do you know my name?*

Terryn retreated, cupping the harvested magic close. His mortal body finished off the melody with a firm resolution of notes, then he opened his eyes, returning his awareness to the mortal world around him. All of this had taken no more than a few seconds. The gates were only just settling back on their hinges, the guards backing away to give the two venators room.

Fendrel grunted, satisfied by Terryn's efforts. He turned to the gate, his legs braced and his shoulders back. "On my lead," he said to Terryn, and raised his pipes to his lips. He began to play the barrier-song spell, but not the variation that would build or sustain the barrier. This intricate line of music was precision itself—a song to gently part those woven threads of music without letting them fray and fall apart, creating an opening just wide enough for the riders beyond to pass through.

Terryn watched the effect of the song spell as it vibrated through the webbing. Then he began to play yet another variation. His shade was quite different from Fendrel's, so the variations used to channel its magic were different. Effective, however. As Fendrel deftly sliced through the strong webbed cords of song, Terryn took the frayed ends and tied them off so that they would not fade away. Working with Fendrel was as natural as breathing. It was almost a relief to step back into this role, supporting his master's work.

The Evanderians on the far side of the spell watched the opening grow. At a nod from the Phasmatrix Domina, they rode forward, one by one passing through the song spell and the gate, into the safety of Dunloch. Among them, Terryn spied a familiar face—a square face with a carefully trimmed beard framing its jaw and a fresh, ugly scar ringing its cheek. A scar very like Terryn's.

Venator Kephan. Terryn's heart lurched at the sight of the man who had, only a month ago, been discovered to be under the Warpwitch's thrall. He'd been sent to Breçar to have the curse broken so that he might return to his work at Wodechran Borough. Had the phasmators of the castra succeeded in gouging out Ylaire's sigil? Or had the curse remained unbroken, hidden much deeper down?

Kephan's eyes flicked to Terryn, and for a moment his face brightened with recognition. Something in Terryn's expression must have given him pause, however, for though he opened his mouth, he didn't speak the greeting on his lips. His brows drew together as he rode on through the gate.

Domina Esabel entered last of all. The moment she was through the barrier, Fendrel shifted the song into a new variation to repair the opening. Terryn followed his lead. As Fendrel drew the threads of magic back together, Terryn secured them until his shadow vision could no longer detect where an opening had been. Their work accomplished, Fendrel and Terryn brought the song to a natural, harmonious conclusion. Then, both sheathing their Vocos pipes, they turned to the Evanderians. Terryn saluted the domina, but her attention focused on Fendrel.

"I trust, Venator Dominus, there is some good reason for this extremity of protection," she said, her voice husky. She was not a young woman, nor even in her prime. Esabel di Conradin, if Terryn remembered correctly, was nearly sixty years of age—proof of her extreme strength and control over her shade. Most Evanderians didn't survive past fifty.

"I will tell you everything, Domina Esabel," Fendrel answered with grim courtesy. "Once you have rested from your journey, King Guardin would meet with you, and we will inform you of what has transpired since I sent my message to you."

The Phasmatrix raised her hand in a single sharp gesture. "I will not rest until I have done what I came here to do, Dominus. Now tell me: Where is this venatrix you claim to be inborn? Take me to her."

The world around Terryn seemed to tilt, to darken.

For a moment, he could not believe what he had just heard. The Phasmatrix's words rang in his head like dull, thudding blows, without comprehension. He stood staring at her, his mouth open, his eyes slowly rounding as understanding took hold.

This was why Fendrel had locked Ayleth up. This was why he had summoned the Phasmatrix Domina from Bédoier.

Flames seemed to erupt before his vision. In his head, Terryn already heard Ayleth's screams.

CHAPTER 5

FOOTSTEPS SOUNDED IN THE PASSAGE OUTSIDE, moving fast.

Ayleth lifted her head, blinking hard, and her heart raced, driving back the fog of the *sòm*. Somehow she knew those footsteps were coming for her. They didn't sound like Venatrix Everild's brisk stride.

No . . . unless she was much mistaken, Fendrel approached her door. With others following close behind him.

Realizing she didn't want to face the Venator Dominus while sprawled on the floor, Ayleth grabbed hold of the spindly chair and tried to pull herself to standing. The door to her room burst open before she'd quite gotten both feet under her. Fendrel's broad shoulders filled the space, and he stared down at her, his eyes sparking with shadow-light.

He stepped into the room, making way for two strangers in red hoods to file in behind him. "There," he said, indicating Ayleth with a wave of his hand. "Hold her fast."

"What—? Wait!" Ayleth gasped, the words slurring on her tongue. The two strange Evanderians, one male, one female, crouched over her and grabbed her arms. They hauled her upright between them, their hands like too-tight shackles.

"Come," Fendrel said and stepped out through the door into the passage beyond.

Ayleth's eyes rounded. "No, wait!" she cried as the Evanderians moved in the dominus's wake. But she was too late. They pulled her into the blood ward on the door.

The blast of the curse knocked her out of their grasps

and sent her flying to the floor in the middle of the room. Burning pain cut every nerve in her body, piercing down into her soul. She couldn't even draw breath but lay in stunned paralysis, every muscle tensed, her mouth wide in a silent scream. Then her body spasmed, and she choked, heaved, and vomited up the contents of her stomach. The pain didn't lessen, but at least she could breathe again.

Fendrel's voice rumbled through her racked awareness. "I forgot. Wait while I dismantle the ward."

The sound of his Vocos playing to cancel the curse sent shudders down Ayleth's spine. By the time it was finished, her vision had cleared, and she pushed up onto her elbows, wiping at her mouth with the back of one hand. The Evanderians closed in on her again, and she didn't try to resist when they caught her elbows and pulled her to her feet.

Fendrel, his face unremorseful, sheathed his Vocos and nodded. "Come."

The blast of the blood ward and the subsequent emptying of her stomach had one good effect at least: She was much clearer-headed than she'd been for the last several days. A mixed blessing. As the Evanderians hauled her too swiftly in Fendrel's wake, she almost wished for the numbing *sòm* to take the edge off her confused fear.

At least she was out of that Haunts-festering room.

They came to the end of the passage, stepping into the open gallery above the main front entrance hall of Dunloch. Craning her neck to peer around the strange woman holding her arm, Ayleth caught glimpses over the railing down to the floor below. More red hoods. A lot of red hoods. Reinforcements from the castra come to witch-hunt, perhaps. Would she be permitted to join them?

Fendrel led the way to the huge front staircase, moving so swiftly that his black hood fell back from his head, revealing his pale hair tied back in three tight braids. Ayleth's stomach heaved with dizziness as the Evanderians dragged her to the top of the stairs, but she had no time to collect herself before they started their descent. Her feet tripped over themselves, and she would have fallen headlong if not for the iron-hard hands holding her upright.

Many faces waited down below, upturned to watch her. For a sickening moment, she relived three nights ago, when she had stood alone at the top of this same staircase, struggling to descend while wearing the voluminous skirts of that crimson gown. Only Terryn had watched her then, his ice-cold eyes gleaming with amusement.

Some instinct compelled Ayleth to search for those eyes now among the crowd waiting below. As though feeling a cold wind rising from his direction, she looked to the shadows by the entrance door. A figure stood there, drawn back from the rest, his hood pulled so low that she could not see his face. But she knew it was Terryn. For some reason she couldn't name, her heart lifted, however slightly.

Her relief lasted no more than a moment before she stumbled down the last few steps and collapsed to her knees. The Evanderians on either side made no effort to lift her up again but continued to hold her arms at an awkward angle while she panted, trying to catch her breath.

A pair of travel-worn riding boots moved into her line of vision, the silver spurs encrusted in mud from the road. An age-roughened voice spoke over her head. "This is the venatrix?"

"Indeed, Domina," Fendrel responded from Ayleth's right. "Ayleth, Venatrix di Ferosa, lately of Drauval."

"And who is at watch over Drauval Borough these days?" the old voice asked.

"Hollis, Venatrix di Theldry."

Ayleth stiffened at the sound of her mistress's name. A surge of rage pulsed from her heart, followed swiftly by a surge of sorrow.

"Ah, yes," the old voice said. "I remember Hollis. She fought alongside you and the Chosen King during the final days of Dread Odile, did she not?"

"She did."

"And following the war, she volunteered to take on the care of remote Drauval. She manages Gillanluòc Outpost without the aid of a hunt brother or sister, does she not?"

"Yes."

"And you think that this brave venatrix—a heroine of Perrinion, your own hunt sister of yore—you believe that she has fallen into heresy?"

At those words, Ayleth's head shot up. She stared at

the woman before her, surprised to see that she didn't wear traditional venatorial garb. Her uniform, though Evanderian in style, was that of a phasmatrix, not a venatrix, and the hood thrown back across her shoulders was white. The Phasmatrix Domina, one of the highest-ranking members of the Council of Breçar. Even as Fendrel mastered all venators in Perrinion, the Phasmatrix Domina was mistress of all phasmators: shade-taken men and women who served to protect both the spiritual and physical health of their Evanderian brethren.

Ayleth's stomach lurched again. Why was the phasmatrix here? It made sense for Fendrel to summon more venators to hunt the Crimson Devils. But why a spirit healer? Could this have something to do with Terryn's curse? But it wasn't Terryn who now knelt at the domina's feet.

And what did any of this have to do with Hollis?

Shaking her head to clear it of the clinging *sòm* fog, Ayleth spoke through gritted teeth. "Hollis is no heretic."

A thin gray eyebrow slid up the domina's parchment-pale forehead, mounding wrinkles. "You will speak when you are spoken to, Venatrix di Ferosa."

Ayleth opened her mouth, prepared to protest, prepared to pour out a gabble of words in defense of her mistress's honor. But her tongue cleaved to the roof of her mouth. The more she struggled, the more tightly her throat constricted. She glared up into the Phasmatrix's eyes and knew it was her doing, her shade that prevented her from speaking out.

Movement on her right drew her eye as one of the red-hooded figures stepped forward, throwing back his hood. Ayleth's eyes widened in surprise. Venator Kephan stood before her, his face ravaged with the same ugly scar that scored Terryn's face, only his was fresh, black stitches still visible over raw, puckered skin.

"Domina," he said, saluting respectfully, "this young woman . . ."

The phasmatrix turned an implacable gaze Kephan's way. "Have you something to say, Venator du Tam?"

Kephan drew a short breath, nostrils flaring. "I just wanted to say that this woman saved my life and the life of her hunt brother only last month. It was she who stopped me when, under the Warpwitch's thrall, I tried to kill them both. If not for her, I would still be Ylaire di Jocosa's slave."

"Stand down, du Tam," Fendrel growled. "Whatever personal gratitude you may feel for this girl, it has no bearing on the case at hand. Stand down, I tell you."

Kephan's eyes flicked from his dominus to the phasmatrix and back to Ayleth. His brow puckered, but he backed away, bowing his head so that the shadow of his hood hid his scarred face once more.

The domina addressed herself to Fendrel again. "Well, Dominus? What have you to say?"

Fendrel swallowed. Though he was of equal rank with the phasmatrix and physically loomed over her in strength and height, he looked somehow childish beside her upright, narrow figure.

"I do not like to cast a slur on my former hunt sister," he said darkly. "I know only what my own tests have told me, the very tests for which I seek your verification."

"Yes, I read of your findings," the domina answered. "And I saw the vial you sent to the castra. A strange test to perform under the circumstances described. *Oblivis* poisoning does not relate in any obvious way to that which you claim to have found. What led you to make this venatrix undergo such a disagreeable examination?"

Ayleth's already racing heart seemed to double its speed. She remembered that test. Part of her had wanted to believe it was nothing more than a dream, an extension of the other fevered dreams she experienced while recovering from the *oblivis*. That shimmering needle hovering above her eye, that penetration, that pain.

Fendrel's face was like stone. "Something . . . struck me as . . . *off* about her," he said slowly. "Something I cannot describe or put a name to. But I have learned over the years not to doubt my instincts. So I performed the test, and I am confident that I read the results correctly."

"Let us hope not, Dominus," the Phasmatrix answered. So saying, she knelt, bringing her head level with Ayleth's. "Let go of her," she said to the Evanderians, who obeyed at once, releasing their hold on her arms.

Ayleth glared up at them, rolling her shoulders, but the Phasmatrix caught her by the chin. Ayleth froze under that icy touch. The domina tilted her head this way and that, and her eyes glowed with the strange light of her shade, gleaming with a color Ayleth could not discern without Laranta's power ascendant. An Apparition shade, if she had to guess, a mind-manipulator. Like Hollis's. She felt the ugly plucking on the edge of her awareness as the shade sought to infiltrate her mind. The *sòm* in her system made this difficult, serving to block outside shade presence as much as it suppressed Laranta.

But the Phasmatrix wielded the power of her shade with great skill and did not seem unduly frustrated by the barriers she encountered. "Where did you study before you began your apprenticeship?" she asked suddenly, her eyes not meeting Ayleth's but looking beyond them into her head.

"Castra Vielhir," Ayleth answered at once. The familiar lie came all too easily to her lips.

"And yet," said the Phasmatrix musingly, "I find no memories of Vielhir inside you." Her stern face hardened. "What age were you when you came to Venatrix di Theldry?"

"Seven."

"Young to begin an apprenticeship." The Phasmatrix sat back on her heels, still holding onto Ayleth's face but no longer peering so deeply. "Your story doesn't hold together well, Venatrix. Still, when you tell me your mistress is no heretic, I see that you believe your own words."

"Hollis di Theldry is a truehearted servant of Evander," Ayleth stated firmly. "Her loyalty to the Order cannot be doubted."

"And what of yours?"

Ayleth opened her mouth. But she couldn't answer. She knew too well the games she'd been playing these last weeks since leaving Gillanluòc. She knew the liberties she'd given her shade. Did this mean she was not loyal to the Goddess and to the teachings of the Saint? Her whole life had been devoted to the cause of Evander. Surely a few stumbling steps along the way didn't equal outright heresy.

But would she now commit to honoring the Saint's teachings to the letter, from this day forward? Would she commit to maintaining the dire bindings on Laranta which Hollis had always urged? Would she forever punish her shade merely for existing inside her?

Of course she must. Her shade was a parasite, a

malicious, remorseless parasite.

All lies. Lies Ayleth could not bear to speak. She closed her eyes and bowed her head.

"Interesting," the Phasmatrix said. Then she stood abruptly, her travel-worn cloak wafting in the swiftness of her movements. A sharp clap of her hands, and the two Evanderians moved in, caught Ayleth by the arms again, and drew her upright.

"Interesting," the domina repeated, "but ultimately pointless without the test itself. Hold her steady. And you"—a motion to another Evanderian standing close at hand—"take hold of her head. Don't let her move."

Ayleth tensed as the third Evanderian stepped behind her, taking her head firmly in both strong hands. She felt not only mortal strength in that grasp but shade power as well.

Laranta! she called impulsively, reaching out for the strength of her own shade. *Laranta, come to me!*

But her shade made no answer, and the Phasmatrix's eyes burned. "Don't seek to summon your powers in my presence, girl," she snarled. "Remember, I'm in your mind. You condemn yourself. Now stand still!"

A terrible paralysis came over Ayleth's limbs. It did not matter that the two Evanderians held her arms, that the third one clutched her head. The power of the Phasmatrix's shade was more than enough to freeze her in place. She could not even blink as she watched the Phasmatrix peel off her glove and hold out her hand. One of her aides rushed to her side, placing a gleaming implement in her palm. Ayleth recognized it at once. It was the same strange tool Fendrel had used on her eye.

A scream built up in Ayleth's breast, but she could not release it, so tightly did the Phasmatrix's shade hold her captive. *Laranta! Laranta!* she cried again, despite the warning she'd been given. She couldn't help herself.

Moving with viper speed, the Phasmatrix Domina stepped in close, caught Ayleth by the back of the head, and spiked that needle straight into her unblinking eye. The pain was enough to break the hold of the shade on her.

Ayleth reacted, lurching back, the scream finally escaping her lips. The Evanderians held her tight, but she thrashed in their hold, managing to throw off one and swing a punch at one of the others. Her blow missed, and the Evanderian who'd held her head caught her by the shoulders, twisted her around and forced her flat on the ground face down, kneeling painfully into the small of her back. She writhed but couldn't escape, and the other two Evanderians came down heavily on her arms, crushing her. She squeezed her eyes tightly shut against the pain and roared in frustration, powerless.

"Yes, an unpleasant test to be sure," the Phasmatrix Domina's voice growled. A moment later, Ayleth heard a clink of crystal. Opening her unhurt eye, she looked up and saw the Phasmatrix carefully applying the drop of blood on the end of her needle into a bottle of gently swirling liquid. A strange, faintly glowing liquid. This time, she recognized what it was.

Eitr. Pure *eitr.*

Her pain forgotten, the sluggishness of the *sòm* long vanished, Ayleth watched in mingled fascination and fear as the domina swirled the liquid. *Eitr* was the strangest substance known to man, neither element nor alloy, neither vegetable nor mineral, but a living material that grew and changed and sometimes even seemed to learn. Deposits were found in the most ancient sites, ruins, and temples, and had apparently once been bountiful throughout the world in ages before the Goddess called humanity to life. Phasmators theorized that it was the shavings left over from when the Goddess carved out reality into existences.

Rarer than gold, rarer than diamonds, rarer than oblidite. Ayleth gaped in wonder to see even such a small amount contained within that vial.

The domina's shade was at work—magic surrounded the bottle and manipulated the liquid *eitr*, calling to life its otherworldly properties in ways Ayleth couldn't begin to fathom. Some strange alchemy of the physical and the spiritual, the tangible and intangible. The liquid in the bottle worked up into a storm of energy, which pulsed through the ether so that even untaken mortals must feel it.

Then, as suddenly as it had begun, the storm ceased. The pulsing stilled, and the *eitr* settled down . . . and transformed.

The Phasmatrix upturned the bottle over the palm of her hand, pouring out a stream of silver dust. "There you have it, Dominus Fendrel," she said in a voice devoid of emotion. "There is your answer."

"She is an inborn then. Just as I thought," Fendrel said, standing above Ayleth like an angel of doom. He turned and barked to the Evanderians lined up in the hall, "Make ready the pyre at once."

Ayleth's heart stopped. She could not believe what she heard, could not make the Dominus's words fit into her brain. Then, with a convulsion of pure terror through every limb, she screamed.

"No! No, you're wrong! It can't be!" Her body bucked, almost against her will but with strength enough that the man kneeling on her back fell to one side and she nearly pulled free of the other two. "No, please! I'm not inborn! Don't do this! *Don't do this!*" She was weeping, retching, half-mad with fright. She hardly knew what she did, what she said.

"Take her back to her room and secure the blood wards," the Phasmatrix Domina said, speaking through the roaring in Ayleth's head. "We will begin the preparations immediately. The execution will take place at dawn."

The Evanderians lifted Ayleth from the ground,

twisting her arms behind her so that she couldn't strike out at her captors. She struggled, but the strength that had surged through her in that first bolt of horror now drained away, leaving her limp and lifeless in their grasps. Her mind whirled, and she craned her neck as they carried her toward the stairs, searching for some sign of help.

Her gaze landed for a mere heartbeat on Terryn's face, deathly pale beneath his low-drawn hood.

CHAPTER 6

FENDREL SAT ON THE EDGE OF THE BED IN THE humble bedchamber he had claimed for himself in Dunloch. As the king's brother, he could have his pick of many fine rooms, but fine rooms did not suit the Black Hood. He was a man of the road, a man weatherworn from hardship and loss. He could never make himself comfortable on silk cushions.

So he sat on the narrow bed, easing the leather bracer off his left arm. He'd tied the fastenings tight against the bandages underneath, and removing that pressure made him grimace in both relief and pain. He rolled back his sleeve, revealing white bandages stained black.

He didn't have much longer.

He faced the truth grimly as he unwrapped the bandages and inspected the three ugly puncture wounds. Black scabs of blood oozed with shade blight, and darkness like ink ran through his veins. It wouldn't be long now before he'd have to choose who would deal him the Gentle Death. It wouldn't be long now before he would be forced to accept his ultimate fate and pass on his legacy.

He hissed, gently pressing a damp cloth against the wounds. Even that slight touch hurt, but Fendrel scarcely felt it. His thoughts tormented him with pain much greater.

Terryn was meant to be his legacy. Terryn was intended to step into his place. The law of Evander forbade venators of the order from siring children; any child produced of a shade-taken parent would necessarily be inborn, an abomination like the girl they would kill in just a few hours.

But when he'd found Terryn in the aftermath of the Battle of Cró Ular, Fendrel had known: Here was the boy he would train up according to the rightness of Evander's law. Here was the man who would someday don the Black Hood in Fendrel's place and stand at the side of the Golden Prince, even as Fendrel had stood at the side of the Chosen King. Here was his son.

But it was all coming undone—

The door to the bedchamber, which Fendrel knew he had locked, burst open, striking the wall and shuddering so hard the hinges threatened to break.

"What have you done, Fendrel?"

Fendrel blinked once, slowly, and drew a long breath. He carefully rolled his sleeve back down to cover the wounds on his arm, fastening it at the wrist. "Terryn. This is not an unexpected visit."

His former apprentice strode into the room, soul seething. No trace of the shade, at least. Even in his distraught state, Terryn was a good venator, keeping tight control over his indwelling spirit. But the power of Terryn's own soul was enough to give lesser men pause.

Fendrel raised his gaze to meet Terryn's. The light of

the setting sun poured through the west window, shining on the lad's dark skin, which had gone deathly gray. The lines of his jaw strained, and his eyes were huge and staring.

"Ayleth is no inborn," he said. "You've plotted to kill her from the start. You've done something. You've rigged the test."

"Is that what you think?" Fendrel asked blandly. "That Domina Esabel is so easily fooled in her craft? You saw her perform the *dachr* test with your own eyes. You saw the girl's soul-tears turn to dust when mixed with *eitr*. You know the truth."

Terryn shook his head wildly. "I know you hate her. I know you would do anything to kill her, though I don't understand why. Does it have something to do with Venatrix di Theldry?"

At that name, Fendrel felt the blood drain from his face. He slapped his leather bracer back onto his left arm, tightening the fastenings until the pain was great enough to drive back rising emotions he dared not face. "Hollis di Theldry will be dealt with according to the law. She has already been summoned to Breçar to account for her actions. She knew the risks of harboring an inborn . . . but training one in the secrets of our order? That is treachery beyond forgiveness, beyond redemption. She will pay the price."

She would face death. More than that, she would face the Haunts. The law of Evander offered no mercy to those who strayed from the path. Hollis would be killed, and her soul, along with that of her shade, would be driven through to that realm of chaos and torment, there to suffer eternally for the evil she accomplished in this world.

It was the will of Evander.

Fendrel stood, looking down into Terryn's ashen face. "It's time you learned, boy," he said, spitting out the last word. "It's time you realized that no feeling of yours—no love, no lust, no longing—has a place in this work of ours." He put a heavy hand on Terryn's shoulder, squeezing tight, his fingers digging into the fabric of his jerkin. "The girl will burn. Be thankful at least that her soul will be saved."

Terryn lowered his gaze. Then, his lip curling back in a vicious snarl, he caught Fendrel by the arm, swung him around, and threw him against the wall. Fendrel's face pressed into the stone, and Terryn, twisting his master's arm painfully back, leaned against him, breathing hard.

"Let her go. Speak to the domina. Put an end to this. Now."

Fendrel's nostrils flared. For an instant, he relaxed in Terryn's grip, just enough that he felt some of the pressure go out of Terryn's hands. Then he flung himself back, putting a foot into the wall to add to his force. Terryn was knocked off balance just enough, and Fendrel whipped around, catching the young man by the throat. With a swinging motion, he hurled Terryn into the wall, holding him fast.

"Is this how you want it all to end, Terryn? Will you die now, a traitor to the cause? You've given me reason enough to kill you where you stand. So answer me, and answer me carefully: Are you Evander's servant? Or are you the slave of this witch-girl? You cannot be both, so which is it, boy?"

Terryn couldn't answer. Fendrel's fingers pressed in too hard, pinching his throat so that he couldn't even draw breath. But the flashing light had gone out from his eyes, replaced by horror. Not horror of Fendrel himself, no . . . This was a much deeper dread.

"Ah. You understand now," Fendrel said. He loosened his hold on Terryn's throat enough that air was no longer obstructed, but kept the young man pinned in place. "You understand the seduction of witches. Dread Odile herself . . . she was once a member of our Order. But she fell into heresy and drew many after her. The poisonous words of a single witch can bring nations to their knees. It has happened before. It will happen again. Don't let yourself be turned, my boy. Don't let yourself stray from what you know is right."

Terryn's eyelids lowered. The vein in his forehead stood out starkly beneath the dark hair falling in his face.

Fendrel let his hand move from Terryn's neck to his shoulder and took a single step back. "Come dawn tomorrow," he said, "the pyre will be lit. Stand with me then. Stand with me and offer up the screams of this inborn witch-girl to the Goddess as penance. The stench of her smoldering corpse will be incense in your nostrils, purging your brain of those lustful thoughts which threaten to lead you astray. Stand with me then, Terryn.

And we'll forget all of this. We will continue on our lifelong mission. We will serve and we will honor the Goddess with our service until our very last breaths."

Terryn trembled beneath Fendrel's hand. With a sudden shake, he pulled away, stepping past his master and moving to the door. Fendrel called out to his retreating back, "You know what you must do."

The young venator paused in the doorway, half turning back but not quite looking Fendrel in the eye. "You're wrong," he said, his voice low, broken. "I don't know anything anymore."

He pulled the door shut behind him, leaving Fendrel once more alone.

The sun set. Night fell.

Soon would come the dawn.

Terryn found a quiet stairwell, part of the network of hidden passages that allowed servants to move through Dunloch without disturbing their royal masters. Most of the servants had abandoned their posts following the attack three nights ago, however, so there was no one to disturb Terryn in the quiet, shadowy space.

He sat ten steps up, beneath a narrow slit of window. Cold air blew in around the poorly fitted glass panes, but he didn't care. He cradled his heavy head in his hands.

Was it possible that he was doubly cursed? Ensorcelled by this beautiful inborn girl, just as Fendrel said? This girl who had been his companion for many weeks now. This girl by whose side he had fought and bled and suffered and triumphed, never realizing what she truly was.

But that was a lie. He'd known all along there was something not right, something dangerous about her.

It must have been her inborn state he'd sensed that made him so uneasy in her presence. His soul had reacted to the wrongness in her very nature. That must be the reason . . . That must be why even looking at her made his blood turn to lava in his veins, made his lungs tighten until he could scarcely draw breath.

He pulled at his hair, gritting his teeth, fighting the anger and the horror and the other, more terrible emotions rising inside him. If he could have pulled his head from his shoulders and dashed it into the stone steps, he would gladly have done so.

As a servant of Evander, he knew the law. If Ayleth was indeed an inborn, as the evidence confirmed, she must die. By fire. It was the only way to save her soul. If he truly . . . He swallowed painfully, his throat thick. If he truly *cared* for her, he'd be the one to light the blaze.

A low moan escaped his lips, and he doubled over where he sat, his eyes squeezed tight. In the darkness inside his head, he saw her again—saw her dancing in a flame-red gown, her shoulders bare, her hair loose and flying, rebelling against the traditional steps of the song and creating her own unique movements, strange and lithe and graceful. Only now, those swirling skirts caught fire, and the blaze engulfed her. Terryn heard her screams as her skin blackened, flaked away—

"There you are."

Terryn started upright, staring without comprehension at the face below him. It took a few breaths before he was able to recognize Kephan entering the stairwell.

"I had to call up my shade to catch a trace of you, you're so well hidden," the venator said, drawing the door shut behind him. He climbed the narrow stair until he stood only a few steps lower than Terryn. He leaned his back against the wall, arms crossed. "The dominus informed us all of the attack the other night," he said. "Of what . . . what happened to you."

Terryn twisted his heavy head to one side, raising dull eyes to meet Kephan's. He could see the question there in the venator's gaze, the question he didn't want to ask. If Terryn's curse was still active after all this time, was Kephan's as well? Despite the ugly scars on their faces, were they both as enthralled to the Warpwitch as ever?

"We'll hunt them down," Kephan said, but without much conviction. "We'll find and kill those witches. There are some impressive hunters in the domina's entourage."

"There won't be any *we*," Terryn growled.

Kephan sighed but didn't argue. He knew as well as Terryn how foolish it would be to risk the two of them going out on the hunt. Not when, in a flash of Anathema magic, they could be instantaneously transformed into deadly enemies.

The silence lasted a little too long, long enough that Terryn wondered why Kephan remained at all. He looked up at the other venator again and caught the man's gaze fixed contemplatively on his face.

"I'm . . . so sorry about di Ferosa," Kephan said.

Terryn looked away again, studying the wall.

"It does make one wonder what Venatrix di Theldry was thinking," he continued. "Taking in an inborn. Training her in the secrets of our order. But then . . ." He shrugged.

Was there a breath of doubt in that unfinished sentenced? A tremulous question suspended in the ether between them?

Terryn's hand moved to his breast, to something tucked out of sight inside his jerkin, and rested there. He ground his teeth until his jaw ached.

"Perhaps," Kephan continued in a musing tone, "she thought if she trained the girl in proper control of her shade, she could be made safe. At least for a time. Put off the necessary death as long as possible. After all, is an impulse of mercy so very wicked?"

Was it mercy that had motivated Hollis di Theldry? Or cowardice. Terryn couldn't say. He had stood in the same position himself only a month ago, when he held Nilly du Bucheron in his arms. And he still didn't know what he would have done if the choice had not been taken from him. He still didn't know if he'd have found the will to do what the law required.

In his secret-most heart, he hoped not.

Kephan reached out and grasped Terryn by the shoulder. "It's dark times we've been born to, my friend. An age of sacrifices."

"Too many sacrifices," Terryn breathed, not intending his words to be overheard. But he'd forgotten about the Feral shade Kephan carried, augmenting his senses. He felt the venator's eyes sharpen their focus.

"Do you think so? Then what will you do? Is one more sacrifice one too many?"

He didn't continue. Silence fell between them. At last, Terryn looked up and saw the question still hovering in Kephan's eyes. What was he asking exactly? Was this an invitation? To . . . what? Revolt? Was Kephan offering to fight for Ayleth? Against Fendrel, against the Phasmatrix Domina, against thirteen other highly skilled venators of the Order . . .

It would be suicide.

Kephan watched him silently for some moments, as

though reading the thoughts passing through Terryn's head. He sighed heavily at last and took a step back down the narrow stairwell. "We all must own our choices, du Balafre," he said. "Even those we are forced to make."

He turned his back on Terryn, heading down the stair. The fading light from the narrow window shone on his coppery hair.

"And what is your choice?" Terryn called to the back of his head. "You wear the red hood as I do, du Tam. After everything, you are still loyal to the Saint."

"Am I?" Kephan turned a swift glance back over his shoulder at Terryn. Then he opened the door at the bottom of the stairwell and stepped out, shutting it behind him. Leaving Terryn alone in the shadows.

CHAPTER 7

BACK IN HER ROOM. HER HORRIBLE, HIDEOUS, HELLISH room.

Ayleth sat on the edge of her bed, her fingers gripping the soft mattress so hard that her nails started to tear through the fabric. Nothing but horror awaited her, nothing but horror filled her head. Flames danced before her vision, and already her skin shuddered with imagined agony that could not come close to the reality in store.

Her hand crept to her waist, to that place where her

Vocos pipes used to hang from a sheath. But they'd taken all her implements and weapons away long ago. Instead, she caught a fistful of her own shirt, right above her heart, and bowed her head. If only she had some means of reaching Laranta! If she could liberate her, let her rise, let her take full possession of their shared body. If only she could speak to her one last time . . .

Inborn. It explained so much.

This was why Hollis had suppressed her memories. Somewhere beyond that webbing spell must be recollections of her life before Hollis found her. Things Hollis did not want her to know about herself for her own safety's sake.

Hollis must have found her on the hunt, realized what she was, and . . . made the insane choice to shelter an inborn child. To train her. To protect her.

And, Haunts-festering-damned fool that she was, she had run away! Right into the arms of the man who would recognize her for what she was and do what Hollis could not. Ayleth closed her eyes, sinking down into her own head. She should have listened to her mistress. She should never have left Gillanluòc.

"*Laranta*," she whispered, straining to catch some trace of her shade. "*Laranta, I'm so sorry. Laranta, come find me.*"

At the far end of their connecting soul tether she felt her shade move, stir. Laranta sensed her distress and wanted to come to her, to offer comfort. But she couldn't. Without her Vocos pipes, Ayleth couldn't hope to summon her. They'd dosed her with *sòm* again, and neither she nor Laranta could penetrate that fog.

Ayleth opened her eyes, returning to the waking world. To this room which suddenly felt small and close. To the darkness of a night that would pass much too quickly. She had to fight the soporific effects of the *sòm,* hold onto her last hours of life. A candle and flints lay on a table nearby, but she didn't have the will to light it. No fire. Not tonight.

Rising from the bed, Ayleth walked as near to the window as she dared. The blood wards had been reactivated, and she knew better than to get too close. She could see nothing down below. Were the Evanderians venturing beyond the barrier spell to gather wood for her pyre? Or would they find sufficient quantity to burn a grown woman here on the island? Were they even now mounding the wood and kindling around a sturdy stake?

It was just as well, she decided, that she could not access Laranta. If she could, she would fight. She knew she would. How could she simply submit to the flames? With Laranta's power coursing through her, she would battle everyone in the yard, and they would be forced to bring her down with poisons, forced to deal the Gentle Death. Then the Haunts would open and drag her to torment.

No.

She'd glimpsed the Haunts. She knew the truth. Evander's law was mercy. Better to die by the flames than to suffer for eternity.

But Laranta . . .

Tears filled Ayleth's eyes, burning on her cheeks as they spilled over. Laranta would be driven to damnation. Alone. Without understanding what had become of the two of them. Believing Ayleth to be her enemy, the one who bound her, who suppressed her with poison. The one who meekly allowed them to be led to their fate.

Ayleth's chest compressed so tightly, she could

scarcely draw breath. Her ears strained to catch any sounds outside that window, sounds of construction, sounds of wood and kindling being gathered. She concentrated so hard that she neglected to listen to nearer sounds and so did not recognize the coming footsteps until they were right outside her door.

Her heart jolted as the door latch turned, the lock clunked. She whirled into a defensive crouch, her breath catching in her throat, her hands clenched into fists. The door opened.

Gerard stepped through.

"Your Highness!" Ayleth gasped. "Is it . . . time?"

Gerard, his face stricken, raised both hands to reassure her. "No, no. No, it's not yet midnight. I demanded they let me speak to you." He looked back over his shoulder to some unseen guard standing without. "Give us some privacy. Please."

A hand moved. Ayleth caught a glimpse of an iron spike and a bracer but otherwise saw nothing more of the Evanderian standing in the shadows. Whoever it was caught the door and drew it firmly shut, leaving her alone in the presence of the Golden Prince.

They stared at one another. Gerard looked like one who had gazed into the Haunts for far too long, so harrowed was the expression on his face.

"Ayleth," he said at last. "I . . . am doing what I can. And I won't stop, I swear."

Ayleth rose from her crouch. She stood tall and put her shoulders back. She would not crumble in the presence of the Golden Prince. She would be brave. She would make him proud.

"You have been a good master," she said in a whisper. It was the most she could manage for fear her voice would break. "You gave me what I wanted: a chance to prove myself."

"You did," Gerard answered. In the darkness of the chamber, with only a sliver of moonlight to illuminate the room, it was difficult to read his expression. Were those tears she saw shining in his eyes? "You have more than proven yourself. You, Ayleth, Venatrix di Ferosa, are a noble soul, a true servant of the Goddess in every respect."

"No." The word came out as a small puff of breath before her lips. "I'm an inborn. Until I am purified, the

Goddess must turn Her face from me."

All in a rush, the courage she had managed to muster failed her. She sank to her knees, not in genuflection but in brokenness. Sobs caught at her throat, and she choked on them, unwilling even now to give them power over her. Both hands pressed to her heart, and every muscle in her face tightened in the effort to push down the swiftly rising hysteria.

Gerard crossed the room, kneeling in front of her. She felt his hand rest on her shoulder. "Tomorrow dawn, I will be there," he said. "Fendrel and the domina won't see me tonight, but I won't let them do this without a fight. I will stand on the pyre myself to stop them. You saved me. More than once. You saved . . . you saved Cerine. Tried to save her. You gave everything you had. You don't deserve this. Inborn or otherwise, I don't care. You don't deserve this."

His words flowed over her, a waterfall of comfort that soaked into the dry, dead soil of her fearful soul. She knew the truth; and by the tone of his voice, she knew he knew it as well. He had no authority over the castra. Only the king himself might sway the domina and dominus from their purpose. But Guardin had already made clear his distrust of Ayleth.

She shuddered, then forced her head up to meet the prince's earnest gaze. "It has been my honor to serve you. You will be a mighty king."

His face twisted with pain at her words. Two tears escaped, spilling down his too-beautiful face. And what a wonder that was! What a wonder that the Goddess's prophesied Golden Prince would gaze on her with such compassion. Would care for her. Would mourn her, even. It was enough to bring the faintest of smiles to her lips.

Gerard stood abruptly. "I must go," he said roughly. "I'll speak to my father. I'll make him see reason."

Ayleth sat back on her heels, arms wrapped around her middle, and tilted her face up to him. She didn't say anything at first, merely looked. Slowly, her brow constricted into a frown. The prince turned to the door, reaching his hand to the latch. But he paused when Ayleth said, "It's strange. I was told . . . I was told you would kill me."

"What?" He turned and looked back down at her, his eyes bright in the moonlight. "What did you say?"

"The little Seer." Ayleth tilted her head as she studied him. "Nilly du Bucheron, the inborn child. She gave me a vision. I saw you with your sword drawn. You were sad, but you didn't hesitate. You cut off my head and . . . I was grateful." Her frown deepened, and she averted her gaze from the prince's confused face, studying the floor instead. "I would have preferred that death, I think."

Silence lingered too long. At last, without a word, the prince opened the door and stepped out, drawing it shut behind him. Ayleth heard a bolt drop, but it didn't matter. Bolted or otherwise, the blood wards would never let her through.

She remained kneeling on that hard, cold floor for she could not guess how long. The minutes seemed to fly by too fast and simultaneously creep along in an eternity of terror-filled waiting. She almost longed for the dawn and the end. But such an end! How could she face it?

At some point she rose and drifted to the bed, where she lay down and stared at the canopy overhead. A recent memory came to her out of nowhere, a memory of lying here, not so many nights ago, wracked with pain from the aftereffects of *oblivis* poisoning. Someone had pulled the spindly chair close to her bedside that night. Someone whose face she could not see, but who had held her hand throughout the long, dreadful hours. Someone . . . someone . . .

Would he be there at dawn along with the prince? Would he also fight for her? She knew better than to hope. He would remain silent, just as he had in the presence of the Phasmatrix Domina. He would stand alongside the Venator Dominus, a true Evanderian through and through.

Now that he knew what she was, could he even bear to look at her?

Tears steadily poured down her cheeks. She closed her eyes tight. How she longed for Gillanluòc! How she longed for Hollis, for Chestibor, for the wild, lonely roads in the mountains of Drauval Borough. How she longed to go back and undo her mistakes, to heed Hollis's commands, to stay quietly where she belonged, far from Dunloch and the intrigues of the kingdom. Hollis had been trying to protect her. Hollis knew what she was, knew that the minute she engaged with the castra, her secret would be discovered. And Hollis herself? Surely she would be hunted down as well. The castra would not show mercy—

A *thunk* rattled the wall.

Then a heavy sound of collapse. Like a body falling.

Ayleth opened her eyes and sat up in the bed, staring at the door. Had she imagined those sounds? The heavy bolt creaked as it lifted, and the door latch moved. Ayleth sprang to her feet, one hand gripping the post of her bed for support as the door swung open and a figure stepped inside.

"Terryn!"

His cloak fluttered like wings behind him as he turned and swiftly shut the door. Then he faced her, holding out an armload of items that her confused mind could not at first recognize. Terryn crossed the room and laid them out on her bed, one at a time. Her pipes. Her scorpiona. Her poisons.

She raised her gaze and met those ice-cold eyes beneath the low-pulled hood. "What are you doing?" she demanded.

"What do you think?" His dark-as-midnight voice rumbled in her gut. He reached inside his cloak and produced a faceted crystal flask. "This first," he said, tossing it to her. She caught it and lifted it to eye level. Her jaw hung stupidly open. "Drink it," Terryn said. "It's the antidote to the *sòm*. You've got to be sharp if we're to have a Haunts-damned prayer."

Her fingers trembled so hard she almost dropped the flask as she pulled out the stopper. Tilting back her head, she drained the contents in a gulp, trusting that the dose was correct. It burned on the way down. She coughed and gagged but would not let herself heave it up. Almost at once she felt its effects: The *sòm* melted away.

Deep down inside her, Laranta stirred.

Terryn caught up her Vocos pipes, drawing them from their sheath. "Summon your shade," he said. "As much of its power as you dare. Go on."

Ayleth took the pipes, but rather than lifting them to her lips, she reached out her other hand and gripped Terryn by the elbow. "What is this? You don't actually think you can break me out of here."

"No," he answered. "But I can sure as Haunts try."

"You . . . you'll be ruined." She squeezed his arm tightly, a sudden frenzy of hope and fear roiling in her head like a storm. "They'll catch you and they'll kill you. They'll damn your soul with mine. You can't do this. You can't! You've got to—"

Terryn caught her by the back of her head, his fingers snarled in her hair, digging into her skull. She gasped as he yanked her toward him, and for a heartbeat his eyes flared brilliantly before her vision and his breath was hot on her face.

Then his mouth pressed hard against hers. All thought fled her mind, all reason, all fear. Everything vanished in a roar of confusion and heat, a bolt of lightning that shot straight to her core and flared through every limb. She tensed, ready to yank herself free.

But instead, she let go of his arm and grabbed him by his neck, pulling him closer, pressing her body into his. His other arm wrapped around her, and for an instant of pulsing power so heady it made her stronger even than when her shade's might surged through her limbs, Ayleth knew what it was to be fully alive.

The instant passed. He broke away.

"Now move," he growled, his lips hovering just above hers.

CHAPTER 8

GERARD STOOD OUSTSIDE HIS FATHER'S DOOR, A CANDLE held high in one hand. The echoes of his knock faded away, answered only with silence. The prince ground his teeth, hissing a sharp breath.

"Father," he called, not caring whether any listening ears behind doors or around corners overheard him. "Father, let me in. We have to talk."

Still no answer. Gerard put his ear to the door and could swear he heard footsteps pacing inside. His father had not shown his face since the arrival of the Evander-ians, not even to greet the Phasmatrix Domina. When Gerard collared one of the king's servants, the poor man had shaken his head and said Guardin had ordered everyone from his chambers and would admit no one.

Gerard scowled at the door. He tried the latch again, but it would not yield. "Please, Father," he urged, lowering his voice slightly. "You've got to let me in. You can't keep me in the dark. Not over this. If there is some reason why Ayleth must die, you have to tell me."

No answer. And really, what did Gerard expect? Being an inborn was reason enough for anyone to die according to Evander's laws. As prince, Gerard had studied the writings of the Saint and knew as much as anyone could who was not a member of the order. He understood the theory, understood the logic: Burn the body to save the soul.

But now . . . now that he knew how willing the Saint had been to twist his interpretations of sacred text . . . In light of that knowledge, how could he accept any Evanderian law at face value? The whole teaching was compromised. Dangerous.

"Evil," Gerard whispered. The shadows in the corridor seemed to draw in closer, deeper, ready to devour him and the small light of his candle. Drawing breath was difficult, as though the air itself had turned to poisonous fumes.

Gerard turned his back on his father's door and slumped against it. His mind churned, struggling to wade through the lies, struggling to make sense of this new reality. Struggling to think of something, *anything* he might try to save his loyal venatrix. Briefly his thoughts flitted to Terryn. Would he find an ally there? Would Terryn dare to stand against Fendrel, against the will of the castra itself? Terryn's feelings for Ayleth ran deeper than mere admiration. But how much deeper?

No. He shook his head, rubbing a hand down his tired face. It wasn't worth considering. To draw Terryn in on this would be to risk his life as well. Much as it pained Gerard to think of Ayleth's execution, the idea of losing Terryn was a hundred times worse. How could he face this world alone? He closed his eyes, feeling the hopelessness of his situation press down on his shoulders, ready to crush him.

"Your Highness?"

Gerard cringed at the sound of his chancellor's voice. Yves was the last person he wanted to speak to just now. But he pulled himself upright and lifted his lantern to shine on a care-lined face. Yves's skin was very pale in the glow, his eyes rounded with terror that never seemed to leave him these days. "Yes, what is it?" Gerard demanded, not trying to disguise the impatience in his voice.

"It's the gate." Yves twisted his hands nervously, his beard trembling with each word. "Captain Achard just sent word: The venatrix has returned."

"What venatrix?" Gerard asked, frowning. "You mean . . . Everild? Venatrix di Lamaury?"

Yves nodded and licked his dry lips. "There's more. It would seem the venatrix has been wounded and . . . and . . ."

"What, man? Speak up!"

"And Lady Cerine is with her."

Gerard arrived breathless across the bridge, the cold night

air knifing down into his lungs. Torches illuminated the world around the gate, and at least six guardsmen on duty milled about on ground level with more in the flanking towers above.

One of their number, Captain Achard, separated from the rest. "Your Highness," he began.

Gerard cut him off. "Show me!"

The captain stepped back and indicated the spy slot in the heavy gate doors. It was already drawn back, and Gerard, still panting hard from his run, sprang up to it and peered out.

He could not detect the barrier spell he had been told surrounded Dunloch. No one without shade powers could. So it was strange and terrible to see the slim form pressed up against the invisible barrier, slapping her hands futilely, like she would against a solid, invisible wall. Moonlight shone down on her face.

Gerard recognized her at once. "Cerine!"

She couldn't hear him. The barrier allowed sound to travel in but no sound to pass out. He slammed a fist against the gate, then turned to the captain behind him. "Why do you not open to her?"

"We are under orders from the Black Hood," Achard replied. "We're not to open the gate to anyone. Even if we did, she cannot pass through the . . . the magic."

"Has anyone sent word to the Black Hood?"

"Yes, Your Highness. We expect him at any moment."

Growling inarticulately, Gerard turned back to the spy slot. He'd thought he would never see her again. When the Phantomwitch *evanesced* out of Dunloch, taking Cerine, he hadn't dared to believe . . . But she was alive! And from what the moonlight revealed, unwounded. Her wedding gown was in tatters and her face ravaged by terror, but she was alive.

"Cerine," he whispered again.

Her voice cried out, carrying through the barrier. "She tried to save me! She tried to save me!"

Only then did Gerard remember that Chancellor Yves said Venatrix Everild had returned as well. Where was she? Gazing out beyond Cerine's desperate gestures, he saw something fallen to the ground just behind her. A body.

"Stand aside!"

His uncle's sharp voice shot through Gerard like a

bolt. He leapt back from the gate, turning to meet the approaching figure of the Venator Dominus. "It's Cerine," he said, his own voice harsh with fear.

"So they say," Fendrel answered, shouldering Gerard aside to peer through the spy slot himself. Gerard felt he would burst with mounting impatience. He wanted to grab his uncle's shoulder, to shake him, force him to open the gate and his song spell. But Fendrel was not to be hurried.

"Captain Achard, what did you see of their approach?" he demanded, still gazing out, his eyes intent.

The captain drew in behind them, standing close to Gerard. "Spotters in the flank towers spied them coming through the trees. The lady seemed to be supporting Venatrix Everild up until they reached the barrier. Then the venatrix fell and has not moved since. We saw no wounds."

Fendrel squinted, no doubt using his shadow sight, which wasn't limited by the shadows of night. He didn't speak, and his face betrayed nothing save for a swift flaring of his nostrils.

Cerine's voice carried again through the darkness: "She

tried to save me! She tried to save me!"

"Uncle," Gerard said, taking hold of Fendrel's arm, "you've got to bring them in. The witches might come at any moment." The Phantomwitch might have an anchor planted somewhere near, enabling her to *evanesce* anywhere in the vicinity. She could appear behind Cerine in a heartbeat and drag her away, never to be recovered.

Fendrel drew back from the spy slot, his face so deeply lined that he appeared much older than his years. "It could be a trap."

Gerard took a step closer to his uncle. "Or it could be that Everild risked everything to bring back Cerine, and it will all be for nothing when the witches catch up with them."

He could see that Fendrel felt much the same urgency. Everild was his right-hand lieutenant, after all, his trusted comrade through many hunts, many battles. She had served at his side these eight years at least.

"She might be alive," Gerard urged. "She might be bleeding out."

Fendrel rounded on his nephew, his lips twisted back from his teeth, which gleamed in the torchlight. "Don't try to force my hand, boy. I know what that girl means to you. But I know better than you what Inren and Ylaire are capable of."

Gerard felt the blood drain from his face. He drew back, his hands clenching into fists. He may be prince, but he had no power here. He could do nothing but stand firm, silently urging Fendrel to act, to try.

Fendrel backed away from the gate, looking up at its great height. His hand moved to the Vocos pipes on his belt. "Open it," he commanded. "I will go in closer. And you"—his eyes flashed to meet Gerard's again—"will stand back."

Gerard nodded despite the protests on his tongue. The guards hastened to obey the Venator Dominus, and the heavy gate creaked open, just enough to let a man through. Fendrel stepped into the road leading up to the gate, his Vocos out and gripped in his right fist. Gerard drew as near to the opening as he dared without directly disobeying his uncle's command. He watched as Fendrel approached the invisible barrier.

Cerine saw him coming. She drew back several paces, her hands falling to her sides, her eyes huge and glistening with tears. Then she threw herself forward, pounding at the barrier with both fists. "She tried to save me!" she screamed. "She tried! She tried!"

Fendrel pointed. Cerine could not hear him speak through the barrier, but she obeyed his gesture, backing away until she stood behind the fallen body on the road. Gerard, his angle improved, now saw Venatrix Everild's face, still and pale in the moonlight, her broken nose wrapped in bandages, her red hood thrown back over her shoulders.

Fendrel seemed to be studying what he could of both the fallen venatrix and Cerine through the barrier. Gerard could not detect any rise or fall of Everild's chest. The men had seen her walk to the gate, so she was alive not long ago. She might still be saved if Fendrel would only hurry.

Again Gerard's gaze lifted to Cerine standing several paces beyond the venatrix. Her hands were folded, her head bent. She looked as patient as a stone saint in a chapel, revealing none of the desperation with which she had cried out only moments ago.

At last, Fendrel raised his pipes. Gerard strained his

ears, though he knew it was futile. The music played on that instrument could not be perceived by mortal senses; it sounded in a realm of spirit beyond Gerard's reach or awareness. Neither could he discern the effect that song had on the barrier spell, though he saw by the way Fendrel swayed that it took effort for his uncle to work this strange magic of his.

"Come on," Gerard breathed. "Come on, come on."

Suddenly, Fendrel lowered the pipes and turned to call back over his shoulder, "Captain Achard, send one of your men."

Gerard lurched forward a single step, but a hand on his shoulder held him fast. Achard's voice barked just behind him: "You. Go." That firm grip pulled Gerard aside, making room for one of the guards to hasten through.

Shaking off the captain's hold, Gerard returned to the opening, determined to see what he could. Achard hovered at his back, ready to restrain the prince again if he must.

The guard hurried to Fendrel's side. Gerard could just hear his uncle's voice rumble, "Stay close to me. Take the lady and hurry back inside. We don't know how long we have."

The guard nodded and, at a word from the Venator Dominus, shot out down the road, passing through where the barrier had once stood. Fendrel followed at his heels, knelt beside Everild's body, and hauled the sturdy venatrix up and over his shoulder. The guard scooped up Lady Cerine, and within moments, both of them hurried back toward the gate. Fendrel stopped before reaching it, set down the venatrix, and turned to use his Detrudos pipes to once more close off the spell. But the guard carried Lady Cerine back to the gate, her arms wrapped around his neck.

Captain Achard was not swift enough to stop his prince this time. Gerard sprang through the gate and met the guard with arms outstretched to relieve him of his burden. "Cerine! Cerine, are you all right?" he cried.

She moaned in his grasp, struggling. He quickly set her down on her feet and supported her by the elbows. Her stained face raised to his, her eyes so round, he could see the whites ringing her pale blue irises. "She tried to save me!" she cried, choking on the words so hard that she doubled over, her body shuddering as though she would vomit. Gerard touched the back of her head. He felt utterly helpless and utterly relieved all at once.

Cerine recovered herself and stood upright again, clutching Gerard by the arm. "She tried to save me," she said, her voice calmer this time. "She . . . tried . . ."

"I know. I know, Cerine," Gerard said, putting his arm around her, a familiarity he would never have dared attempt even a few days ago. "Come. Let me help you inside. Can you walk?"

She shook her head vigorously but leaned heavily on his arm as he led her out from among the guards, away from the gate, and back to the bridge. Her breath came in short, sharp gasps, and she kept shaking her head. "She tried. She tried. She tried. She tried."

The poor girl was lost in hysteria. Whatever her ordeal had been, she certainly wasn't capable of discussing it now. "It's all right," Gerard murmured gently. "You're safe now. You're safe in Dunloch. Nothing can penetrate Fendrel's barrier, I swear. Not even the Witchwood gets through his spells! You're safe. They can't reach you anymore."

Cerine whimpered. Her whole body sagged as though all the strength went out from it in a rush. Realizing she was about to faint, Gerard caught her up behind her shoulders and knees, holding her close. She was such a delicate little thing, carrying her was hardly more difficult than carrying a child. She shook her head again, tears falling from her eyes, but wrapped her arms around his neck and sank her face into his neck and shoulder. She was alive. Alive! And in his arms, safe and sound.

Perhaps the Goddess was still merciful after all.

"Let me get you inside," Gerard said.

CHAPTER 9

"WHAT THE HAUNTS WAS THAT?"

Ayleth hurled the words at Terryn's back as he strode across the room to the chamber door. He didn't answer, merely opened the door and vanished outside. "Terryn!" she called after him in a tight whisper that was as loud as she dared under the circumstances.

What in the Goddess's own Haunts-damn world did he think he was doing? He must be out of his mind. She was due to die in hours . . . to be burned alive at the stake, for festering-Haunt's sake! Her world had just crashed around her, a world made up of Hollis's lies and her own stupid beliefs, all stripped away to nothing, and he had the nerve to go and do something like . . . like *that*.

"Terryn!" she hissed again and stomped as close to the door as she could before the ugly prickling of the blood wards drove her back. "Terryn, you can't just *leave!* What in the Haunts do you expect me to— Whoa." She backed away rapidly as Terryn reappeared in the doorway, moving awkwardly as he dragged a body into the room. A body wearing a red hood. With a dart of poison still stuck in his throat.

"Who is that?" Ayleth asked, staring stupidly as Terryn propped the man against the wall.

"Venator du Gontier," Terryn answered, folding the man's hands demurely in his lap. "Your guard for the night." He cast a glance over his shoulder. "Why haven't you called up your shade?"

Ayleth couldn't speak. Her brain fogged over as though drugged with more *sòm*. She couldn't take her eyes off that dart in du Gontier's neck. Terryn had taken down a fellow venator, one of his brethren. With Evanderian poison.

He was a dead man.

"Venatrix!"

Terryn's sharp voice snapped her back into the moment, and Ayleth tore her gaze away from the inert venator. "It doesn't matter," she said. "With or without my shade, I can't get through the door. I can't even get near it."

"That's why I need you to call up your shade," Terryn said, reaching inside the front of his jerkin. With a rapid shake and a flourish, he whipped out a long rag stained with something dark. Ayleth stared at it, uncertain what it was she saw. Then she realized: blood. Shade-blighted, blackened blood. Fendrel's blood. How Terryn had come by such a thing, she couldn't begin to guess, but it was exactly what she needed. Exactly what Laranta needed.

Realizing Terryn had pressed her Vocos into her hands, she snapped the pipes into position and put them to her lips. With a fleeting prayer to the Goddess that no venators with ascendant shades were close enough to hear, she began to play the Song of Summoning. Her hands shook, and she wove the first variation too quickly, stumbling over the notes. Laranta didn't respond.

Though impatience roared in her veins, Ayleth drew a deep breath and closed her eyes. She let the spell song flow through her, then plunged down with it into the realm of her mind, stepping in spirit back into the dark shadows of the pine forest.

She was naked again, as she always was when she walked in this realm. The Summoning melody swirled around her, moving through the pines like a breeze. Ayleth cupped her hands around her mouth and called, "*Laranta, come to me! Please!*"

Laranta stirred, deep in the trees, beyond Ayleth's sight.

"*Laranta, I'm sorry. I never should have used the iron poison on you. I never should have bound you at all! You've always trusted me, always helped me, always—*"

Her voice broke, and in the mortal world she struggled to sustain the song.

"*Please,*" she continued, no longer shouting into the trees. It didn't matter, not here. In her own mind, only she and Laranta existed. She could shout, she could whisper, she could say nothing at all. Laranta would know. Laranta always knew.

"*I swear.*" She bowed her head, pressing her hands to her heart, "*I swear, Laranta . . . I will never bind you again.*"

The shadows moved. Ayleth felt the shift without looking. The darkness came together into shape and form, and the massive head of her wolf shade hovered mere inches from her face.

Mistress, Laranta said. *I help?*

Ayleth gasped. In the mortal world, her hands ceased playing the pipes, not even bothering to resolve the melody of the spell song. Her mental image of herself wrapped bare arms around the wolf's dark neck, which was like trying to hug a cloud of smoke. Laranta shook her head, embarrassed, and dissipated entirely. But it didn't matter. She was back, she was near.

Nothing but fire would ever part them again.

Ayleth opened her eyes, leaving behind the pine forest, and returned to the hateful prison bedchamber. Terryn watched her, his face a study, the scar on his right cheek standing out starkly in the moonlight. Now, with Laranta risen inside her, Ayleth could study him with shadow sight and see how his own shade's powers glimmered on the edges of his soul. He must have unbound more of his shade from its suppressing songs than was his habit. She could feel how the binding spells strained to keep the spirit contained.

Terryn risked more than the wrath of the castra to come to her.

"Are you in control?" he demanded, his voice dire with disbelief. He knew that she had not finished the spell song, that she had placed no restraints on her shade.

"I am," Ayleth answered with confidence. "We are ready."

Terryn nodded. He had little choice but to believe her despite everything his training had taught him. He had poisoned a fellow venator. He was no better than a heretic himself now.

He held out the bloodied rag to Ayleth, who took it at once. "*Laranta*," she spoke inside her head. "*Come.*" Her shade poured out from her mind in a stream of darkness, manifesting before her vision in the shape of a wolf. Terryn could not see her, but he sensed her and drew back half a step. Ayleth ignored him and held the rag up to her shade's nose.

"*There's a curse on the door,*" she said. "*A blood-curse, anchored with my blood and the blood of this man. Can you find the anchor?*"

Laranta sniffed at the rags, her eyes bright and interested. Then she turned and padded over to the door, passing through Terryn on her way. He shivered and pulled even farther back. Ayleth followed her shade, studying the intricate weave of curse webbing that blocked her from approaching the doorway. She'd not been able to see it before, with Laranta suppressed. Terryn might not be able to see it at all, even with his shade called up, for it was a ward set for her and her alone.

But all curses had to be anchored somewhere; otherwise, they simply dissipated into nothing.

Laranta approached the spell webbing but yipped and jumped back when she came too close. Apparently the ward was strong enough to affect shades as well as mortals. "*It's all right, Laranta,*" Ayleth said, though her heartbeat quickened. "*Find the anchor. That's all you have to do. Just find the anchor.*"

I smell it, Laranta growled, her eyes bright. *I smell it in the floor. Underneath.* She fixed her gaze on the spot, and Ayleth, using her shadow sight, looked as well. There she could see where all the complex, winding, woven threads of spell song sank down into a single floorboard.

"There!" she said, pointing it out to Terryn. "There, that board."

Terryn sprang into action at once. He pulled his knife from its sheath and pried at the board. It came loose more easily than one might expect—probably because it had been pulled up recently by Fendrel when he planted the curse anchor. Sure enough, when Terryn slid the board up into his hands, Ayleth could see the stain of a bloody handprint—Fendrel's, presumably, used to seal the anchor in place.

She nodded grimly. "Destroy it."

Terryn held the board between his hands. Suddenly, light flared up in the veins of his arms, so bright it shone right through his sleeves and leather bracers. It pulsed in a shimmering stream of power, out through his fingertips and into the board, which sizzled, burned, and disintegrated into a pile of ash.

The curse broke.

Ayleth gasped in relief and took one lunging step forward. Terryn sprang up before she could take a second and put out a still-glowing hand to stop her, wincing with obvious pain. "Get your weapons," he said, biting out the words. "Put on your hood."

Ayleth nodded her understanding and returned to the bedside. Her best bet was to disguise herself as what she was, or what she had been: a venatrix. With all the Evanderians come to Dunloch that day, she might be able to pass through their midst undetected. If she was extraordinarily lucky.

She pulled on the jerkin, donned the quivers of poisons, and fastened her scorpiona onto her right wrist. Her hand hovered momentarily over the left bracer with the spike. To make her uniform complete, she should wear it, but . . . no. Never again. She would hide her left arm under her cloak if she had to.

In truth, she knew the disguise wasn't going to be enough. While mortal eyes might be deceived by the outward uniform, and the hood could cover her face, she couldn't disguise the shade inside her. The shades of the venators and venatrices now walking the halls of Dunloch would recognize a stranger in their midst. If they were well trained, well under the control of their masters, they would sound an alert.

But if they were suppressed just enough—or if they hated their masters enough to resist control—they might let her go. They might.

Ayleth buckled the belt holding the sheaths for the Vocos and Detrudos pipes. More tools she would never use again, but she would wear them for show at least. *"Laranta,"* she spoke inside herself, *"you need to go low. Be as quiet and small as you can. Don't attract attention. Do you understand me?"*

Her wolf shade streamed back into her mind and collapsed down into a small, crouching shape in the center of the pine forest. *I am small, Mistress,* she said. *Very small.*

Probably not small enough. Laranta was a potent spirit, brimming with power and presence. But she was obedient, and as long as she made no sudden moves, perhaps no other shade would notice her.

Ayleth pulled her hood over her head and onto her shoulders, drawing it up to cover her straggling hair. Only then did she turn and face Terryn again. He no longer brimmed with shade magic. His face was strained, the ugly scar standing out stark against the pallor of his cheek. But he had mastered the power inside him. For now.

He met her gaze for two breaths. Then, without a word, he stepped out into the passage. Ayleth had little choice but to follow him.

What a relief it was to cross that threshold with no wards knifing at her very soul! Once through, she pulled the door shut behind her. No doubt the household of Dunloch had been forbidden to come anywhere near this room, but if anyone should happen to look down the passage, they shouldn't see anything amiss. Other than the lack of a guard, perhaps.

She followed swiftly in Terryn's footsteps. Every floorboard seemed to creak with its own clamorous tune, but that may be only the imagining of her jumping nerves. "I hope you have a plan," she whispered, the words scarcely audible, her voice was so low.

Terryn answered through tense lips, "Yes. Get out of Dunloch alive."

He proceeded several paces down the passage, but

Ayleth caught him by the sleeve. "We can't just walk out the front door." She nodded to one of the other bedchambers on their left. All the chambers in this wing were presumably empty. Who would want to bed down so near to a condemned inborn's prison cell? "We're safer going through a window. These aren't warded."

Terryn looked as though he would protest. He lacked her experience scaling the walls of Dunloch keep. But he nodded once and reached for the latch of the nearest door. Opening it quietly, he peered inside. "Empty," he whispered, and opened the door wider, stepping through. Ayleth moved to follow him.

Laranta's voice exploded suddenly in her ear: *Shade, Mistress! Shade, shade, shade!*

CHAPTER 10

CHANCELLOR YVES SENT STRONG MANSERVANTS OUT to relieve the prince of his burden before he reached the doors of the keep, but Gerard refused to let Cerine go. "Lay a fire in her room," he barked to one man, and to another, "Bring food and blankets and fresh clothes."

Cerine was icy cold in his arms and trembling like a leaf. She was in shock. *Evanescing* in the clutches of the witch was bad enough, but who knew what other horrors she had endured at the hands of Inren and Ylaire over the last few days?

He didn't wait for Fendrel to follow, though he spared a fleeting prayer for Venatrix Everild, that the Goddess would show her mercy. She must have undergone a great deal to bring Cerine home, and she may have already paid with her life.

"She tried to save me," Cerine whimpered again as Gerard carried her up the porch steps toward the open front doors. She raised her head from his shoulder and looked around. With a little moan, she bucked hard in his gasp, writhing so that he almost dropped her. She opened her mouth and uttered a wordless scream.

"Cerine, it's all right," Gerard said, careful to keep his voice calm. She clung to his shoulders, shivering violently. "You're safe now. You're safe, Cerine. I've got you."

Chancellor Yves stared at them as though they were both possessed, and the servants withdrew several paces, their faces white with dread. No one wanted to get too close to a witch's captive. Who could say how much shade taint such an unfortunate person might carry with them?

Gerard adjusted his grip on Cerine. He didn't care

what the servants thought, what they feared. He wasn't going to let her go, not now that he had her back. He would never let her go again. "Let me get you to your rooms," he said. "You need to get warm."

She whimpered and let her head droop again as they crossed the threshold into the entrance hall. She made no other sound or protest as he hurried across to the broad stairs. His own urgency gave him strength, and she was such a light burden. He bore her up to the second-floor wing where her rooms waited, empty since the morning after her capture.

A servant had managed to strike a light on the hearth before Gerard entered. Others put out food and fresh blankets. Gerard carried Cerine to the bed and laid her down carefully, resting her head on the cushion. She shivered, clutching at the rags of her wedding gown, her head shaking back and forth.

"She tried to save me. She tried to save me. She tried to save me."

"Hush, hush," Gerard murmured, stroking her forehead. His eyes could not seem to take in enough of her face, wan and fear-stricken though it was. Was she truly here? Or was this all nothing more than a desperate dream?

Her hands flailed suddenly, drawing his attention to the raw wounds on her wrists. The witches had bound her, had drawn the rough cords much too tight, biting into her flesh. "Water. And a cloth," Gerard ordered, and a servant hastened to obey. While he waited, Gerard took Cerine's hands in his, clasping them gently but firmly so that she couldn't accidently strike herself. "Cerine, darling. Hush now. You're safe; you're safe."

She sat bolt upright in the bed, clutching his hands so tight, he thought the bones of his fingers might well break. Staring into his face, she shouted with enough volume that anyone in the west wing of the castle must have heard, "*She tried to save me!*"

Gerard tried to free his hands, but she wouldn't let him go, not even when he stood up. He almost pulled her right out of the bed, so fierce was her grip on him. "*She tried to save me!*" she screamed again and again. "*She tried to save me!*"

"Cerine, please! Stop!"

A pounding of footsteps behind him, and Fendrel

burst into the room. "Let go of her, Gerard," he said, lifting his scorpiona armed with a dart and aiming it at Cerine's chest.

Instinct surged through his body, and Gerard jumped between his uncle and Cerine, who still clutched his hands. "What are you doing?" he cried.

"Step back," Fendrel growled. His firing arm shook, and he brought his left arm up to steady it. "Everild's been dead. *For hours.*"

Gerard gaped. He didn't understand. "That's impossible! It's not been an hour since the guards saw her and Cerine walking . . ."

His voice trailed away to nothing. He turned from his uncle to look down at Cerine. She was sobbing now, tears streaming down her face as she continued to wail that same phrase over and over. And suddenly Gerard realized what she'd been saying.

Tried. *Tried.*

Everild didn't succeed. She didn't save Cerine.

He stared into the face of the woman he loved. And he watched as she suddenly doubled up, her whole body spasming, heaving. Her throat strained, and her face turned purple as she choked and gagged. She leaned over the side of the bed, and everything poured out, all the contents of her stomach. Gerard leaped back . . . and watched a faceted black stone roll across the floor.

Fendrel sprang to Gerard's side, grabbed him by the shoulders, and yanked him back behind him. Cerine crumpled up on her side, sobbing, her fingernails tearing through the short hair on her scalp, leaving lines of blood.

"It's too late," Fendrel said. "The anchor is activated. The witches are in Dunloch."

CHAPTER III

"WHAT'S WRONG?" TERRYN PEERED BACK AT AYLETH through the open door of the chamber he had just entered.

Ayleth backed into the center of the passage, away from the door. Part of her mind urged her to hurry after Terryn, to make their escape out the chamber window. But Laranta's wild voice in her mind continued to warn, *Shade! Shade! Shade!*

Someone was near. Someone was close. A venator?

Had her escape from her room been discovered already?

"*Laranta,*" she spoke in her mind, "*give me your—*"

Something struck her between the shoulders, knocked her clean off her feet. She hit the ground hard, turning her face only at the last moment to avoid breaking her nose. Laranta's power shot through her limbs, and she tucked into a roll before the whole of her body had landed. The second blow struck her in the ribcage. She gasped, the breath knocked out of her, and landed hard on her shoulder.

"*Laranta!*" she cried.

Her wolf shade roared in her head. A burst of unnatural strength shooting through every limb, Ayleth lashed out with one hand and caught a booted foot before another kick could land. With a vicious twist, she yanked her attacker off balance. A body crashed to the floor beside her. She saw it fall. But it made no sound as it landed.

No time to think of that. No time to wonder why Terryn had not leapt in to help her. She was up at once, ignoring the pain in her ribs and back, throwing herself on top of that dark figure, her hands reaching for the throat. She caught a glimpse of a strange man's bearded face, she felt the tensing of his neck under her fingers. Her fist drew back for the first strike—but hit the floor where his head should have been.

Ayleth swallowed a yelp of pain. But Laranta's power was too ascendant for her to pause even for a breath. She leapt to her feet, searching for some sign of her attacker, but the hall was empty.

Grunting, muffled sounds came from the open chamber. Ayleth sprang to the door. Had her attacker somehow slipped out of her hold and gone after Terryn instead?

No, not one attacker. Two men grappled with Terryn, slammed him into the wall, knocked over furniture. Streaks of light shot up his arms, his shade power building to fight them off. But that power, once turned loose, might be more dangerous than the attackers themselves.

Ayleth launched into the room. She snatched one of the men by his neck and the back of his shirt. With Laranta's strength, she swung him like a straw doll, ramming him face-first into the wall, hard enough to knock him unconscious. Hard enough to kill.

But he dissipated in her hands, like vapors. And suddenly, there were two of him, one on each side of her, grabbing her arms.

"Haunts!" she cursed, and flung herself backwards, attempting to yank herself free. They held on, but she pulled them both off their feet. They wrenched her arms, but she wrenched back, swinging them into one another.

They broke into dust and smoke as they connected. And reformed as three.

They turned and looked at her, craning their necks in sequence. The same man, three times over, his teeth flashing in a smile through what she realized wasn't a beard at all but a hideous fungus covering his jaw and neck. The rest of his face was shadowed by a blood-red hood.

"Get down!"

Terryn's voice. She cast a wild glance back over her shoulder and saw him braced with a man clinging to his back and another wrapped around his waist. One of them got an arm around his neck. But Terryn's upraised arm aimed at the three men in front of Ayleth. Blinding light gathered in his palm.

She threw herself to the ground before the brilliance of the light shot into her foes. Their mirrored bodies flared up like torches of pure white fire then burst and scattered in the air. This time they did not reform.

Ayleth, scrambling on the floor, whirled and lunged at one of the men holding onto Terryn. She had to discern what kind of shade this man was using that could multiply its host at will. She'd never encountered anything like this power, and didn't know what poison to use. She yanked the man off of Terryn's waist, and Terryn doubled up, hauling the man on his back over his head and onto the floor. Again, the body made no sound as it struck, merely vanished in a cloud of dark vapors.

Terryn, rubbing at his neck, rasped to Ayleth, "Hold him!" His hand moved to the quivers of poisons across his chest.

Ayleth twisted the man's arms behind him, forcing him down to his knees. She pressed one foot into the small of his back so that he couldn't move. Terryn slipped a dart from its quiver, strode toward the man, and plunged it into his neck.

The man broke and vanished, slipping out of Ayleth's grip. The dart fell uselessly to the floor.

"No, no, no!" Ayleth swiped at the vapors, but it was no use. She turned this way and that, expecting the man to reappear at any moment, or several of him at once. But nothing came. The room was empty.

"What was that?" Ayleth demanded in an urgent whisper, turning to Terryn. Then she gasped, her eyes widening still more. Light still pulsed in the veins of his arms, mounting faster and brighter with every beat of his heart. His shade was rising, too fast, too fast! If he did nothing, it would surely tear his soul right out of his body and take full ascendancy.

Ayleth saw his right hand reach for the iron spike on his left bracer. "Don't!" she cried. She reached out and caught his hand. "You'll need your shade's powers! Don't suppress it now!"

His eyes seemed to vibrate in their sockets with the intensity of pain and power coursing through him. When he closed them, more light burned through the lids. He bowed his head, struggling against the swelling magic inside, his lips twisted back from his clenched teeth.

Ayleth reached for his belt, slipping his Vocos pipes from their sheath, and pressed them into his hand. "Use it," she urged.

His hands shook so hard she feared he would drop the instrument. The first few notes of the Suppression spell song cracked and slurred as he played, but he found the variation and managed to make it through several measures. At first nothing seemed to happen, and Ayleth feared the iron spike would be necessary after all. But Terryn was a master of his pipes—she'd never met anyone his equal. He moved from variation to variation, smooth and seamless despite the pain he must be experiencing.

Slowly, the power inside him faded back, still potent, but no longer on the verge of breaking free. Ayleth watched what took place in horrified fascination. She had never seen such a powerful shade contained and controlled within a mortal body before.

No man, no matter his strength of will and conviction, would be able to contain such a force for long. And yet . . . and yet . . .

"Terryn," she said, just as he finished resolving the last

notes of the song spell. "Terryn, you've got to let your shade loose."

He dropped the Vocos from his lips, breathing hard. He didn't seem to have the strength even to look at her.

"I know it's heresy to say it," she continued, taking hold of his arm. "But . . . well, I'm an inborn. Apparently I was born a heretic, whether I like it or not. It doesn't matter anymore." She knelt in front of him and tried to make him meet her eyes. But he turned away, his breathing too hard, sweat beading his pale brow. "You've got to let your shade loose," she said. "Suppressing it like this . . . will kill you. The suppressions themselves, that's what's causing you this pain! Power like that *cannot* be contained. It'll tear your soul to shreds if you keep trying to hold onto it."

He shook his head. He could barely stand, much less form any sort of an argument.

"Listen to me." Ayleth slid her hand down his arm, around the scorpiona to touch his fingers. She hesitated only a moment then gripped his hand and squeezed. "Please. I've glimpsed the spirit you carry. I don't believe it will harm you."

"Does it matter?" Terryn lifted his head with an effort, his ice-cold eyes lancing into hers. "Does it matter what you *believe?*"

She couldn't answer. In truth, she couldn't know for sure. Continuing to suppress the shade would kill him sooner or later, but letting it loose? It might destroy him in an instant. She had only her guesses and hopes, no foundation solid enough to support risking a man's life . . . Terryn's life.

As her head dropped forward, her gaze fell upon the unused dart. Letting go of Terryn's hand—trying not to notice how his fingers sought to catch at hers before they pulled away entirely—she caught up the dart and held it closer to her face for inspection. It was tipped in Apparition poison.

"That venator we just fought," she said, looking at Terryn sharply. "He carried an Apparition? A mind-manipulator? Those images we saw of him, they were merely projections?"

Terryn stood upright. He drew one more long breath into his lungs before snapping his Vocos shut and sheathing the instrument. "That was no venator."

SYLVIA MERCEDES

Ayleth blinked up at him, then slowly rose from her kneeling position on the floor. "He wore a red hood."

Terryn shook his head. "That man was not among the Evanderians who arrived today." Grim lines hardened his expression. "I know who he is."

"Who?"

"The Legionwitch."

Ayleth's stomach dropped. Reacting to her host's emotion, Laranta snarled, confused but ready for anything. Ayleth didn't try to quiet her. "Scias du Sibb," she breathed. "Another Crimson Devil."

Terryn nodded. He swiped the dart from Ayleth's hand and slotted it into his scorpiona, adjusting the firing mechanisms.

"But he . . . he was trapped," Ayleth said. "Wasn't he? He fled beyond the Great Barrier during the Purging. He's trapped in the Witchwood. He couldn't escape unless . . . unless . . ."

Of course. The Phantomwitch. She could *evanesce* in and out of even the most powerful barrier spell. Just so long as she had an anchor planted within range on the other side. With Inren once more ascendant and Fayline

170

suppressed, there was nothing to stop her from fetching her brethren.

From bringing all of them into Dunloch.

Terryn watched Ayleth's face, no doubt seeing how her mind ran through the possibilities and probabilities, one after another. He shook his head. "That was Legionwitch. We must assume he and the other surviving Devils escaped the Witchwood, and we don't know how many of them have breached the castle. I have to . . ."

His voice trailed off. But Ayleth finished for him, knowing what he meant to say. "You can't escape with me. You have to warn the others. You have to help." Help those who intended to burn her alive.

She grimaced and raised her scorpiona arm, setting the trigger to firing mode.

"Ayleth." Terryn closed the distance between them, reaching for her but not quite touching her. "Go. Climb out the window, get out of here. If Dunloch is breached, you might be able to get away during whatever fight comes. This is your chance."

He'd called her by her name. She couldn't remember ever hearing him call her anything but "Venatrix" or "di

Ferosa" before now. But she wasn't a di Ferosa. She wasn't even a venatrix, not anymore. She was only herself. An inborn, an abomination. A disgrace to the Order, to all of humanity.

But the way he said her name . . . sounded like a gift.

She smiled suddenly and ferociously. She caught him by the front of his jerkin, pulled his face down, and rammed her lips into his. It was not the tenderest of moments—their noses collided and her teeth jarred—and Ayleth spared the briefest regret that she'd never have a chance to practice her sorry kissing skills with this man, that this kiss was likely to be their last, and that in this final moment she'd probably just bruised his lip.

But his hand came up to cup her cheek. Such a gentle gesture in contrast with the roughness of her kiss! Her breath caught at that touch, and for a wild instant, she forgot about witches and heresies, forgot about flames and poisons. Heat flared in her chest and coursed through her limbs, and she only wished there could be time: time to lose herself to this outrageous feeling, time to lose herself to these strong arms and supple lips, which responded to her attack with delicious interest.

She pushed him away so hard, he staggered back two paces. "Find the prince," she said. "Get him to safety." Plucking a dart from her quivers, she slotted it into her scorpiona. "I'll hunt down the Legionwitch."

CHAPTER 12

FENDREL CAUGHT GERARD BY THE SHOULDER, PULLING him away from the bed. "We must go. Now," he said.

Gerard shook off his hand and instead reached for Cerine. He wrapped an arm around her shoulders, not speaking, simply holding her, his face pale with fright. The girl herself sobbed uncontrollably, lost in her hysteria. Blood trickled in thin rivulets from the corners of her mouth.

Fendrel looked at the scene, his mind running swift

calculations. Gerard would not leave the girl, that much was certain. And she would be nothing but a liability— too weak to run on her own, not to mention a carrier of ensorcellments. The way she kept repeating that same sentence implied that her tongue was not hers to control, not fully. She was under a witch's influence.

And Inren's curse anchor lay on the floor beside the bed.

Fendrel snatched it up, holding it to catch the light from the fire. There were ways to destroy these things, but nothing he had readily available to him. He strode to the nearest window and crashed it open so hard a pane of glass shattered. Then he hurled the stone out into the shining waters of Loch du Nóiv. He almost believed he heard the *plop* as it sank down under the moonlit waves.

But, as good a throwing arm as he had, he could not throw it a mile away. The Phantomwitch could *evanesce* anywhere within the vicinity of one of her anchors, the threads of magic connecting her to it always drawing her back from the Haunts through which she moved. In the blink of an eye, she could appear in this very room.

Fendrel whirled away from the window. He had to get

the prince to safety, had to get him to the vault. But he couldn't take the cursed girl too, not without too great a risk. Lifting his scorpiona arm, he aimed the poisoned dart at the girl's exposed neck where she crouched in the bed. The Gentle Death worked as effectively on un-taken as on shade-taken mortals, and it was mercifully swift. His finger began to squeeze the triggering mechanism.

Gerard looked up and, with a cry, sprang between Fendrel and his mark. "If you kill her, I will kill you."

Fendrel's heart seemed to still in his throat. He read in his nephew's eye that Gerard meant what he said: He would act without hesitation. Haunts damn it, this was why Evander forbade his servants from falling prey to love! Love invariably drove a man to foolishness, to ruin. Love broke a seasoned warrior, turned him into nothing more than a weak and useless child. Fendrel knew this. He had long ago steeled his heart against such feeble feeling, such vulnerability. But . . .

But he loved his nephew. And if he took the shot, the shot he knew he must take, Gerard would never forgive him. He would try to kill Fendrel, and while he would not succeed, he would carry hatred of his uncle all the way to his grave.

Fendrel lowered his weapon. Knowing as he did so that he'd already lost the coming battle.

"Get her up," he growled. He strode across the room and caught Cerine by one arm. "We have to get you to the vault. You and your father both. Before it's too late."

Gerard nodded without question. Gripping the girl hard by her other arm, he helped Fendrel pull her off the bed. She was limp in their grasps but somehow managed to stay on her feet. Gerard drew her arm around his neck, then met Fendrel's gaze and nodded.

Fendrel answered the nod and slipped the Gentle Death dart from his scorpiona. He slotted instead an Evanescer poison. If Inren appeared, he would take her down in a single shot. And Dunloch had reinforcements now, the fourteen Evanderians who'd come with Domina Esabel. The Phantomwitch was a formidable foe, but even if she brought Ylaire with her, surely they could not be a match for such a force. Not the two of them alone.

"Stay close behind me," Fendrel said, moving swiftly to the door. Gerard half carried Cerine behind him. She sobbed, her head and shoulders shaking, her face bowed.

At least she seemed to be making some effort to stifle the sound. Perhaps, despite her hysteria, she was somewhat aware of what took place around her.

Fendrel stepped out into the passage, his right arm up, scorpiona ready and supported on his bracing left arm. Gerard hastened in his footsteps, dragging the girl with him. The familiar halls of Dunloch seemed suddenly haunted, deadly. In the east wing, on the opposite side of the keep, a guard was posted outside the blood-warded door of the witch-girl's room. Most of the other thirteen venators and venatrices would be in the paved courtyard at the base of the north tower, preparing the pyre, arranging the wood and kindling, while others assisted the Phasmatrix Domina in the unique preparations necessary for the killing of an inborn.

Or they might be dead already. The Phantomwitch moved fast.

His shade reacted to his fear. Fendrel felt its power rise like the pounding of his own pulse in his throat. It was pleased when he was afraid. Fear threatened to break his concentration, allowing the shade that much more opportunity to work its way through the binding song spells.

But Fendrel had long years of practice at controlling his fear. He blinked once and hard. When his lids rose, the fear was gone, locked away in the deepest, darkest corner of his mind, so remote that it might as well not exist at all. His shade writhed with frustration but could do nothing more.

Shadow-light sparked in Fendrel's eyes, and he did not view the world as stone and mortar, things of matter. Instead, with every step he took, he sank deeper into the spirit realm, observing the overlay of strange lights and patterns in the world beyond mortal perception. A shade approached. Just at the end of the corridor, around a bend. Not a shade Fendrel recognized, certainly not one of those that arrived with the Evanderians.

A figure stepped into view at the end of the passage.

Fendrel took his shot.

The dart sped through the air and struck the exposed hollow of a throat.

A deep voice rumbled in a reverberating chuckle: "Oh, Fendrel, Fendrel, my old friend. Did you just shoot me with an Evanescer poison? You should know better than to fire without first making sure of your target."

Fendrel gasped.

So Inren di Karel had not *evanesced* into Dunloch alone.

The chuckle turned to a snarl, and shadow-light flared bright, momentarily illuminating a face Fendrel recognized. A handsome, dark face, with sharp cheekbones and long black hair that hung loose over his shoulders. Save for the darkness of his eyes, he might easily have been mistaken for Terryn.

But then the mouth twisted in a ferocious smile, and the face no longer looked like Terryn's at all.

"You and I, Fendrel, we are old friends. You should call me Gillotin, Venator Dominus du Visgarus, according to my rank."

"You are no venator," Fendrel snarled. "You betrayed Evander's Order when you fell for Dread Odile's poisons and lies." His hand moved slowly, smoothly, going for the Anathema poison he carried on his chest. He knew this man, knew the shade he carried. The first of Dread Odile's Crimson Devils, he had long since abandoned his original body, shifting hosts multiple times over the centuries of Odile's reign.

This host—this handsome figure, broad of shoulder and still strong despite his years of captivity in the Witchwood—would be his last.

"That's one way to look at things," the Corpsewitch grinned. "One might as easily say old Evander betrayed humanity when he initiated the slaughter of innocents and called it the Goddess's will." He tilted his head even as he lifted both hands, one holding a knife. He sliced a long cut down his scarred palm. "I like my interpretation better."

"DOWN!" Fendrel roared and threw himself back into Gerard and Cerine. Not a moment too soon—the Corpsewitch flung out a splatter of blood, and with it a blast of Anathema magic that slashed just over their heads. Curse bolts struck the stone walls of the passage, leaving deep gouges. Dust and debris rained down over their heads.

Fendrel shook himself off and sprang to his feet. He didn't pause to check on Gerard and the girl. He could only hope they'd avoided the blast when he knocked them from their feet. The dark figure of the Corpsewitch stalked toward him down the passage, his shade lashing out from the depths of his soul in a burning Anathema glare.

"Get to the vault!" Fendrel shouted over his shoulder. With peripheral awareness, he believed he sensed Gerard rising to his feet, pulling Cerine along with him. "Go, go!" he urged. He had to trust the boy to retreat back down the passage, to go around through the servant's stair.

The Corpsewitch laughed again. "Don't go, little shiny prince! We need you and that fine blood of yours."

Fendrel's heart stopped. They knew. They knew what lay hidden in the depths of Dunloch Keep. They knew, and . . .

With a warrior's roar, Fendrel drew his knife, sliced his palm open, and hurled out a streak of fresh dark blood in a scythe-like arc. With it flew a curse—a deadly curse that could tear a body into shreds. He didn't care in that moment if he dealt a violent death. He must kill this man. He must stop him now, before a single moment more passed. His curse hurtled down the passage.

The Corpsewitch put up his hand, already scored with two more fresh cuts. The power of his Anathema shade burst out from the center of his palm, blocking Fendrel's blast. The thwarted magic exploded off to each side, tore through the walls. Parts of the ceiling fell, raining down stone and plaster.

Fendrel squeezed his hand to bring forth more blood and prepared to hurl another bolt. But the Corpsewitch's other hand was already up, and his curse flew swift and fast, like an arrow loosed from the bow. It struck Fendrel in the arm that held his knife.

"Got you!" The Corpsewitch grinned. He closed his hand into a fist, and Fendrel felt all control, all mastery of his limb vanish. It no longer belonged to him.

The Corpsewitch twisted his wrist—and Fendrel's arm bent. His knife slashed at his face. He was only just fast enough to put up his left arm and catch his own wrist, straining. The Corpsewitch approached, his laugh deep as it reverberated in that broad chest. He smiled like a fiend, twisted his wrist, and manipulated the threads of power coursing from his blood into Fendrel. He tried another angle, attempting now to make Fendrel stab himself in the throat. Fendrel only just fended it off. He backed into the wall.

"It's too late, my old friend." The Corpsewitch

clenched his fist and squeezed. Then he wrenched again, twisting the knife so that it almost slipped free of Fendrel's grasp. "We're already inside. You can't stop us now."

Fendrel gritted his teeth as his mutinous arm pulled back and then slammed again, the very tip of his blade tearing into his flesh.

CHAPTER 13

FIRST, A STAKE WAS ERECTED AND SECURED IN THE
center of the paving stones on the back courtyard
overlooking the lake. Then, six red hoods, men and
women alike, worked together to assemble the massive
mound of wood and kindling needed for an execution
pyre. It was backbreaking work, and the sun had long
since set before the stacks of fuel rose high enough.

Kephan stood apart from his brethren. He leaned
against a retaining wall near the base of the tower and

watched them at their work. Venator du Harsent cast him ugly looks, and Venatrix di Javis asked if he was too afraid of breaking fingernails to offer assistance, her voice dripping with sarcasm.

Kephan made no response. Neither did he make a move to assist. He watched the pyre rise, and his heart pounded in his throat as though he watched his own scaffold being raised.

Movement drew his eye. Kephan looked up to see Domina Esabel and her two attending venators approach the stone steps leading down to the courtyard. The domina's white hood gleamed bright and spectral in the light of the moon. She spied Kephan where he stood, and one eyebrow slid up her lined forehead.

"Kephan, Venator du Tam," she said, and nodded down to where the other Evanderians worked. "You do not join your brethren in their labors?"

"I have no stomach for it," Kephan answered even as he offered a respectful salute.

The domina's face tightened. "We none of us relish the task to be accomplished. But when souls are imperiled, we must rise above and do the good work to which we are called."

"Burning alive the young woman who saved my life?" Kephan's chest tightened, and he turned away, looked again at that stake. "I don't know that I would call it a *good* work, my Domina."

Kephan felt Esabel's gaze on the side of his face, studying the pattern of scars ringing his cheek. "You care nothing for the eternal good of your hunt sister's soul?" she said, her voice soft and silken and dangerous. "Perhaps, Venator du Tam, you are more compromised than we first realized. We shall revisit your case when tomorrow's work is done."

So saying, she moved on down to the pyre. Her two cohorts cast Kephan uneasy looks as they followed her. Kephan crossed his arms and leaned back into the wall. He heard the domina call out to Venatrix di Javis, but he couldn't distinguish her words through the roaring in his temples.

He realized suddenly that the day was at hand, the day his service in the Order of Saint Evander ended.

He grimaced and swallowed hard. "Don't act surprised, old boy," he muttered to himself, his voice chiding. "You knew it would happen eventually."

He had long known that he would one day be faced with a task too heinous, that he would one day be asked, in the Goddess's name, to commit an act no man of conscience ever could. And that would be the day he died. He'd believed the day had come several months ago, when word arrived from the castra confirming Nane's tests and ordering the death of little Nilly du Bucheron. Kephan had honestly believed he would die fighting Nane. Of all people! Nane, who was his very heart, but who served the Order with unflinching resolve.

But circumstances had arranged themselves in such a way that Kephan lived and Nane died. A fact for which Kephan could never forgive himself. He bowed his head. Torchlight flickered red on the paving stones beneath his feet, dancing around the edges of his shadow.

"At least the child lived," he whispered.

Ayleth would not be so lucky. She was doomed. Whatever last stand he chose to make, he would make it alone. He would fight his brethren to save the young venatrix, a girl he barely knew. He'd rather hoped to find an ally in Terryn; he'd hoped that the weeks Terryn served at Ayleth's side would soften his ice-cold heart, teach him a measure of compassion. But Terryn had been carefully molded by Fendrel over the years. He couldn't possibly break that mold now.

"So you'll do it alone," he muttered. "And they'll kill you, and they'll damn you for what you did. And then they'll burn the girl notwithstanding. What an idiot you are, Kephan!"

It didn't matter. He'd do it anyway.

"I'll see you soon then, Nane," he whispered, the words scarcely audible in the night. But though his heart trembled, his resolve firmed.

The torch nearest to him sputtered suddenly, spitting sparks. Kephan looked up and saw the flames lash again, hissing angrily as drops of rain fell. Frowning, Kephan peered up at the sky, which had been clear and full of moonlight only moments ago. Thunder growled in the distance. A storm rolled in fast, gathering across the lake and mounding in the sky above Dunloch.

Another drop landed on Kephan's cheek. He yelped, startled. It burned! Was it actually rain he'd felt, or a spark from the torch?

Another drop fell. Someone shouted. Someone cursed. Then the heavens opened.

Burning, searing pain fell on Kephan's face, his hands. He cried out and yanked his hood up over his head, wrapping his cloak tightly around himself. It was some protection, but he felt smoldering heat as the fabric burned away.

Screams erupted down below as the torches went out one by one. Frantic shadows moved, then footsteps pounded on the stairs as the venators fled the storm. One voice rose above the rest, almost unrecognizable in its pain. Though his feet turned to race to the shelter of the castle, Kephan turned despite himself, looking back down to the courtyard. Domina Esabel lay prostrate, twisting and writhing on the stones, her hood and cloak torn away.

"Haunts damn me!" Kephan snarled and rushed down after her. His cloak still offered some shield at least, but when he reached out his hands to grasp the domina, the rain burned into his skin, searing to the bone. By the last of the torchlight remaining, he saw her mutilated face. Something liquid streamed from her eye-sockets, and he hadn't the courage to look more closely.

Heaving her up with one arm around his shoulder, Kephan half-carried, half-dragged the woman up the steps. The door into the keep was still open, and he dove inside, dropping the domina in a heap of limbs. He tore off his soaking cloak and hood, throwing them away. His eyes wide and wild, he saw Venatrix di Javis nearby, along with a few of the others. How many? He wasn't sure. Not all of them.

"Help her!" he snarled to di Javis, who, shuddering, sprang to the domina's side and began tearing at her outer garments, trying to spare her more burning. By the light of the nearest lantern, Kephan saw Esabel's pale skin melted and blackened in large patches. She was hardly recognizable anymore.

He turned to stare through the doorway. The rain was already dissipating, but the attack wasn't over. Something more rolled in over the surface of the lake—a huge wall of mist. It poured right through the spell barrier and swarmed up the shores of the island.

Kephan growled a vicious curse and darted a hand out just far enough to catch the door handle and pull it shut, slamming hard. That should help, though the seals were not secure enough to prevent the mist from creeping in around the edges, spreading subtle poison.

He knew whose work this was. "The Stormwitch," he hissed. "He's escaped the Witchwood. And how many others with him?"

There was no time to puzzle it out, no time for hesitation. Kephan whirled on Venatrix di Javis, Venator du Harsent, and the others there in the passage with him, all coughing, gasping, and writhing in pain. His own body screamed from innumerable small wounds, but he pulled himself upright and drew his scorpiona from its holster.

"Di Javis," he barked, "stay with the domina. Keep her safe. Du Harsent, you're with me. We've got to get to the king."

Guardin du Glaive paced his room with a rapid stride. He crossed in front of the desk that had been brought from a study into his private chamber, which was now mounded with multiple open volumes, many with pages half torn. He couldn't bear to look in that direction, however, so he paced from his fireplace, where a bright blaze glowed, back to the window overlooking the stone courtyard and the lakeshore below.

Every time he came to the window, he paused again to inspect the progress being made. The Evanderians were swift and efficient—a stake stood tall, mounded with enough fuel to burn at least three fully grown bodies to ashes. Lamp oil had been added to the kindling so that it would light swiftly, flaming high and fast. No chance for the accused to die of asphyxiation before the fire itself did its cleansing work.

Guardin's gaze lifted from the pyre to the lake and beyond to the horizon. A storm was rolling in. Would a heavy rainfall soak the wood too much for the fire to be struck? He must hope not. He must hope the clouds would roll on by, not interfering with the work to be done.

Oh, Goddess above, would dawn never come?

His heart shivered in his breast, and his whole body quaked. He turned away from the window again, pacing back across the room to his door. There he stopped and listened. Gerard had not returned, thank the Goddess's grace. He couldn't bear to speak to his son. Not now. Not until it was done. Not until he knew she was gone from this world and all was safe once more.

She must die. The fulfillment of the prophecy must be protected. At all costs.

A cry rang out from the lakeshore.

Guardin turned to his window. His brow pulled into a knotted frown. Quickening his stride, he hurried back to push open the window and gazed down into the yard. At the sound of falling rain, he cursed. The storm had broken after all. He must pray that it would pass swiftly, that it would not soak the kindling—

A drop struck his hand. He cried out, drew back. His eyes widened as he stared at the skin on the back of his hand, which blackened and bubbled before his eyes. Surprise and pain swelled inside him with such force, he couldn't even think.

Shouts, indistinct but full of terror, rose to his ears. He thought he heard the formidable voice of the Phasmatrix Domina . . . but then her voice transformed from commanding shouts to screams. Guardin stood transfixed at his window, his wounded hand clutched to his chest.

He tried to make sense of the chaos, tried to make sense of the wild shadows cast by the sputtering torches, which expired one after another. This was no natural storm. This was . . .

"No," Guardin breathed. He backed away from the window. "It can't be!"

Fendrel. Fendrel must be told. He must find and warn Fendrel.

No! No, first and foremost, he must get to the vault. Not even the Phantomwitch could *evanesce* through those wards. He must go at once.

"Gerard," he whispered. What about his son?

He hesitated with his hand on the door latch. All of his warrior's training crashed down to nothingness in the face of this terror. He knew what the storm outside meant. He knew who had come to Dunloch, who had somehow breached the barriers. And if one of them got through, the others had as well.

He couldn't fight such foes. He hadn't the weapons to stop them. He must get to the vault, trust Fendrel to find Gerard, and—

"Going somewhere, pretty king?"

Guardin whirled and watched the crack in the worlds open up before his eyes. The Phantomwitch, wearing the shapely, nearly naked body of young Liselle di Matin, stepped through swirling darkness into his chamber.

CHAPTER 14

THE CRASH OF CURSES IN THE WEST WING REVERBERATED through the stone halls.

Terryn skidded to a halt just as he reached the open gallery overlooking the entrance hall. His hands gripped the waist-high rail for support, and shadow-light sparked in his eyes. The bloody aura of Anathema magic danced before his vision, radiating out from one of the passages across the expanse of the hall.

"Fendrel," he whispered. Surely that must be Fendrel

using his shade power. But on whom? Strain his gaze though he might, Terryn couldn't detect the number of shade souls present, not at this distance. He would need to summon up more of his shade's powers, and that he dared not do.

Sounds plucked at his mortal hearing—guardsmen shouting to one another, the clank of armor and bright ringing of blades. There were screams as well, screams of pain, more distant, as though coming from the back of the castle. Were the un-taken men and women of Dunloch trying to fight witches? Fools! Even if one of them somehow managed to land a killing blow, the violence of death would merely propel the indwelling shade spirit into a new host.

Terryn hesitated. He wanted to race down the stairs, rush to the assistance of those defenseless untaken. But no. He had to find Gerard.

Cursing, he spurred himself into motion, sprinted along the gallery, and made for a door to a servant's passage in the wall. He burst through the door, nearly running into a cluster of terrified serving girls. They screamed and covered their faces, but he pushed through them and ran on through the corridor, often obliged to turn his shoulders at an awkward angle, so close did the walls press in on either side.

He rounded a corner and slammed into another body obstructing his progress. The person fell back with a cry, blind in the near-complete darkness of the passage at night. But Terryn, looking with shadow sight, saw his face. "Gerard!"

"Terryn, is that you?" Gerard's voice, taut with terror, reached out to Terryn like a man grasping for a last lifeline. "Fendrel's in trouble! He's holding off a shade-taken in the passage outside. Not Inren. I don't know who it is, but he wore a red hood! Have the Evanderians turned on us?"

Terryn shook his head, unwilling to take the time to explain. "Fendrel can handle himself. We've got to get you to safety. That's all that matters." He caught Gerard's outstretched hand, pulling him upright. Only then did he see that the prince wasn't alone. "Lady Cerine?" Terryn gasped, too surprised to believe what he saw.

She didn't answer. Her soul, visible to his shadow eyes, vibrated like the plucked string of a lute, humming with a single ongoing note of pure fear. And there was more besides. Around that humming spirit something wound, something constricting and dark, like the tentacle vines of a poisonous black plant.

She was under a compulsion.

Terryn gripped Gerard's arm tighter and pulled, dragging him painfully through the too-tight space of the servant's passage until he stood on Terryn's other side, away from Cerine. "Terryn, no!" Gerard protested.

"She can't come with us," Terryn said darkly. He put up his hand. In his veins, pure white light burned, mounting in pressure and power. He didn't let it loose, not yet. He had no wish to hurt the lady. "She's cursed."

"Please, Terryn," Gerard persisted. He pulled at Terryn's arm. "It's not her fault."

"It doesn't matter. The curse is activated. She could turn on you at any moment."

"As could you!"

Terryn jerked his head around to see the prince's eyes, which were white-ringed as they strained to perceive him in the shadows. "She is no more likely to turn on me than you are. And she is far less dangerous."

Terryn couldn't answer. His throat seemed to close up against all words.

"I won't leave her." Gerard took a step closer to Terryn, his teeth bared in a fierce snarl. "I won't leave her, Terryn."

For three terrible heartbeats, neither moved, neither spoke. But there was no time to linger, no time to argue. The prince had to be protected.

"All right," he said. "Come." He put out a hand and caught Cerine's elbow. She made no protest, no sound at all; she scarcely seemed to breathe. He pulled her closer, then stepped around to take the lead in front of Gerard, letting the prince put his arm around Cerine's shoulders. "Stay behind me," he said. "Follow close and don't lag. Can she keep pace?"

"She will," Gerard answered grimly.

"Dunloch has been breached," Terryn said as they made their way along the dark passage, back toward the door by which he had entered. He bypassed that door, pulling it quietly shut as they went, and led the way to the spiral stair, which took them down to the ground floor. They had to get to the portrait gallery. Though he had never seen it, Fendrel had told Terryn there was a vault there, a safe room with blood wards on it that could protect the prince or others of his blood. "I don't know how many witches are here," he continued. "I met one at least, but Inren must have brought others with her when she *evanesced* in."

He couldn't say more. Even if he dared risk being overheard as they crept through the passage, he didn't want to give voice to his own fears. But the truth could not be denied: If the Phantomwitch had come to Dunloch, she had no doubt brought Ylaire with her. The Warpwitch. Whose sigil still marred Terryn's soul, down beneath the ugly scars on his cheek.

It didn't matter. Once he got Gerard to the vault, none of it would matter. Even if the Warpwitch found him and broke him bone by bone, if Gerard was safe, his work was done. And Ayleth . . .

No, he wouldn't think about her. Not even with the burn of her rough kiss hot on his lips. He must purge all thought of her from his mind. She could handle herself. She always had. She always would.

They made it to the bottom of the spiral stair. The

door hung open. Others had fled through it not long before—the serving women Terryn had run into earlier, perhaps. He peered out, his scorpiona upraised and ready. The shouts and cries of guards seemed too close, but no one was in sight. His shadow senses discerned more blasts of Anathema magic upstairs, and possibly other shade disturbances, less distinct and farther off. But here the way looked clear enough. Peering ahead with shadow sight, he saw no trace of shade souls through the walls.

"Come," he said and stepped out of the passage into a storage room. They were still in the servants' quarters of the castle but not far from the portrait gallery. Terryn led the way, his scorpiona outstretched before him, armed with the Gentle Death.

Creeping like thieves in the night, the three of them stepped out into a sumptuous marble hall. To the left lay the portrait gallery. Terryn beckoned with a quick nod and stepped light and fast toward that gallery.

"Wait!" Gerard's voice was a tight gasp.

The sound sent a thrill of horror up Terryn's spine. He whirled and saw Gerard stumble as he sought to catch and support Cerine. She fell hard, landing on her hands and knees, her head bent and shaking. Something in her quivering soul flared suddenly and brilliantly, blinding to Terryn's shadow sight.

Anathema magic. It rippled through her soul, rolling out from an implanted sigil in her cheek, and over-whelmed her physical body. She screamed and collapsed on her face as her bones broke. Spines jutted out through her back, tore her gown, dripping with blood.

"Cerine!" Gerard fell on his knees beside her. He clutched her arms with helpless hands as though he could somehow hold her together. "Goddess, no!"

Terryn lunged. He was only just in time to catch hold of her wrist as her arm swung in an arc. One instant slower, and the razor claws tearing through the ends of her fingers would have slashed Gerard's throat open. Terryn twisted hard, and she fell, her arm bent painfully behind her. But even as she went down, the rest of her body bent, broke. Her jaw unhinged, and her scream became a roar.

Drawing back his arm, Terryn punched her face hard, knocking her flat. She fell in a bundle of mutated limbs, choking on her own hideous voice. Terryn sprang back and pushed Gerard behind him. He raised his scorpiona.

With a wordless shout, Gerard grabbed Terryn's arm and pulled. His aim went wide; the Gentle Death flew over Cerine's misshapen shoulder and struck the far wall.

Terryn's eyes flashed to Gerard's face. The prince didn't say a word, but his face spoke volumes—threats of violence and death.

From the corner of his eye, Terryn saw Cerine gathering herself, already recovered from the hit she'd taken. She sailed through the air, and Terryn only just had presence of mind enough to hook a foot behind Gerard's legs and knock him flat on his back. Cerine flew over the prince and landed on all fours several feet beyond. She whipped her hideous face around and hissed. A long, purpled tongue protruded through a cage of teeth.

But, warped though she was, she was neither large nor strong.

Terryn cursed again, vainly wishing he possessed some of Ayleth's shade-augmented strength just then.

Cerine sprang. She aimed at Gerard, not Terryn, driven by the compulsion of the curse. Her claw-like hands tore at the prince's face, but Terryn caught hold of her neck and one of the spines on her back, whirled her around, and smashed her into the wall, knocking the breath out of her. She collapsed, a pitiable bundle of limbs and bones.

Before Terryn could catch his breath, she was up again, lashing out. Terryn put up an arm. Her razor claws tore through the leather of his bracer and grazed the skin underneath. The force of her momentum knocked him off his feet. He landed hard with her on top of him, slavering, raging. Foam flew from her unhinged jaw; blood dripped from the savage teeth that had torn through her gums. Her long tongue whipped in his face, and her hands scrabbled for his throat. He punched her face again and again, but she didn't go down.

Suddenly the pressure lifted from his chest. Terryn coughed, gasped, and propped up on his elbows, his vision swimming. He shook his head and saw Gerard standing braced with Cerine in front of him. One arm wrapped around her neck while the other held the back of her head, locking her in place. She writhed, but he'd angled his body so that her spines couldn't tear into his torso. Her hands lashed at the air wildly but never quite struck him . . . as though she still had some small measure of control, as though she fought the curse-compulsion driving her to tear him apart.

Terryn saw Gerard's lips moving, but he couldn't hear whatever he said over Cerine's wild slavering and struggles for air. Then her eyes rolled back. The monstrous body sagged limp in Gerard's arms. Terryn watched the raging Anathema magic in her soul fade as she fell unconscious.

Gerard released his hold around her throat and tenderly lifted her hideous frame in his arms, cradling her like a child.

Terryn clambered to his feet, breathing heavily. "Gerard," he said. "We can't take her."

The prince looked up at him. A long cut ran down the side of his face, oozing blood. His eyes were hollow with fear, but a spark of defiance gleamed in their depths.

"You have to put her down, Gerard," Terryn said. "She's still cursed, and she'll—"

In the shadows beyond the prince, a figure stepped out from behind a pillar between them and the portrait-gallery door, a tall man wearing the uniform of the prince's guard.

Terryn immediately leaped to put himself in front of Gerard and Cerine, between them and the stranger. He slammed another Gentle Death dart into his scorpiona, squared his shoulders, and aimed his weapon at the man's heart. His shadow vision jumped and whirled, struggling to discern a trace of shade. But the man's soul was somehow . . . confused. Blurred.

"Declare yourself!" Terryn cried.

"Oh, my sweet little pet," the man said, his hard mouth breaking into a huge, savage smile. "Do you not recognize me in this body? I needed something stronger than that old priestess, though I've never enjoyed wearing a male form."

All the life seemed to go out of Terryn's body. His lungs constricted, incapable of drawing air. Then, with a spasm and roar, he sighted his scorpiona, squeezed the trigger—

And at the last moment aimed up, shooting the poisoned dart directly into the ceiling.

The man raised a blood-streaming hand clenched into a tight fist of control. "That's right, dear one," the

Warpwitch spoke through the stolen mouth. "You don't want to hurt me, now do you?"

CHAPTER 15

THE NIGHT AIR SURROUNDING DUNLOCH CASTLE WAS filled with inexplicable tension.

The lone rider making her way through the parkland gardens of Dunloch toward the island keep felt that tension down in her bones, down in her soul. Wary, she drew rein on her horse as she came within sight of the castle turrets and slipped a set of Vocos pipes from their sheath on her belt. A few lines of strange music later, shadow-light gleamed in her eye.

She collapsed and re-sheathed the pipes. "Walk on," she murmured to her mount and continued on down the road through the trees. Whatever waited at the end of this road, it was best to ride forth and meet it, not linger indecisively here in the middle of the night.

Within a few more paces, the humming of a barrier-song spell pricked in her mind.

She pulled her horse to a halt again, her brow tightening. This was unexpected. A barrier spell? Here? Around the castle? She knew of the Great Barrier not many miles from here, binding back the Witchwood . . . but what could possibly have motivated a venator to raise such a stout defense around Dunloch in this time of peace?

"What did she do?" the horsewoman whispered.

She spurred her horse's sides, urging it into a trot, then a canter, swiftly progressing down the road until the castle bridge came into view. The massive gate loomed, ominous in the moonlight. Torchlight flickered within the flank towers, but she saw no sign of guards on duty.

Something was definitely not right here.

The barrier-song spell gleamed to her shadow vision, a

complex weaving of magic force. Arcane magic, she thought, mingled with Anathema threads. Reaching out with her own shade's perceptions, she touched the webbing, testing its quality. Her mouth turned down into a deeper frown. There was familiar magic here. A weaving of such complexity, such density, could be the work of only one man. One powerful venator . . .

So he was here. At Dunloch.

So he must know already what she had done.

So. So, so . . .

What had he thought when he realized the truth? What action had he taken in response? Had the years softened his hard resolve? Had he learned to see reason beyond his own fixated fanaticism? Had he realized her intention?

Or had he already killed her Ayleth?

With a sweep of her cloak, the horsewoman swung down from her horse and braced herself before the spell. Every barrier had its points of weakness, and Evanderians were trained to find those points, to use them according to necessity. Her quick eyes, bright with shadow-light, studied the complex weaving and found a place where it had been opened recently.

She lifted her Vocos to her lips and began to play. Power rose from the depths of her soul.

Kephan led the way, Venator du Harsent close on his heels. They'd paused scarcely long enough to loosen the bindings on their shades, and now, with shadow sight gleaming in his eyes, Kephan couldn't help wondering if he ought to call up more power. His Feral shade not only augmented his mortal senses but simultaneously offered him a range of unnatural senses for which mortal language had no name.

With those senses he felt unrelenting, overwhelming danger on all sides.

Du Harsent paused behind him. Kephan stopped, looked back, and saw his fellow venator arming his scorpiona. "What are you doing?" he demanded.

"That rain." Du Harsent looked up at Kephan, his eyes shimmering with magic. "That was the Stormwitch's work. He's an Elemental shade-taken."

This was true. And if they encountered the Stormwitch somewhere in these passages, Elemental poison would be necessary to take him down. But if they encountered any other witch bearing any other type of shade, the wrong poison would serve only to anger and empower them.

Kephan decided not to argue. His shade senses felt the palpable terror coursing through du Harsent, who, as one of the Phasmatrix Domina's aides, had led a rather sheltered existence for an Evanderian. But Kephan chose not to follow du Harsent's lead. Instead, he loaded his weapon with Anathema poison. Something told him, if the Stormwitch had come to Dunloch, the Warpwitch was near as well.

Their ears filled with screams, with sounds of battle in different parts of the castle. They emerged from the passage into a pillared hall outside the portrait gallery and hastened on to the great entrance hall. There they stopped dead in their tracks, their breath catching in their throats. Six members of the household guard were pinned to the far wall, huge spears of crystal protruding from their armor, from their faces. The crystal pulsed with magic.

"The Crystalwitch," Kephan hissed, backing out of the great hall to take cover behind another pillar. "She's here too."

Du Harsent cursed and fumbled to switch darts yet again. Kephan simply used his shadow vision to scope out the room. No sign of life—the guards' souls had long since fled their mortal remains. No shade was near either.

A door opened. Five figures tumbled out from a servants' hidden stair, their eyes wide, their mouths open in silent screams of terror. Du Harsent started in surprise and swung his scorpiona, taking aim. Kephan was only just fast enough to knock his hand aside so that the dart flew over one young woman's head and struck the wall. She gave a choking scream and fled with the other four into the shadows.

Kephan cast du Harsent a hard glare. Du Harsent gave him only a half glance back before fumbling for another dart. Kephan didn't wait to see which poison the venator would choose this time. He turned again to the cavernous entrance hall and strode out from behind his pillar toward the huge front stair.

An explosion shook the walls overhead, up in the west

wing. Kephan paused again at the base of the staircase, every muscle in his body jumping with the instinct to flee. He suppressed the urge and headed up the stairs. The king's suite was in the west wing. Whatever terrible altercation was currently taking place, Kephan knew he must face it if he hoped to reach his sovereign. He heard du Harsent at his heels, breathing hard. He wasn't entirely grateful just then for the trigger-happy hunter's assistance.

Suddenly, his shade vision flared bright. Kephan stopped so abruptly that du Harsent ran into his back before stumbling back several steps. A figure stood on the landing. A little figure, child-sized, but brimming with ascendant shade light.

Kephan stared at her, unable to move.

"Watch out!" du Harsent snarled. He jumped in front of Kephan like a shield and took aim with his scorpiona. "It's ascendant!"

Kephan glimpsed the black fletching of the Gentle Death loaded in the weapon. "No!" he cried and shoved du Harsent violently to one side, knocking him against the marble banister. "She's a Seer. Look at her . . . she's harmless."

Du Harsent, his firing arm caught in Kephan's grip and pinned awkwardly to his side, scowled ferociously. "Doesn't matter. She's a taken—she's one of *them*. A monster."

"A Seer," Kephan said again, his voice tight. "Don't you understand? She's inborn."

That last word got through to du Harsent. He froze in his struggle. To give the Gentle Death to an inborn was to damn her soul. Not even a man as volatile as du Harsent wanted to be guilty of such an act. "Fine," he growled, and the tension went out of his arm.

Kephan relaxed his grip and stood back. Du Harsent squared off, looking up at the landing and the child still standing there, so small, so solemn. He drew his knife. "No time for fire," he said. "This will have to be violent enough."

He took two lunging steps before Kephan caught him and swung the other venator wildly off balance, using the summoned strength of his Feral shade. His eyes, augmented by shade power, saw a flash of du Harsent's face just as the man hit the banister and flew over. He saw the shock, the fear. The betrayal.

In that flash, it was like seeing Nane's face again . . . the last time Kephan ever saw him alive.

Du Harsent disappeared from sight, and a thick-sounding thud followed. Kephan leaped to peer over the handrail, down to the floor below. The venator lay still, his arms and legs spread like a star. Using his shadow sight, Kephan searched for signs of the man's soul and, to his utmost relief, saw that it was still tethered firmly to his body. He wasn't dead then. What the extent of his injuries might be, Kephan couldn't guess. But he wasn't dead. Neither would he be killing children anytime soon.

A distant shout followed by a bellow of rage drew Kephan's attention back upward. The child stood just where she had been, watching him. Oblivious to the horrors around her. She blinked down at Kephan.

He shook himself, then hastened up to the landing, taking the steps two at a time. The little girl watched him come, her eyes rounding slightly. Jade-colored light streamed from their depths.

"What are you doing here, child?" he demanded in a low whisper. "How did you get inside?"

"The witches." The girl tilted her head up at him.

"They brought me to see the way."

"Witches?" Kephan clenched his teeth against a curse. "How many witches? How many are here?"

The girl shook her head slowly. The green shadow-light in her eyes flickered and then intensified, swallowing up her pupils and irises in brilliant disks of green. When she spoke again, her voice was no longer that of a child but a strange, multitudinous voice, echoing against itself over and over again: *"Blood to blood. Bone to bone. The queen will rise to claim her own. Blood to blood. Bone to bone. The queen will rise to—"*

A scream rent the air. An unnatural, horrible sound, coming from the east wing this time. Kephan drew a sharp breath through his nostrils. There was no time to linger. Moving swiftly, Kephan caught up the little girl and tossed her lightly across his shoulder. The words continued in an unstoppable torrent, pouring from her lips. *"Blood to blood, bone to bone, blood to blood, bone to bone . . ."*

"Thank you, I've got the general idea," Kephan growled. He turned on the landing and raced up to the west wing, away from that last horrible scream. He couldn't take the child with him into a fight. But he couldn't leave her standing there for either witches or Evanderians to find. He tried a series of door handles, finding most of them locked. When he found one that gave, he pushed the door open and, after a brief scan to make certain the room beyond was empty, dropped the girl on her feet inside.

"*Blood to blood,*" she said, reaching her skinny arms up to him. "*Bone to bone. The queen will rise—*"

"Yes, I know, she'll rise to claim her own." Kephan pressed a silencing finger to her mouth. "You stay here, and you stay *quiet.* I'll come back for you. If I can."

With those words, he pulled the door shut and hurried back down the hall toward the open gallery above the stairs. He paused at the rail to check the firing mechanism of his scorpiona.

A crash of magic exploded in the air behind him. Kephan whirled, gazing across the open space and across the balustrade into the east wing and the shadows beyond. A voice shouted somewhere close: "Stop, or I'll fire!"

"Ayleth?" he whispered.

CHAPTER 16

SCREAMING ECHOED FROM THE LOWER LEVELS AND even from outside. Ayleth's senses, heightened with Laranta's unnatural perceptions, picked up every sound even through solid walls of stone. So many screams, so many frightened voices coming at her from all sides.

Her instinct urged her to run *toward* the screaming, to throw her power against whatever evil being harried the defenseless folk of Dunloch. But she must focus. The hunt was on. She would save more people if she took down the Legionwitch now, before he could send his powerful illusions to batter and break unsuspecting minds.

"*Laranta, find the Apparition,*" she commanded, pulling back her shade's scattered awareness and focusing it to search for one clear sense. Not a scent, not a sight, not a sound, but a *perception* unlike any of these. Clearer. Bolder. A perception of shade.

Crouched low in the forefront of Ayleth's mind, Laranta growled with eagerness, ready to burst out in her smoke-like wolf form and bound down the passage ahead. But that might alert the Legionwitch to Ayleth's approach. Too risky. "*Steady, girl,*" Ayleth said.

Her eyes, filled with Laranta's sight, stared down the corridor, perceiving the world of spirit overlaying the stone and plaster and tapestries. She detected a few mortal souls shivering in terror behind closed doors. Otherwise, this passage seemed to be empty of spirits, except—

Shade! Laranta barked in sudden warning.

Ayleth turned, her scorpiona upraised, armed with a poisoned dart. She shot at the figure just passing before her view, landing a hit in his thigh.

"Haunts!" a harsh voice cursed, and the man went down on one knee. Ayleth whipped out a Gentle Death, slotting it into place as she strode swiftly down the hall. Her shadow vision roiled with sudden, mounding power. Too late, she realized she'd hit a shade-taken, but not an Apparition. In her haste, she'd used the wrong poison.

She flung herself to the ground, covering her head with her arms as a blast of raw, wrathful shade force shot over her head and splintered the walls on either side of her. All the wood paneling from head-height up broke into roughened spears of wood and shot through the air. She was quick enough to avoid the worst of it, but hissed with pain as several smaller splinters bit into her exposed hands; and she felt the impact of at least one larger splinter drive into the back of her jerkin, not quite able to penetrate the stout leather.

Her mind whirled with swift calculations, faster than mortal thought. She'd used the wrong poison and enraged the shade, temporarily empowering it. But in this blast of power, she had opportunity to see what exactly her mistake had been, what shade type she actually faced. The brilliant flare from the center of the man's soul was unmistakable—an Elemental. But which element did he harness exactly?

She was rolling before the debris cleared, her hand reaching for her quivers. Pulling herself up into a kneeling firing stance, she took aim at the man, whose arms were outstretched, his jaw clenched as he struggled to pull his shade back under his control. His eyes fixed on her—and she recognized his face. He was no witch. This man was one of the Evanderians she'd seen in the great hall earlier that day, when she'd been brought before the Phasmatrix Domina.

A venator.

"You!" he cried, pointing one hand directly at her.

"Stop or I'll fire!" Ayleth barked. She watched his eyes flick to the end of her scorpiona, saw him wondering whether or not she'd loaded correctly this time. She could bring him down in a second unless he was quick enough with his powers to ward off the shot.

"Listen to me," Ayleth said, keeping her weapon aimed straight at his throat. "The Phantomwitch has penetrated Dunloch. She brought others with her."

"You think I don't know?" The venator's eyes flashed. "You're one of them, aren't you? Inborn! Have they come to save you? To take you back with them?"

"Don't be stupid." Ayleth took a careful step toward him. "I've fought the Phantomwitch before and killed one of her hosts. I may be inborn, but I'm still the Goddess's servant. And I can help you stop them. We can help each other."

"Witch," the man snarled, his hand trembling. "Heretic. I'll never join you." His power mounded, roiling almost out of control inside him, though how it would manifest Ayleth still could not guess.

"Stop!" she cried. "I will shoot you!"

"Shoot me then," the venator spat.

Ayleth squeezed the trigger.

Something struck her arm. Her shot went wide, and Ayleth gasped, yanking hard, trying to pull away. But something had wrapped around her wrist, and when she looked, she saw that it was a solid wooden branch, living and growing right out from the splinters along the wall. Using Laranta's strength, she broke its hold, but another branch stretched out from behind her, and caught her other arm, while a third wrapped around her ankle and a fourth reached for her neck. Ayleth broke these too, but they kept coming, one after another, pulsing with magic.

"No! Clodio, don't!"

Ayleth could scarcely see through the thicket of branches, but she recognized the voice at once. "Venator du Tam?" she gasped, ducking around one lashing branch only to be struck in the side of the head by another. Her vision spun, but she saw the square figure of Kephan appear at the end of the passage.

The other venator looked at him and snarled. "Have you finally turned heretic after all these years, Kephan? Thrown in your lot with this witch girl? We always knew it was just a matter of time." With this final word, he wrenched his arm, and another branch darted out from the wall at Kephan's side.

Kephan dodged the bough, squared his stance, lifted his scorpiona, and shot. His dart flew true, striking the other venator in his thigh. The venator roared. The flash of power Ayleth's wrong dart had given him flickered, and his whole soul lurched, trying to fight the effects of the Elemental poison now coursing through him. He sank to his knees.

Ayleth tore through another branch, trying to reach the end of the passage. "Venator du Tam!" she cried. He turned to her.

A shadow moved behind him. Then another. And a third.

Three figures manifested out of thin air and, before Ayleth could cry out a warning, began pummeling Kephan with their fists. He dropped under those blows, surprised, then roared to his feet again, his Feral shade power flowing through his arms. He struck back, knocked two of the figures flying.

Three more appeared in their place. And others as well, surrounding him and the other venator, who could not fight back as the paralysis poison took effect. He disappeared behind a wall of brutal men, all twins of each other, all kicking, tearing, punching, biting.

Shade! Laranta howled.

"*A little late now,*" Ayleth snapped. She ducked back into the weird splinter forest, expecting one of the Legionwitch's projections to appear behind her at any moment. She saw Kephan toss several more to the ground, but they simply vanished like vapors, and more appeared in their place.

Ayleth swiftly slotted a new Apparition poison into her scorpiona. "*Where is it?*" she demanded. "*Where is the shade?*"

Near, near, Laranta urged, straining her senses away from the battle taking place at the end of the passage. Instead, she shifted her awareness up to the ceiling. The Legionwitch wasn't on this floor, Ayleth realized. He was above her, working his shade's influence from a safe distance. Wherever he was, he could perceive the venators he now attacked, but she must be standing just outside his range of awareness. She would have to keep it that way if she wanted to save Kephan.

"*All right, Laranta,*" she said. "*I need you to go down again. As small as you can. Hide yourself so that he can sense no other shade near.*"

Without a murmur of protest, Laranta obeyed, more swiftly than she would have obeyed the commands of the Vocos pipes. She sprang back into Ayleth's mind and curled into herself, reduced to a tight ball of magic, simmering with potential but momentarily innocuous.

Ayleth turned and ran back down the corridor, pushing through the branches and roots springing out from the wall, and made for the servant's stair at the end of the passage. She flung open the door and climbed the stair three steps at a time. Her body felt weak and vulnerable without Laranta's strength surging through her, but that didn't matter.

The door into the third story made no sound as Ayleth pushed it open. She thought she heard grunts and thick sounds of blows from below, but without Laranta's augmenting senses, that was probably imagined. Her mortal eyes struggled to see much in this dark corridor. She moved down the hall, turned a slight bend.

A man crouched before her. He pressed one hand into the floor while his other hand clutched at his forehead as though it pained him. Even without Laranta ascendant inside her, Ayleth felt the potency of magic shimmering in the air around him, an invisible aura in the ether. She braced herself to take the shot.

The floorboard under her foot creaked.

The man shot upright, whirling, his hand outstretched. The shadows of figures appeared up and down the hall, a dozen and more, all turned aggressively to throw themselves at her. But they froze. The man himself, his eyes round and staring, dropped to his knees.

"My Queen!" he cried. "You are awake!"

Ayleth blinked.

Then she took the shot.

The dart sped down the hall, between all those phantom forms, and struck directly between the Legionwitch's eyes, which widened still further in utter shock. He raised both fists, and the illusions of himself staggered, jolted. Some of them took swings at Ayleth's head. One managed to land a hit on her shoulder that sent her reeling, but the others missed as the witch lost control of his projections under the influence of the poison.

Ayleth, her shoulder smarting, marched down the passage. She removed a Gentle Death from its quiver. The man stared up at her—a pale, freckled youth, like some fresh-faced farm boy. A newly stolen body, belying the true age of the poisonous spirits housed within. A black tattoo marred his forehead, still scabbed from recent application. Ayleth recognized it instantly, even if she did not recognize the boy's face—the five vertical lines rising from a single horizontal slash. The mark of the Crimson Devils.

Shadow-light whirled in his eyes and streamed from their tear ducts, slowly fading as the shade succumbed to the effects of the poison. "My . . . Queen . . ." he gasped.

"I'm no one's queen," Ayleth snapped. She jammed the Gentle Death into his throat.

The man went down like a sack of potatoes. Ayleth stepped back and watched as the snarled souls inside him struggled weakly against the death they could not resist, a death so gentle that it offered no power. Eventually the souls stopped struggling. Two souls only—the witch and his shade, bound inextricably together. The original soul belonging to this boy's body was long since gone, ousted and left to wander revenant in this world.

Ayleth's hand moved impulsively to her Detrudos. But she stopped. Even as she felt the yawning, tearing cleft in the world open in the air above her, even as she felt the drawing in of putrid breath that was the Haunts seeking to reclaim its own, she did nothing. She would not try to save the spirit of this man, to separate the witch's soul

235

from that of his shade. She merely watched as both souls, flailing ineffectively, were drawn up and away, flashing one last brilliant burst of terrified magic just before vanishing into the void.

The Haunts reclaimed another lost soul . . . and gained a new mortal soul in the process. It was a just end for a monster like the Legionwitch.

With a curse that was almost a prayer, Ayleth got to her feet, rushed back down the stairs to the floor below, and pushed through the eerie forest of splinters to where two bodies lay. Kephan was still partially upright, his shoulders leaning against the wall, his elbow supporting his torso. The other venator lay still on the floor, blood pooling beneath him. Ayleth's shadow sight detected no sign of a living soul in that body, human or shade.

"He's dead," Kephan gasped. Ayleth crouched beside her former hunt brother. "Careful!" he warned her as she tried to help him sit up. "I've got some broken ribs, I think. Nothing that can't be mended—my shade protected me from the worst of it."

"Thank you for stopping him," Ayleth said. As soon as she spoke the words, they felt wrong. The man had been Kephan's brother-in-arms, after all. And he was now dead.

Kephan gave her a look. "How did you get out of your—" His voice broke off, and his eyes widened until the whites ringed his pale irises. "It . . . it's happening!" he said, then moaned and clutched at his cheek.

"Venator?" Ayleth put out a hand, but he smacked it away, and when he did so, she saw the scars on his face. More than that, Laranta's shadow vision revealed to her the pulsing, searing glow of the sigil flaring to life just beneath those scars.

"She's here! She's here!" Kephan cried. "She'll take me over. You've got to go, girl. Go!"

Ayleth sprang to her feet, taking several steps back. Kephan groaned and buried his face into the floor, his body twisting with pain. Any moment, he would warp into something monstrous. Any moment he would spring up and attack her. Any moment—

"Terryn." Kephan lifted his tortured face, looking up at Ayleth. "It's not me she wants. It's Terryn . . . and she's got him!"

A scream tore through the castle, louder than all

others. A tearing, shrieking, otherworldly scream of a soul in mortal agony.

Ayleth turned, the blood draining from her face. Then, with a snarl, she whipped a Feral dart from her quivers and plunged it into Kephan's neck. The paralysis took hold, and he slumped on his side, momentarily spared the warping of Ylaire's curse. Ayleth backed away. "Sorry, Venator," she whispered.

She took off running as fast as Laranta could carry her.

CHAPTER 17

"THIS IS WHY I PREFER TO WORK WITH CORPSES."

Fendrel felt the increase of power coursing through his arm as Gillotin's voice purred in his ear. Only the strength of his own Anathema shade battling to suppress the curse kept him alive. The tip of his knife pricked at his own throat, but by sheer force of will he turned it to the side so that it plunged into the plaster wall, digging down to the wood and stone beneath.

Fendrel sought inside his soul for a grasp on his own

shade. If he could channel that power inside him into his cursed arm, maybe he could nullify the curse. Not break it—breaking it would require more pain, more time, more precision than he had available to him. But if he could just render the curse impotent . . .

His shade shrieked, resisting his reach. It lashed against the binding spells repressing it, pulled at the strands. He couldn't battle both it and the Corpsewitch's curse.

"Corpses don't fight back, you see," the witch said. He circled Fendrel, one fist pressed casually into the small of his back, while the other, streaming with blood, twisted at the curse strand imbedded in Fendrel's right arm. "That venatrix I found at the barrier, for instance. She was nice and malleable as soon as she was dead. With only a little help from the girl, she walked to the gates of this castle like she was a living being. Such an excellent carcass! Is she still around? I might like to use her again before she rots away."

Everild's face, rigid with death, flashed before Fendrel's vision. He snarled and wrenched at his own wrist, ready to break the bone if he had to.

Footsteps pounded on the stair. The Corpsewitch and Fendrel both turned their gazes in time to see a venatrix appear no more than five paces from them at the end of the passage. "Dominus, the Phantomwitch—" she began.

Fendrel roared, "Get down!" but too late. His own arm moved against his will, throwing the knife with expert precision. The blade embedded straight into the woman's heart. The impact knocked her back several paces. She stared down at her chest, dropped to her knees.

As she fell back in death, the spirits inside her exploded out in a violent propulsion of magic. The shade she'd carried roared away, out of Fendrel's sight, searching the near vicinity for a new host body to inhabit. Some serving girl. Some kitchen boy. Some unlucky stable hand. Some poor, unprepared bastard, about to be overcome by a power never intended for mortals to bear.

The instant it was gone, her body moved. Threading curse-strands wove through her limbs, visible to Fendrel's shadow vision. Blood poured down her torso as she got to her feet and swayed where she stood.

"Ah, see?" the Corpsewitch cried, his handsome dark

face beaming with delight. "This is what I'm talking about. So obliging, so agreeable."

The venatrix lurched two steps. Gillotin twisted his hand again, like a puppet master manipulating a string. She took another step, this time more graceful, with all the coordination of life. She pulled Fendrel's bone knife out of her breast with a great gush of heart's blood. Fendrel watched in horror as the venatrix turned and looked at him through her dead eyes.

Then she was running at him, blade swinging. He roared, letting go of his own hand just long enough to deflect her blow then kicked her solidly in the stomach so that she fell in an unnatural heap of dead limbs.

His right fist swung at his face again, no longer armed but still intent on his destruction. It landed a blow before he caught it again with his left hand. Blood rushed from his nostrils, down his face and mouth. Running, fresh blood.

That was all he needed.

Slamming his own right hand into the wall hard enough to momentarily stun it, he dragged his left hand down his face, smearing palm and fingers with blood.

Then he flung out a curse just as the venatrix was climbing to her feet, striking her full on. She flew backwards at the impact, hitting the far wall, her dead body cut in a dozen places, one leg nearly severed at the knee, one arm hanging from a bloody stump.

"Impressive!" The Corpsewitch applauded politely and rubbed his bloody hands together in delight. "You always were such a talent, old friend. A formidable opponent in those final days of our glorious war. But tell me, can you fight yourself and three more?"

Footsteps behind him. Fendrel turned, his jaw dropping in horror. A young page, a serving woman, and one of the prince's under-secretaries lunged down the hall. Their faces were gray with death, devoid of all expression. No malice, no bloodthirst. Simply empty. And deadly.

His right hand struck again while he was distracted, sending Fendrel staggering. The three dead moved in, none of them strong, none of them powerful. It didn't matter. They piled on him while he still fought his own hand, the page tearing at his stomach, the serving woman clawing at his back, the secretary reaching for his throat.

Their hands grasped and pulled, their empty faces swam before his vision. He kneed the dead page, slammed the woman into the wall with his shoulder.

The secretary's fingers closed around his windpipe, and when he tried to grab at them, to pull them away, his right hand tore at his own eyes. He pulled at his shade, and the strain of its power tore at the restricting song spells, the only things preventing it from destroying his soul and fully inhabiting his body. To draw on more power without first strengthening those restrictions was suicide. But the secretary's fingers tightened, and he could not draw breath. Darkness closed in around his vision. What choice did he—

A voice appeared in his mind: *"Don't be stupid."*

A dry, sardonic voice.

A voice he knew.

His eyes, staring into the dead face of the secretary, swiveled to one side. The Corpsewitch stood within three paces, his bleeding hands upraised, squeezing the air as his puppet-corpse squeezed Fendrel's throat. But behind him . . . behind him . . .

The Corpsewitch's eyes widened as his own shade

suddenly became aware of what approached. He dropped his hold on Fendrel, letting the dead secretary's fingers go limp, and swung around.

An Anathema dart grazed his cheek. Beyond him stood the short, spry form of a venatrix, her scorpiona upraised.

"Haunts damn you, bitch!" the Corpsewitch screamed, touching bloody fingers to that place on his chiseled cheekbone where the poison had just touched. Not enough to bring him down, but enough to affect his control on his shade. He lashed out at her with a curse, flinging it with a spattering arch of his own blood. But the curse went wide and slammed into the wall several feet from where she stood.

She whipped out a second dart and slammed it into the scorpiona. With a wrench of power, the Corpsewitch dragged the dead serving woman between him and the venatrix. He didn't have enough control to use her as a weapon, just enough to make her his shield. The venatrix's second dart struck the dead woman's eye instead of its intended target.

The Anathema inside the Corpsewitch flailed against

the poison coursing down through its host body to affect the soul within. Fendrel saw the shade like a dozen bloody tentacles stretching out from the center of the host, thrashing and writhing in frustration.

The Corpsewitch, squeezing his hands tight, plunged another curse into the ground at his feet, unfocused but powerful. It tore into the flooring and shook the walls. Both the venatrix and Fendrel fell to their knees, and the dead page boy and secretary collapsed inert, all the curse-threads gone from their limbs.

Using the serving woman still as his shield, the Corpsewitch fled down the passage. The venatrix hurtled after him, but within a few steps she hit that final curse and rebounded off it. The air seemed to ripple like torn and blood-dripping rags. Any novice could see that the curse wouldn't last more than a few moments. But for those few moments it was effective, and the Corpsewitch vanished down a side passage, staggering in retreat.

"Haunts damn it!" the venatrix hissed, striking at the curse barrier with the iron spike on her bracer.

Fendrel pulled himself upright to stare at her from his seat on the floor. "Hollis!" he cried.

She turned to him. Her eyes flared. "Well met, Venator Dominus," she answered coldly. "You've got a curse on you still."

Fendrel opened his mouth. A thousand things he wanted to say piled up on his tongue in one instant. Words of wrath and confusion, sorrow and gladness. Words of urgency and command.

Instead, he looked down at his dull right arm and grimaced at what his shadow sight told him. The curse Gillotin had landed was still implanted. It wasn't a deep implantation, wouldn't last more than a day. But in the meantime, he couldn't use his arm—and he couldn't risk having it suddenly turn on him again.

Hollis left the temporary curse barrier and hurried to kneel beside him. She reached out with both hands, carefully touching his arm as though it bore a physical wound. Fendrel felt the potency of the shade drawn up inside her, right to the limits of the suppression spells.

"I can put a block on your mind," she said, meeting his gaze for a mere instant before focusing on his arm again. "I can make you forget you have a right arm. If you don't remember, the curse should not be able to work. It will be as though you don't have an arm at all. It won't last for long, but—"

"Do it." Fendrel bit out the words sharply, clenching his teeth hard to prevent himself from saying anything else.

She nodded. Suddenly, her hands clasped the sides of his face, and she gazed deep into his eyes, beyond his mortal gaze, her shadow vision plunging straight through to his mind. He winced but didn't pull back. He didn't like for her to see the torturous strains he suffered in his ongoing efforts to control his shade. He didn't want her to see the doubts that racked him, the fear that underlay every command decision. Steeling his will against hers, he suppressed all of these thoughts and feelings, refusing to give her access.

She didn't press. With the precision of an experienced markswoman, she sent her Apparition powers straight through to that place in his mind that controlled his body. This was one of the first skills Apparitions were trained in at the castra, and Hollis was no novice in her craft.

"There," Hollis said, and Fendrel shuddered at the sensation of her shade slipping back out, like a cold finger trailing across his brain. "You're safe for the moment."

Fendrel nodded. He stood up, swaying a little. His throat felt bruised, and his gaze shot briefly to the dead man and the dead page lying on the floor nearby. The Corpsewitch had escaped. And . . .

"Guardin!" Fendrel gasped. All the questions he'd wanted to hurl at Hollis evaporated in an instant of roiling, rushing terror. "I've got to get to my brother."

He was in motion the next instant, leaving the corpses and the fading curse barrier behind and hastening another way, across a small upper landing to the king's suite of rooms. Hollis followed at his heels, demanding, "The king is here as well? What's going on, Fendrel? Why are—"

He didn't hear her. He couldn't have answered anyway. Blood pounded in his ears, and his shade roared in his soul. He saw the closed door to his brother's suite and threw himself against it. Bolted fast. Maybe . . . maybe . . . .

Lifting his left arm, Fendrel swiped at the fresh blood still flowing down his face. With a cry, he flung a curse at that door. The hinges shattered. The door sagged and fell.

"Fendrel!" Hollis cried again, but he ignored her. Stepping on the door, he rushed into the firelit room, turning this way and that, his eyes darting from his head.

The chamber was empty. Guardin was gone. Leaving his door bolted from the inside.

"She has him," Fendrel breathed. He whirled to face Hollis, who tilted her head back to stare up at him. "The Phantomwitch. She has him. They're making for the vault."

CHAPTER 18

PAIN SHOT THROUGH TERRYN'S LIMBS, RACING THROUGH his veins like fire. Anathema magic seared his blood, straight to his soul, overwhelming his will with the urge to succumb, to obey, to bow the knee to the compulsions of the curse caster.

"*Terryn!*" Gerard's voice. But so far away.

Terryn's vision sparked, flashes of magic exploding in bursts before his dazzled gaze. Unable to bear the sight, he closed his eyes and beheld instead the stone-hard landscape of his mind. The curse flooded in over the horizon like a molten river of blood, pouring into all cracks and crevices, seeping into the depths of his spirit.

He fled from the torrent. The image of his spirit-self stumbled as he ran, keeping only a few steps ahead of the onslaught that would drown him. Before him, a few paces away, loomed the bulging, stone-encased draconian shape of his suppressed shade.

There was nowhere else to run. The blood-magma of the curse was going to sweep over his head, and he would succumb to its will—to the will of the Warpwitch who controlled it. Desperate, Terryn ran to that bulge of stone and scrambled up its hard, sloping side onto the spine-like ridge. The molten blood swept in around, splashing up against the stone and rising, rising. It would catch him. There was no escape.

The stone shifted beneath him. He staggered, desperate to catch his balance. A voice rumbled from the end shaped like a massive head.

Do you know my name?

Terryn opened his mortal eyes. The world around him exploded with red Anathema light. The Warpwitch, wearing the body of the guard, strode toward him, bloody hand outstretched, teeth bared as she twisted at the curse thread binding Terryn to her.

"Come on, little pet," she crooned through the man's mouth. "You only hurt yourself by fighting."

His bones seemed to be breaking inside him. He fell to his knees, not in subservience to the witch, but simply because he could no longer stand. Where was Gerard? Where was Cerine? He couldn't search for them. The pain was too much. His arms spasmed, and every finger tensed. The cords in his throat stood out as he threw back his head, screaming through clenched teeth.

He closed his eyes.

Once more he stood in his mind-scape. The blood-curse rose swiftly, steaming with heat that would melt the skin from his bones were this body not a mere projection. The mass beneath him stirred again, and only by catching hold of a stone-encrusted spine did he save himself from a fall.

You know my name, said the voice. *Tell me.*

"No!" Terryn screamed. "*You'll destroy me! Fiend of the Haunts, you'll destroy my soul!*"

My name, said the voice. *Tell me my name.*

Terryn's mortal eyes opened again. The Warpwitch stood over him, not an arm's length away. If he had the will, he could knock the guard's body off his feet, could pummel his face, could stab a poisoned dart into his throat. But another jolt of pure agony shot from his head down his spine, out to every extremity. He felt his broken bones beginning to reknit in a new, horrible shape.

"Give in to me now, boy," the guard said. His face smiled with the strange, seductive slyness all hosts of the Warpwitch wore. "The more you fight, the more you suffer. You'll never break my curse on you."

A sudden movement just behind the guard's shoulder.

Terryn's gaze swiveled, alerting the Warpwitch at the last moment. Her host body started to turn just as a fist swung and struck her hard in the head. With a yell, she fell under the blow, her large man's frame landing with a thud.

Gerard stood over the Warpwitch, unarmed but undaunted. His face twisted with rage, he kicked the guard in the head, kicked him again in the ribs, kicked again harder, and harder. The Warpwitch snarled viciously, spitting foam and blood from her host's mouth. Terryn saw the build-up of Anathema magic in the center of the guard's soul. He tried to scream a warning, to urge Gerard to flee. But his mouth would not obey him.

The Warpwitch raised the guard's hand to his mouth and bit down savagely, drawing fresh blood. She hurled it, and along with it a blasting curse that sent Gerard flying down the hall, landing flat on the hard floor, and skidding several more feet.

"Stupid boy!" The Warpwitch spat out a broken tooth as she pulled her host body back upright. One arm had dislocated in the ferocity of the prince's assault and now dangled uselessly. Limping, she stalked down the passage toward the prince. "Stupid little princeling bastard. We need your blood, but we don't need you. I think your head will do well enough all on its own!"

Gerard didn't move. Had the curse killed him? Stunned him? If he wasn't dead already, the Warpwitch would kill him in the next few moments. Moments . . .

Terryn blinked, and for an instant, he stood in the landscape of his mind again. Burning blood-magma stretched from horizon to horizon, and scarcely more than a foothold remained here at the top of the stone mound.

Say my name, the voice in his head urged, faint beneath the flood of the curse. *Say my name. Say it!*

Terryn bowed his head. This was the end then. He would die. He would lose his soul. He would never attain the Goddess's Light, but would be ousted from his body to wander revenant until he faded to nothing. Utter oblivion was his doom.

But he would save Gerard.

He opened his mouth. In the mortal world and in the world of his mind simultaneously, he spoke the name— the name he'd known from the moment the foreign spirit entered his body, from the moment just before he, with the help of Fendrel and the Council of Breçar, bound and suppressed it beneath this stone casing. The name he'd known but been forbidden to ever speak, to ever think, to even acknowledge its existence. The name of his shade.

"*Nisirdi!*" he screamed.

The stone beneath his feet broke. White light shot from each crack in beams so brilliant, they could cut through skin and bone. More light burst through the blood-magma, driving it back in waves from the bulge of stone.

Glad to meet you, mortal man, said the voice.

The stone dragon lifted its head.

Terryn's mortal eyes flared open. The Warpwitch crouched over Gerard, yanking him up by the front of his shirt. The prince's head lolled to one side, bleeding from various wounds. The witch drew back a hand, curse magic mounding in the space between curled fingers.

"Ylaire!" Terryn cried.

Startled, she turned the guard's head to stare at Terryn.

"NO!" she shrieked in the man's stolen voice.

Dropping the prince, she flung out her bloody hand, catching at the curse thread attached to his soul, straining to regain control. White light pulsed through Terryn's veins, purging the curse. The Warpwitch twisted the connecting thread, pulled at the place of anchoring, the sigil implanted in Terryn's cheek. Terryn felt the curse's power still resisting the rising magic of the shade.

You need to release me, mortal, the voice said in his head. *I can break the curse if you'll let me.*

Terryn's hand fumbled for his Vocos. The Warpwitch,

realizing what he was doing, leapt up and ran at him, a knife flashing in the guard's hand. She managed to drive her host body three paces. But before she could take a fourth step, Terryn blew a one-note blast on the Vocos—the single, piercing note that, when played, broke all other spells. It shrieked through his senses, sliced through his soul, obliterating the last of the binding suppressions on his shade.

On Nisirdi.

Power burst from every pore of Terryn's body, burst from the core of his spirit. He screamed, not in pain this time, but in terror. This power was much too great. This power was much too full of all the light, all the strange music of Arcane magic.

Out from his chest rose a being of angelic majesty. Terryn's dazzled mind, unable to comprehend what it saw, crafted a shape, a form, to try to understand. He beheld a mighty dragon—glorious, pure, shining like all the stars of heaven. It unfurled wings of prismed radiance, shaking off the last dust of the stone-like suppression spells. Its slender, horn-crowned head arched at the end of a long, serpentine neck, and spines like silver knife blades gleamed down its back and the endlessly coiling lengths of its tail.

The Warpwitch drew up short, the host body she wore skidding to a stop. The guard's eyes rounded as Ylaire gazed up at that ascendant being. Whatever form that mortal mind conjured to understand the incomprehensible, it filled the witch with utter horror.

The light-dragon lunged.

The Warpwitch flung up a bloody hand, and out from the center of the host body sprang her Anathema shade, lurching to meet that other, tremendous power. Terryn's confused shadow vision discerned something like a snake, dripping with blood, striking at the dragon's neck, attempting to latch hold and wrap round and round the dragon's body, limbs, and wings. But the dragon caught the snake in its outspread arms, enveloping it in an embrace of mighty wings.

The strangeness of the encounter was too much for Terryn's mind to even try to understand. He looked away before his spirit broke with pure insanity, and his mortal eyes landed on the Warpwitch.

She saw him at the same moment. And they were *her*

eyes he beheld in that man's stolen face. The same eyes that had gazed into his when he was a small, helpless child, as she caressed his cheek before tearing into it, implanting him with her sigil. The same eyes that had laughed at him from Lady Mylla's gentle face, the same eyes that had mocked him as he suffered under her compulsions.

Her shade, wrapped in the light and power of Nisirdi, could not help her now.

Though pure Arcane magic poured from his body, streaming from his eyes, his nostrils, his fingertips, Terryn still possessed some tiny measure of control. He could feel his soul slipping under the ascendant power of his shade. But he had a few seconds left. All the time he needed.

He pulled out an Anathema dart, leapt at the Warpwitch, and plunged it into the guard's open, screaming mouth.

She tried to run. The host body she wore was strong, but Gerard's blows had weakened it. Terryn caught hold of the guard's broken arm and refused to let go, even as the poison took effect. The man fell, twisting in desperation, still screaming. The Anathema shade, falling under the potency of the poison, melted out from the arms of the light dragon, sinking down smaller and smaller to coil up inside the host body. The light of two entwined spirits—witch and shade—lulled and dulled to almost nothing.

Terryn opened his mouth. Pure white light shot from his throat, and he smiled through it and said, "Sweet dreams, Ylaire."

He fell on his knees beside the guard's body and stuck the Gentle Death alongside the other dart, right into the man's swollen tongue. The world rocked around him as reality tore in two, and he felt the cold-burning blast of the Haunts on his skin. The hellish gates opened to reclaim yet another escaped shade. Terryn shuddered—but then something moved and blocked him, shielding him from the ugly, poisonous air of that other realm. A vast white wing cupped around his body, gentle as a mother's arms.

The Haunts closed. Terryn fell flat beside the dead guard's body and felt his overwhelmed soul tearing loose inside.

CHAPTER 19

AYLETH SPED DOWN THE FRONT STAIRCASE, FOCUSING Laranta's perceptions through the din of screams and terror and mayhem, focusing on that one voice. Her blood pumped frantically in her veins. Even with shade power driving her, she felt she could not run fast enough, could not possibly arrive in time.

Figures loomed before her mortal vision in the long dark shadows of the great front hall. Her shadow vision almost missed them, for they possessed no shining spirits, but her heart jolted with dread at the sight. They were men. Women too. Three faces she recognized from among the household staff, and two Evanderians.

Each pinned to the wall by protrusions of crystal.

The Crystalwitch was here. Crisentha di Bathia. That made four of the seven surviving Crimson Devils, including the Phantomwitch and the Legionwitch, whom she had just slain. And the Warpwitch. She was here for certain.

How many of them were here inside the keep? And how had they escaped from the Witchwood through the Great Barrier?

The answer presented itself even as she skidded on the polished floor, trying not to look at the dead on the walls. The Phantomwitch. Of course. Now that the Warpwitch had called Inren ascendant, overpowering Fayline d'Aldreda's lingering soul, Inren could easily cross the Barrier and return, stepping through the Haunts. As long as she'd left an anchor stone on the far side. She could have carried all of the devils out. She could have brought all of them into Dunloch as well.

And for what purpose other than to slay the Chosen

King and his son?

Another scream burst in Ayleth's senses, driving these other thoughts far from her mind. She flung herself around the supporting pillars in the great hall and careened into the broad north passage. Just as she stepped into this hall, the world erupted in a blast of shadow-light so brilliant, Ayleth threw up both hands to shield her face. She fell back into the wall, turning her head away, while Laranta howled in her mind, *Shade! Shade! Hunt the shade!*

Ayleth pulled herself back upright and, wincing against the light, peered down the passage again. Through the glare of magic, her physical eyes saw four figures. Nearest was a woman, her head turned away so Ayleth couldn't see her face. Three male figures lay on the floor not much farther down the passage—Prince Gerard, one of the household guards with two fletched darts protruding from his open mouth, and . . . Terryn . . .

From the depths of his soul poured the white shade light.

"No," Ayleth whispered. Then she shouted, "No! Please!"

She knew what this was. The vastness of power emanating from Terryn told her that he had released his shade. Just as she had several times urged him to do. Why, she did not know, but he'd done it, and now this incredible maelstrom of power would tear his soul from his body.

She couldn't let it happen.

"No! No!" she cried, then switched to speaking in spirit instead, throwing her voice out through Laranta, reaching out to that shade. *"Please, don't hurt him!"*

The white light seemed to gather itself into a form—a shape she could almost recognize but not quite. She felt a profound sense of glory, majesty, purity. All things she'd never before thought to associate with shades. And she felt rather than saw the compelling interest of eyes watching her.

I do not wish to hurt him, a voice spoke. Or rather, a song sang, without words but with such complexity and precision that Ayleth understood the meaning, unhindered by the limitations of language. *I do not wish to hurt the mortal man.*

"But you are!" Ayleth said. *"You are hurting him. He can't*

sustain this level of power. He doesn't know how. You'll destroy him, you'll oust his soul. Please, please—for Terryn's sake, reduce!"

I do not like to reduce again, the voice answered, more sternly this time. *I've been captive for so long.*

And what could she say to that? She knew how profoundly Terryn had bound his shade, how he had treated it. He'd believed it his enemy, his nearest and worst enemy, and with good reason. This being—it was so much greater than anything Ayleth had ever before seen.

She could not argue. So she said only, *"Please don't hurt him. I . . . can't bear to lose him."*

The being watched her closely. The brilliance of its glow pulsed with interest and curiosity. Then it said, *Neither can I.*

As it spoke, it reduced. Ayleth watched in disbelieving wonder as the white light coalesced into the shape of a long, elegant beast with magnificent wings. It bent its extraordinary head down to Terryn and seemed momentarily to rest the end of its slender nose against Terryn's heart. Then it shrank and flowed into his limbs and torso, curling down tight and quiet. The white brilliance continued to glow through Terryn's skin for some moments, illuminating the corridor, but vanished at last, leaving all dark and strangely still.

With a wordless cry, Ayleth fell to her knees beside Terryn. She grabbed his shoulders and hauled him upright, and her heart leapt to her throat when his eyes blinked rapidly.

"A-Ayleth?" he stammered, shaking his head and peering at her in disbelief.

Ayleth couldn't speak, couldn't begin to explain. She pulled him close in a swift embrace, but quickly pushed him away again to meet his gaze. He stared at her, his eyes fixed on her face yet not really seeing her. He was trying to comprehend what had happened, trying to make sense of it.

Then he blinked again, and when his eyes refocused, he exclaimed, "Gerard!"

Both of them turned to the prince lying close at hand, covered in a dozen gashes from a vicious blood-curse. Ayleth and Terryn both scrambled to the prince's side, partially falling over the strange guard in their way. Ayleth, glancing at the tips of the fletched arrows, saw that the guard had been brought down by both a paralysis dart and the Gentle Death. Was it possible the Warpwitch had stolen this man's body as a host?

She didn't linger over this thought but hurried with Terryn to the prince. She quickly placed her fingers at his throat. A pulse! He was alive, merely unconscious.

"She was going to kill him," Terryn said, referring to the guard, Ayleth gathered. "I had to . . . I had to—" His eyes sought Ayleth's once more, huge and desperate. And full of wonder. "I let it go."

"You did the right thing." Ayleth rested her hand on top of his. "You're still alive."

Terryn looked down at the deathly still prince. Then, with a shake of his head, he moved to slide an arm under Gerard's shoulders. "We've got to get him to the vault. It's the only way to keep him safe while we hunt down the rest of these devils."

Ayleth nodded and helped Terryn lift Gerard. The prince moaned, seemed to try to rally himself back into consciousness, but ultimately drooped as a dead weight in his brother's arms. His face was torn up, three ugly slashes bleeding profusely. Ayleth drew one of Gerard's arms around her neck to help Terryn support him. Then her gaze landed once more on the unconscious woman.

"Lady Cerine!" she exclaimed. The next moment she choked in horror as she recognized the bloody tatters in the lady's gown, places where spines had protruded and bones had broken and reknitted. A collision of thoughts tumbled in Ayleth's brain—realizations, assumptions, confusions, all mingled into one. They'd used her. The witches used her to get into the castle. How exactly, Ayleth couldn't yet fathom, but they'd done it.

"We've got to go," Terryn urged, his voice thin and strained. "Leave her for now. We'll come back." Before he could continue, two figures rushed into the corridor on the far side of Cerine. Dominus Fendrel and—

"Hollis!" Ayleth cried.

As if this night couldn't get more complicated!

Both dominus and venatrix skidded to a halt at the sight of Terryn, Ayleth, and their burden. Ayleth tensed, half ready for Fendrel to try to shoot her where she stood, escaped prisoner that she was.

Instead, the dominus roared, "To the vault! The vault!" Terryn and Ayleth exchanged quick glances. The dominus was upon them the next moment, grabbing the unconscious Gerard out of their arms and dropping him unceremoniously at their feet. "Leave him! With me at once. To the vault!" he commanded.

Hollis was in her peripheral vision, Fendrel was before her, and the command rang in her ears. Though this same man had only hours ago ordered her pyre to be raised, it didn't matter now. Ayleth's training took over. She fell into step, following him down the passage to the portrait gallery. It was like something out of a nightmare to be at Fendrel's heels, Terryn on her right hand with an unsuppressed shade coiled tight in the center of his spirit, and Hollis—Hollis!—on her left. Could it be that all this was nothing more than a conjuring of her terrified mind? That she'd fallen asleep in that hateful prison of a bedchamber and merely dreamt up this chaos?

Fendrel, his right arm hanging strangely lifeless from his shoulder, used his left to open the door to the portrait gallery, slamming into it with his shoulder. He rushed inside, Hollis at his heels. Ayleth was just starting to follow behind them when a bolt of magic flashed before her vision. She recoiled back into Terryn, who caught her before she fell.

"Hollis!" she gasped.

Her vision cleared. She saw her former mistress recover from a roll and assume a defensive crouch, shadow-light shimmering in her eyes. Her Apparition shade must have warned her of the incoming attack just in time. Fendrel was also unharmed by the blast, which had struck the far wall. From between two large paintings jutted huge growths of crystal, gleaming like teeth. A chunk of plaster dropped to the floor.

The Crystalwitch waited inside, blocking the way to the vault.

CHAPTER 20

HOLLIS GLANCED OVER HER SHOULDER, SAW WHAT had become of the wall, and knew at once who her attacker must be. Her hand moved to her quivers, pulled out a paralysis dart, and slotted it into her scorpiona.

After regaining her feet, Ayleth nodded to Terryn and reached for her darts. He followed suit, and the two of them, one on either side of the doorway, peered into the gallery. Another blast of magic flared across Ayleth's shadow vision, and Fendrel only just avoided having his right leg caught in crystal, which sprouted up from the floor in a formation as tall as a man.

Terryn met Ayleth's eyes across the doorway. His angle afforded him a better view down the gallery. Ayleth suspected he could see the Crystalwitch. She watched him, her scorpiona upraised and ready.

Laranta, she spoke inside, *reach out. Find where the witch stands. The shade.*

Her wolf shade's senses stretched into the room—not sight or smell or hearing, but other senses for which Ayleth had no name. They manifested in Ayleth's head, and her mind shaped them into something she could comprehend—a shadowy vision of a figure standing ten paces out from the secret door at the end of the gallery. A figure brimming with power, which launched yet another blast that missed its target but shook the walls.

Ayleth met Terryn's gaze. "Tell me when," she mouthed, trusting him to understand her.

With his back pressed to the wall, angled so that he could see into the room with one eye only, he nodded. His scarred cheek tensed, his jaw clenched. Then his eyes flicked to her, and his lips moved soundlessly: "Now!"

Ayleth sprang into the room and took aim, allowing her shade's senses to guide her. Before her mortal eyes fixed upon her target, she shot—and the dart sped across the gallery, between Fendrel's moving form and outcroppings of crystal grown up from the floor, flying straight on its trajectory to the heart of the witch.

It struck home.

The poisoned tip of the dart bent and broke against Crisentha di Bathia's impenetrable, glittering skin.

The Crystalwitch looked down at the dart. She had changed bodies since Ayleth last glimpsed her in the Witchwood. She now wore the form of a huge, barrel-bosomed woman, her hair spiraling out from her head in solid, crystallized curls. Her massive hands clenched into fists as she looked up directly into Ayleth's face. And smiled.

Laranta's power surged inside her, and Ayleth leapt with such speed and strength that she ran partway up and along the wall, narrowly avoiding the blast aimed her way. She sensed the cold brush of magic, felt how it sought to catch her, to encase her, to send crystals sprouting out from her very bones through her skin. Only her shade's strength and agility saved her. This time.

She came down hard, lost her footing, and landed on her shoulder. Training made her roll quickly behind one of the crystal protrusions in the floor, which made for an effective shield.

She peered out between formations and saw the Crystalwitch take another dart, this time from Hollis's scorpiona, equally ineffective. Hollis dodged a blast, and Fendrel hid behind another crystal projection, his right arm useless at his side, unable even to take a shot. She saw Anathema power mounting up inside him and watched him stand up and fling a bloody curse at the witch's head. It struck, but produced no visible effect other than to make her stagger back two paces.

The Crystalwitch grinned again, her teeth flashing like so many square diamonds. Beyond her, the door leading down to the vault stood open.

I have an idea.

Ayleth shivered, recognizing the voice suddenly appearing in her head: It was Hollis, speaking through the power of her Apparition shade directly into Ayleth's mind.

Venator du Balafre, she said, and Ayleth realized her mistress's voice was appearing in multiple minds at once. *We need a distraction. Can you use your power to stun the witch? This is what I have in mind.*

Ayleth winced as Hollis presented an image, a visual of what she hoped Terryn could do, planted directly into their heads. When the image faded, she looked around at Terryn, still in the doorway, and she saw him nod. He understood. This would mean drawing on his shade's power so soon after nearly being overwhelmed by it. Could he do it? Could he balance the control necessary to channel such power with an unsuppressed shade?

Everyone, Hollis's voice said, *cover your eyes!*

Ayleth buried her face in her arms. Even so, the sudden blinding brilliance of Arcane magic seemed to burn right through, searing her eyeballs, threatening to melt her brain. She could feel that magic, that light, reflected off the many crystals until it filled the whole room.

The Crystalwitch screamed. And Hollis stepped into play. The power of Hollis's shade mounted up from deep in her soul, more ascendant than Ayleth had ever felt it.

She couldn't look at her mistress with the light of Terryn's shade still reflecting off the crystals in deadly power, but with Laranta's senses she felt it swelling, and she knew Hollis must have used her Vocos to loosen most of her restriction spells.

With expert precision, Hollis lashed out with her Apparition, aiming straight for the Crystalwitch's mind. The witch, overcome with pain, wasn't ready for the attack. She screamed again, this time in rage, but Hollis was already in her head.

The heat and glow of Terryn's magic faded. Ayleth dared to raise her head, her eyes dazed with dark spots. She peered around her shield of crystals and saw the witch writhing on the floor, her massive, crystal-encrusted limbs flailing and helpless. Suddenly, the crystal melted away, leaving behind nothing but pale, soft skin.

Fendrel sprang into action before Ayleth even got to her feet. Using his left arm, he pulled out a paralysis dart and stuck it into the exposed flesh of the witch's neck. Crisentha uttered a last furious cry and tried to muster strength enough to shoot a blast of magic into Fendrel's face. But Hollis was still in her head. The witch's arm swung away from her target, and her hand clenched, stifling the blast.

The poison took effect, subduing her, body and soul.

Terryn stepped in behind Fendrel, his hands still glowing with the brilliance of the magic he had just channeled. Once more, his shade curled down tight inside him, trying not to overwhelm him, but the force and magic hummed from his core so that he seemed to carry song with him with every step he took. He pulled a Gentle Death dart from his quivers and knelt over the Crystalwitch.

Fendrel gripped his shoulder. "No," he said. "Secure her. We might need her for questioning." Then he looked back at Hollis, who rose shakily to her feet, weakened by the use of her shade. "Follow me!" he barked and, leaving Terryn with the witch, headed for the open door leading down to the vaults.

Ayleth and Hollis made brief eye contact before they both sprang into action, following the Venator Dominus. Terryn caught Ayleth's eye as she passed him, his expression unreadable. She looked away quickly, leaving him to bind the Crystalwitch according to Fendrel's command.

She reached the door a few paces ahead of Hollis and hastened down the narrow steps in pursuit of Fendrel. He may still want her dead. He may still command that she be burned alive as soon as this battle was complete. But for the moment, she would follow Fendrel du Glaive straight into the mouth of hell if there was some chance he could lead her to stop these witches.

"No past," she whispered. "No future. Only the hunt."

Laranta growled in her head.

Inren di Karel stood in the passage just outside the lower-level vault, which was shut fast against her. Her hand, stained and running with fresh blood, pressed into its smooth surface. Even that touch should have sent her crashing back into the wall. But the blood coating her hand and protecting it from the blood wards wasn't hers.

Guardin knelt at the witch's feet with both hands pressed to his neck, trying to stop the bleeding from an open wound. He would die from this gash if it was not bound. His body shuddered, shivered, and his vision spun.

"It won't work," he choked, spitting out more blood with each word. "The wards . . . the wards . . ."

Liselle di Matin's lovely face smiled down at him, and Inren spoke through her mouth. "I know how blood wards work, dear kingling. I've picked up a trick or two over the years. Only someone with du Glaive blood inside can pass through, is that right? Well . . ." She licked her knife, little caring when the edge cut her tongue. "There. Let's see how that works, shall we?"

Figures moved in on each side of the dying king. Two figures, two witch men. They watched the Phantomwitch with solemn, silent interest as she reached her bloody hand to the bolt, lifted it, and pushed the door open.

Ayleth was only a step behind the Venator Dominus on the narrow stair, her scorpiona up and ready, aimed over his shoulder. In the back of her mind, she wondered exactly what they were doing. If there was a blood-warded chamber below, it made sense to bring Gerard and his father down here where they would be safe while the Evanderians dealt with the Crimson Devils.

Why had Fendrel taken Gerard from Terryn's arms and left him on the floor, exposed and alone in that corridor? Had he guessed the witches would set up a defense here? And the witches themselves, were they simply lying in wait, knowing the king and his son would come here for safety? How did they even know about the safe room? It wasn't as though this was common knowledge? Or was there something else—

Ayleth's mind exploded in roiling clouds of darkness, her senses full of stench and clamor and a feeling like knives scraping her skin. She fell back on the narrow steps, pressing herself against the wall, no longer aware of her surroundings, no longer aware of the danger.

Her mind was filled with nothing but screaming, horrific pain.

The light from Inren's lantern shone into the sarcophagus beyond the door, illuminating the stone table where a corpse lay in funeral state, its hands crossed over its breast. A headless corpse wearing the burnt remnants of a fantastic, bejeweled gown.

Beyond the table, on a pedestal under glass, lay the severed head.

All the hair was burnt away, and the skin was blackened and hideous, especially around the forehead, which had burned all the way to the skull. The eyelids were half closed, but a strange, fluttering sort of sensation gave the impression they would spring open again at any moment. One could almost see the movement of black eyes behind the pale, translucent skin.

"No." The Chosen King's lips moved without sound. He could not speak. He could scarcely keep himself upright, leaning against the wall, his hands pressed to his death wound.

"My Queen," Inren breathed. She took a step. The blood wards ought to strike her down at once, to tear her into a thousand pieces. But she had guessed the weakness of Fendrel's magic correctly. With the smallest trace of Guardin's fresh blood inside her, she passed through the ward untouched.

With cries of delight and eagerness, the two witches

around Guardin closed in on him. Both of them wanted their taste of his blood. They took what they needed and hurried after Inren into the room. "Bring him," the Phantomwitch called to the second man before he entered.

The witch man paused. His movements were sluggish, his face muscles, slack. Someone had managed to graze him with a paralysis dart. But he grabbed Guardin by the elbow and pulled him up. The king nearly fainted. He desperately wished to let unconsciousness come, to fade into darkness and death before he saw what he knew must happen next. But he refused to succumb to that wish.

He would watch. To the end.

Where was the girl though? His sickened brain grasped at this thought with a flicker of hope even as the witch man dumped him on the floor beside the stone slab and the corpse of his enemy. Without the girl, they couldn't possibly accomplish their purpose. And she was nowhere in sight. Perhaps . . . perhaps . . . .

The Phantomwitch pulled a vial made from some faceted black gemstone from the bosom of her tattered gown. "The head, my dear. Bring our queen's head," she said, her voice as reverent as a nun in prayer.

The other witch man stepped over to the pedestal and lifted the glass dome. He dropped it, and it shattered in a hundred shards on the floor. Reaching both hands to that gruesome head, he lifted it with such gentleness, such tenderness! As though he held the most sacred of relics. He carried it to the slab and gently, ever so gently, laid it in place beside the severed neck.

All three witches crowded in. Eager to see, eager to behold the miracle. The curse. The abomination which Guardin had already witnessed once. Twenty years ago . . .

Dark tendrils of *oblivis* reached out from bone to bone, neck to neck, knitting together what should never be repaired. Dread Odile was once more whole.

"Why does she not wake?" one of the witch men demanded, his voice reedy and spraying spit in his eagerness. He hovered over his dead queen, who still lay inert, the spirits within her silent. "Why does she not rise?"

"You forget, brother," the Phantomwitch scolded him

with a sharp glare before once more fixing her worshipful eyes on the face of the dead witch. "You forget the counter-curse. She can only be restored by one of her own blood." She smiled then, unstopping the vial she held. "But, as with all blood-curses, there is usually a work-around."

She caught the corpse's mouth in her hand, pulling the jaw open. Tilting the vial, she watched a thin stream of dark red liquid pour onto that swollen tongue and trickle down that ravaged throat. She kept pouring until every last drop had fallen. Then she shut the dead woman's jaw and dropped the vial so that it crashed on the stone. She backed away, as did the two witch men. Their faces were masks of dread and desire, terrible to behold.

Guardin knew then what had happened. Somehow . . . somehow they had taken the girl's blood. Not a lot. But it didn't matter. Only a little was needed.

Goddess, Guardin prayed even as his life oozed out between his trembling fingers. *Goddess, don't punish my people for my sin. Don't punish my son for my lie. Don't desert us—*

The body spasmed. The arms, crossed at her chest,

flung out to each side, each finger straining. The head tilted, and the back arched.

Dread Odile screamed.

CHAPTER 21

AYLETH SCREAMED.

Fendrel whirled around at the base of the stairs, his eyes flaming with shadow-light. "What is she doing?" he snarled. For a moment, Hollis feared he would let loose the curse he had built up in his palm, cutting Ayleth in two where she lay to silence her.

Acting fast, Hollis leapt down the stairs over Ayleth, placing herself between her former apprentice and the Venator Dominus, and clamped her hands down over

Ayleth's mouth. The girl didn't seem to be aware of her at all and kept on screaming, even as she lost air. At this rate, she would alert every witch within a twenty-mile radius to their presence.

"Mind the passage!" Hollis shot back at Fendrel over her shoulder. Still keeping her hands tight over Ayleth's open mouth, she leaned her forehead against the girl's.

Ayleth! She plunged her shade to the edges of the girl's mind. The Apparition, which had traveled many times into this realm, moved swiftly, searching for an opening. Ayleth's terror made access difficult, but Hollis drove her shade on. *Ayleth! Can you hear me?*

Looking through her shade's eyes, she glimpsed the shadowy forest that made up Ayleth's mind-scape. Somewhere in that forest, Ayleth's soul stood screaming at the empty sky, incoherent. Hollis reached in with her shade, trying to tap the edge of the girl's awareness, just to make her realize she wasn't alone. She found her at last and dove down to reach her.

Then she heard the voice.

COME TO ME! COME TO ME! COME TO ME!

It filled this space like constant, roaring thunder, bursting with bolts like lightning. It was a voice Hollis knew. Too well. Much too well.

Ayleth! she cried again, desperate to reach the girl. Using her shade's power, she lashed it deep inside the girl's mind. *Ayleth, come to me! Follow my voice!*

But Ayleth couldn't hear her. She was utterly given over to her terror, utterly given over to the pounding, pulverizing voice beating down upon her soul. Hollis could detect no sign of the girl's shade, which Ayleth ordinarily kept so close. The voice had driven even that powerful *sensi* spirit back into the deeper recesses of the shadowy forest.

Suddenly, the voice ceased. Ayleth's screaming died away as well, almost immediately. Hollis, using her shade's power, studied the girl standing there in her mind, upright and expressionless, arms limp at her sides.

She opened her mortal eyes to look at the physical form of the girl before her. Ayleth blinked slowly. Awareness flickered in her face and then came fully back to life. She shook away Hollis's pressing hands, grimaced, and rubbed at her forehead with the heel of one palm.

"What . . . what happened?"

Hollis didn't answer. She stood on the stair, turning to face Fendrel down below. The Venator Dominus stood with a curse upraised, prepared for a witch attack at any moment. "Fendrel!" Hollis barked.

He looked up, met her gaze. The color drained from his face. Hollis didn't have to say anything. He already knew.

But she spoke the words anyway: "She's awake."

The powerful warrior, the man of vision, the leader who had commanded the deaths of thousands for the sake of what he believed . . . In that moment, he looked like a lost, frightened little boy.

His jaw firmed. "Get her up," he said, striding up the steps two at a time. He reached out with his left hand. "Get her on her feet! She's our only chance now."

Hollis didn't argue. He was right. She grabbed Ayleth by her upper arm and, with Fendrel's assistance, pulled the tall girl upright. "Hol . . . Hollis," Ayleth gasped. She swayed, and her eyes rolled. "What . . . what are you . . .?"

Hollis snatched a dart from one of the quivers strung across Ayleth's chest. She grabbed the girl's scorpiona, knocked the loaded dart to fall on the stone steps, and slid this new dart in its place. "Elemental poison," she said. "Don't hesitate to fire. The moment you have a clear shot, fire!"

"Fire? At whom?"

"You'll know," Fendrel answered darkly. They descended into the shadowy passage, staggering and stumbling as fast as they could while Ayleth desperately tried to regain control of her own feet. Hollis would not let herself hope they'd make it in time. Hope no longer mattered.

Her hands scrambled for her neck, trembling like leaves. She gagged and choked, coughed and spat, sitting up on the stone slab and heaving between her upraised knees. Nothing came up, but she continued to heave, her long fingers trembling as she stroked and stroked her neck, as though unable to believe it was intact. Then she looked down at her arms, her shoulders, her hands.

"They burned me," she rasped. The voice was like knives tearing through her throat. She gagged again. But her hands clenched into fists, and she shook her head, roaring louder despite the pain. "They burned me! They burned me! They cut off my head and *they burned me!*"

"My Queen—" spoke the Phantomwitch.

With a roar, the spectral thing on the slab lashed out one arm, and a bolt of pure darkness shot from each fingertip, striking the wall just to the right of her servant, blasting a hole through the stone. The chamber shook, the ceiling shuddered.

The witches backed away from the slab, exchanging frightened glances.

Dread Odile stared at her hand in wonder. Then a slow, terrible smile cut across her face.

"I've still got you, haven't I?" she murmured. "My shade, my dearest demon. Even now you can't resist my will. So we can rebuild. We can reclaim what was stolen. We will find our crown, and we will—"

Her eyes and nostrils flared, and she turned her head, her death-brightened eyes fixing on the king where he lay in a bundle of limbs by the wall. He met her gaze, and though his failing heart surged with the desire to stand before her one last time, he no longer had control of his body. His weakened hands fell away from the wound in his throat from which his life's blood flowed. But he met her gaze without flinching.

"You," Odile hissed. She twisted on her slab, tried to climb off, and nearly fell in her efforts. Her shivering fingers grasped the edge of the stone, only just keeping her upright. "You cut off my head and you burned my body. You stole my throne and you slaughtered my people."

He could not speak. He could do nothing except . . .

One corner of his mouth twisted in a faint half grin.

With a shriek of pure rage, Dread Odile lifted her skeletal arm and blasted the Chosen King of Perrinion to oblivion.

Ayleth heard screaming from the end of the passage. Her vision swam, and the world around her seemed made up of nightmarish chaos.

How did she know that voice? Why did Fendrel and Hollis carry her between them, not away from battle, but toward it? She tried to gather herself, to pull free of their arms, to stand on her own.

Ahead she saw the vault door. Lantern light streamed through a gap into the shadowed passage. And then the screaming:

"They burned me! They burned me! They cut off my head and they burned me!"

Her stomach clenched in terror. Laranta howled inside her. She should draw on her shade's power now, throw off the clutching hands that dragged her along, and flee. But no. She was a venatrix. She would not run from a fight.

"Find the shade, Laranta!" she commanded inside.

Laranta wailed, *Shade! Shade!* and her powerful senses lurched out from Ayleth into that room. The witches were there, waiting, shades ascendant.

But there was more. There was . . . a power. Unlike anything Ayleth had ever before encountered.

"You!" the voice roared. "You cut off my head and you burned my body. You stole my throne and you slaughtered my people."

Fendrel sprang into the doorway, letting go of Ayleth's arm and raising his left arm, curse magic building in his palm. Ayleth staggered to his side and looked into that open chamber. Her mortal senses were too confused to comprehend anything. But her shade senses perceived everything in a single crystalline moment of absolute clarity.

She saw the slab and the woman seated upon it, gripping the stone edges so tight that her fingers bled. She saw the witches, three of them with their backs pressed against the wall, their eyes huge with terror, their mouths open with wonder. She saw the king, bleeding out, collapsed on the floor not far from the door.

She saw the power of *oblivis* mounting from the very center of the raging woman's soul. An element not of this world, a force of sheer destruction.

"NO!" Fendrel cried. He lunged, but Hollis caught his arm and wrenched him back, preventing him from flinging himself in front of the king.

Ayleth, her mortal eyes blind, her shadow sight dazzled, saw the utter blackness of *oblivis* shoot out from the woman's center, channeled along her arm, through her fingers. It struck the Chosen King in the heart, shattering his chest into a million flashing particles. Each for a shining instant gleamed like the stars of the heavens, bursting out to fill all the universe with their brilliance. Then they dissipated and fell in a cloud of dust, dull and dead upon the floor.

Guardin slumped over, a gaping hole in his torso twining with tendrils of *oblivis*.

All mortal senses dulled. Ayleth could hear nothing, see nothing, feel nothing. She perceived with unnatural senses how Fendrel flailed and roared behind her, collapsing to his knees, still held in Hollis's grasp. She perceived the witches lunging toward that center slab, hands outstretched to the woman.

She felt the woman look up from the death she had just dealt and stare Ayleth directly in the face. "You're supposed to be dead," she said.

Ayleth saw her own face. Only it was her face as it had appeared in Nilly's vision of her death—hair burned away, a black brand ringing her forehead and skull, her skin peeling like curls of ash. Her own eyes, flaring with shadow-light and death, gazed back at her.

The woman raised her hand, and the power of *oblivis* gathered, roiling into a dense sphere of destruction in her palm, ready to blast forth. Ayleth raised her scorpiona armed with the paralysis dart and took aim.

The Phantomwitch caught the woman by her shoulder. Just before the bolt loosed, a crack in the worlds opened, and the Haunts themselves yawned around the witches. Ayleth took her shot, but the dart sped through a cloud of whirling *oblivis* where the woman on the slab had crouched but an instant before.

The dart struck the far wall with a clatter and fell broken to the floor.

CHAPTER 22

AYLETH STOOD WITH HER SCORPIONA STILL UPRAISED, supported on her bracing left arm. She stared into that space in the empty chamber where her own face had been but a moment before. Her heart thudded in her ears, and slowly, slowly she became aware of other sounds, other movements in the world around her.

Fendrel wrenched free of Hollis's grasp and dove into that chamber. The blood wards did not affect him. He passed through without pause and collapsed on his knees beside the broken body of his brother. As though from far away, Ayleth heard wailing, sobbing, and she realized it came from the Venator Dominus, who gathered the dead king in his arms.

Someone touched her arm. With a start of surprise, Ayleth looked down into the pale eyes of her mistress. Hollis gazed up at her, tears glinting, her expression full of things Ayleth couldn't understand.

"That was Dread Odile," Ayleth said.

Hollis nodded once. But she didn't have to. Ayleth already knew. Dread Odile . . . alive, not dead as Ayleth had always been taught. Not beheaded and burned and gone. Alive. Ayleth blinked. Her vision swam as she tried to maintain her focus on Hollis's stricken eyes.

Softly, gently, she whispered, "Why does she have my face?"

Hollis turned away from Ayleth almost as though she couldn't bear to look at her anymore. Ayleth's head spun. Darkness closed in around the edges of her vision. She followed her former mistress's line of sight, gazing into the blood-warded room.

Fendrel, his right arm hanging limp, somehow

managed to heave the body of his brother up and over his shoulder with his one good arm. Using the wall for support, he got to his feet, the power of his shade shimmering through every limb. He turned to the door, tears streaming through the blood on his face, and for an instant his gaze pierced Ayleth's face with such a ferocious hatred, she feared her heart would stop then and there. His eyes slid away from her the next moment, and he bowed his head beneath the burden he bore and stepped through the doorway, carrying the corpse of the king.

Hollis and Ayleth backed away, giving him room in the narrow passage. Hollis's hand reached out, just touching his dead arm as he passed. "Fendrel?" she said quietly.

He made no answer, no acknowledgement, but moved heavily down the hall. More than once he fell against the wall and had to pause and brace his feet. Though Hollis several times moved reflexively to help him, she restrained herself, holding back several paces. Neither of them spoke of what they had just seen, the impossible apparition which had been all too real but moments ago. In the midst of their horror, neither of them seemed . . .

surprised.

They knew. The realization struck Ayleth in the gut. They had known all along. Dread Odile wasn't dead. And they'd lied. Both of them. Lied through their teeth.

Ayleth's feet moved on their own, for she couldn't find the will to follow the venatrix and the dominus. But follow them she must. It was that or remain here in the darkness of the vault, so near to the stink of death and *oblivis*. Anger and betrayal roared in her head, too confused to transform into the questions she needed answered.

Thumping of boots on stone drew Ayleth's attention. She peered with shadow sight through the darkness ahead, over Hollis's head and around Fendrel's broad shoulders and the body he carried. Terryn appeared at the bottom of the stairway leading up to the castle's main floor, shadow-light brilliant in his eyes, his scorpiona upraised. He started at the sight of Fendrel and took aim, but stopped himself from firing the shot as recognition took hold.

His gaze fell on the dead face of the king. He gasped for a breath, then took a lunging step forward, reaching to help Fendrel with his burden. "Back away, Venator," Fendrel snarled, and pushed roughly past his former apprentice. Terryn flattened himself to the wall, and Fendrel climbed the stair, each laborious step an effort of pure will.

Hollis followed after, but Terryn turned to look back down the passageway. His shadow sight lit upon Ayleth, and she saw his mouth open, his hand extend toward her.

She couldn't look at him. Was he in on Fendrel's deception? He was the dominus's hand-reared protégé, after all, trained to serve, trained to obey without question. Did he know who had rested beneath the floors of Dunloch Castle all this time?

Did he know whose face she shared?

"Ayleth," he whispered, but she passed him without a word, hastening up the stairs after Hollis and Fendrel.

When she gained the gallery above, she saw Fendrel already halfway to the door. Hollis waited for her, standing over the unconscious form of the Crystalwitch. The venatrix nodded, and Ayleth moved to obey without protest, the instinct of years dictating her actions. She bent and caught the witch by the shoulders while Hollis lifted her by the knees. Together, they hauled her from the gallery, between the protrusions of crystals jutting up from the floor, and followed after Fendrel.

Gerard, Ayleth thought suddenly. They'd left the prince lying in the passage outside the gallery. Wounded by a curse blow, bleeding, vulnerable. Had another witch found him and ended his life while he lay unprotected? Had Perrinion lost both its Chosen King and its Golden Prince in the course of one night?

As she and Hollis carried the limp body of the Crystalwitch into the passage, Ayleth looked at once to the place where she had last seen the prince. Her heart gave a thud of pure relief, for she saw him sitting upright, his head resting in one hand, his eyes closed. His face was gashed in three terrible stripes where the Warpwitch's curse had struck him. Lady Cerine lay still where Ayleth had last seen her, several yards from the prince.

At the sound of their approach, Gerard looked up to see Fendrel bearing down upon him with the body slung over his shoulder. He scrambled upright, swayed so hard he almost fell again, but managed to keep his balance. His eyes, huge and round, fixed upon the figures bathed in moonlight.

Fendrel collapsed at Gerard's feet. The body of the king sprawled out across the floor. Gerard drew back several steps. Ayleth watched his gaze travel from the bloody wound in his father's neck down to the gaping hole where the heart should be. She watched the battle of incomprehension and realization war in his spirit, watched self-control struggle against pure horror. He shook his head, harder and harder, as though refusing to accept the reality before him.

"The king is dead." Fendrel's voice filled the passage like the growl of thunder. "Long live the king."

Gerard's face froze. He ceased shaking, and a stillness came over him like a mask falling into place. Ayleth's heart ached at the sight, but she, Hollis, and Terryn immediately echoed Fendrel's words: "Long live the king."

Fendrel drew a sharp, hissing breath. Then he bowed over his brother's body in an attitude of prayer or despair, it was impossible to say which. He placed one trembling hand over the wound in Guardin's chest, as though he could somehow, by sheer force of will, repair the damage and renew the life inside.

Gerard lifted his gaze from his uncle's hunched back and looked to Ayleth and the other two. "How . . . how did this happen?" he asked, his voice thick and full of pain. He looked to Terryn as the one he trusted most of those assembled.

Terryn opened his mouth but hesitated. He'd not seen how the king had died. He'd not seen what took place in that secret chamber. "We . . . we came upon the Crystalwitch guarding the door to—" he began.

"It was Odile."

Hollis raised her bowed head and met Gerard's intense stare. Her eyes were bright points of shadow-light staring out from behind strands of fair hair.

"It was Odile," she repeated. "Her lieutenants breached the vault and reawakened their mistress. Odile then killed the king, and the Phantomwitch *evanesced* her out, along with two other surviving witches."

Though her words were softly spoken, they rang loud in that deathly still air. Hearing Hollis state the matter so clearly made Ayleth want to curl over and be sick on the floor.

But worse still was the expression on Gerard's face. The expression that told her he had known as well. Along with Fendrel, along with Hollis. Gerard, the Golden Prince, the hope of all Perrinion . . . He was in on the lie.

Terryn rounded on Hollis. "What are you saying? Odile has been dead for decades."

The vehemence of his words surprised Ayleth, but a swift dart of gladness followed her surprise. He, at least, hadn't colluded with the others. He was innocent of their deceits. His gaze moved from Hollis to Ayleth, seeking in her eyes some verification of his own doubting words. But she could give him nothing, no matter how she wished to. Terryn shook his head, unwilling to believe. "I was there," he said. "I was there when the Chosen King rode into Dunloch with her head on a pike! I was there when her body was burned. She cannot—"

"She's not dead."

Terryn's eyes darted to Gerard. His mouth opened to speak more protests, which died on his tongue.

"She's not dead," Gerard repeated. He closed his eyes and rubbed a hand down his face, smearing blood from the cuts. "They didn't kill her, Terryn."

Terryn stared at the prince, his mouth slowly shutting. Then he bowed his head. His shoulders hunched, and he retreated into himself as the full weight of these revelations fell on his soul.

Gerard took a step forward, looming above the crouched form of his uncle and his father's dead body. "Now is not the time for questions," he said. "We must regroup. We must pull ourselves together and discern what is best to be done. Venator Dominus— No." He shook his head and lifted his gaze from Fendrel to Terryn instead. "Venator du Balafre, I charge you to find out which of your people are alive. Gather the Evanderians and secure the castle. See to it there are no more witches in our midst."

Terryn's head came up, and for the space of a single heartbeat, Ayleth wondered if he would obey. But he offered a salute the next moment. Then, without a look Ayleth's way, he sped down the corridor, making for the back of the castle and the stone terrace where the Evanderians had labored earlier to erect her pyre.

Ayleth watched him go until she heard Gerard's voice speak her name. "Venatrix di Ferosa, who is this you have brought to me?" She met the prince's gaze and saw that he indicated the unconscious witch lying beside her.

"The Crystalwitch," she blurted hastily. "One of . . . one of Odile's lieutenants."

"Alive?" Gerard asked.

Ayleth nodded.

"Excellent. You and Venatrix . . .?"

"Di Theldry," Hollis supplied. "Hollis, Venatrix di Theldry."

"The two of you secure this witch in one of the back storerooms. We will question her upon waking and discover what our enemies intend to do next."

"We won't need to wait for her to wake," Hollis muttered grimly even as she and Ayleth hastened to obey the prince's command. Ayleth couldn't look at her mistress, but she helped her, nonetheless, to heft the witch back up. If nothing else, it was a relief to have a command to follow, a job to do. Something useful to focus her mind on instead of reliving what she had just witnessed.

Just before she and Hollis reached the end of the passage, she heard Gerard speak once more: "Uncle, see to my father. And speak to no one until you have seen me again."

Ayleth looked back over her shoulder to see the Venator Dominus bowed and broken over his brother's body.

CHAPTER 23

SOUNDS OF SCREAMING AND WEEPING RESOUNDED throughout the castle as Ayleth and Hollis lugged the witch's body into the back passages of Dunloch toward the dark storerooms. Here and there they passed frightened and fleeing household members who looked upon the venatrices with utter terror, no longer able to tell the difference between witches and Evanderians. Neither Ayleth nor Hollis attempted to call out to them or assure them that the danger was past.

The attack on Dunloch may have ended, but the real danger was only just beginning.

"Here," Ayleth said, and kicked open a low door leading down a short flight of steps into an arch-ceilinged, windowless undercroft. Barrels of wine and vinegar-stored meats and vegetables lined the alcoves, but otherwise it was bare. It would serve as a makeshift dungeon.

Hollis and Ayleth dumped their burden in the center of the room. The poison paralyzed her body and soul. Looking at her with shadow sight, Ayleth could see her shade curled up underneath the poisonous suppressions. Nevertheless, Terryn had taken care to bind her hands and legs, and Ayleth sensed the workings of a Detrudos song spell around her as well. The Crystalwitch was an old and powerful worker of magic, with masterful control over the shade indwelling her. It would be unwise to underestimate her strength.

Ayleth backed a step up as Hollis knelt beside the witch, reaching out to take her face between her hands. "Wait," Ayleth said.

Hollis looked up quickly. "I am going to access her

mind," she said. "We need to find out—"

"No. Please." Ayleth's voice squeezed out through the thickness of her throat. "Hollis, you have to tell me. Don't make me ask again, I beg you. Why . . . why . . .?"

Why did she share a face with the greatest villain in all Gaulian history? The monster Dread Odile, the slaughterer and enslaver of humanity? Why had all that Ayleth believed to be true suddenly come undone right before her eyes? The Chosen King who had slain the Witch Queen was instead slain by the Witch Queen. And the Goddess's prophecy was nullified, decimated.

"Why?" Ayleth whispered.

Hollis stood up and backed away from the witch, her hands clenching into fists. Only then did Ayleth notice a certain stiffness in her movements, a slight favoring of one leg over the other. Was she wounded? That would explain why she hadn't come after her wayward apprentice sooner.

Shadow-light flickered in her mistress's eyes as she turned away, moved to the wall, and took a seat on one of the wine barrels. "I have so much to tell you, my girl. So much I must confess. I . . . I don't know where to begin."

"I do," Ayleth said. She crossed her arms, hardening herself against the vulnerability she heard in Hollis's voice. "I know exactly where to start. I am inborn. I know that much already. They have already raised my stake in the yard and intend to burn me at dawn."

Hollis shuddered. She looked frailer in that moment than Ayleth had ever before seen her. But she shook her head, and the frailness vanished almost at once. "They won't touch you now," she said harshly. "They wouldn't dare. Fendrel won't let them."

"Fendrel orchestrated it." Ayleth crossed the dark chamber to Hollis. She wanted to catch the venatrix by her shoulders, to shake her until she got the answers she needed. "He knew I was inborn the moment he saw me. How? How did he know? How did he—? Why do I—?"

Hollis reached out and took Ayleth's hand. A simple gesture, but one that Ayleth could not remember ever taking place between them before this moment. Not even when she was a child of seven, newly come to Gillanluòc outpost. Hollis would grab her arm, grab her wrist, even catch her by her long dark braid. She never held her hand.

She took it now, like a mother gently taking the fingers

of her child, and though Ayleth was taller than her mistress by more than a head, her spirit trembled at that touch. She wanted to melt into Hollis's arms, to be held, to be comforted.

The impulse horrified her. How could she, even after everything she'd discovered, still crave this woman's love and care? How could she still be so stupid, so susceptible? She might as well open her mind wide and invite Hollis in, tell her to block whatever she liked, tell her to manipulate as she pleased.

She wrenched her hand out of Hollis's grasp and took several paces back. Her body shuddered, but she drew back her head, nostrils flaring. "I know you've manipulated my mind," she growled, each word barbed.

Hollis didn't hang her head. No shame showed in her face when she answered only, "Yes."

"You blocked my memories. Of my past. My . . . my family."

"Yes."

Ayleth clenched her fists. Her nails dug into her palms hard enough to draw blood. "Why?"

"Because I killed your mother, Ayleth." Hollis drew a

long breath and blinked slowly, but kept her chin firmly lifted, her expression calm. "I killed her, and I took you, and I knew you would never trust me if you remembered what I had done."

Silence thundered in Ayleth's ears. She could no longer hear anything but the thud of her own heartbeat. She stared at her former mistress, but she could not see her.

Instead, she saw the long, low shadows of almost-memories running through the forest of her mind. She saw the dark gully, the pit, the webbing-spell. And she almost—but not quite—heard the roaring of animals, savage with fury and pain.

"Who . . . who was my mother, Hollis?" she asked, her voice thin and small.

"Her name was Olecia di Mauvalis," Hollis replied, "Princess of Dulimurian and only child of Dread Odile."

This wasn't exactly a surprise. The moment she'd seen that face in the vault, she'd known there must be some connection. But hearing it stated so baldly took the breath out of her lungs, the strength out of her limbs. Ayleth sank to the ground, one knee drawn to her chest, the other leg extended before her. She thought she might be sick and hung her head, waiting for the dizziness to pass. Her long braid fell over her shoulder and dangled beside her cheek.

A rustle of movement, then Hollis was beside her, one hand on her shoulder. "Ayleth, please. There's so much and . . . and so little time! I didn't have a choice. Your mother would have killed me, and then no one would be left who knew you were alive. We need you, Ayleth, and—"

"Give them back to me."

Hollis withdrew slightly. Her hand on Ayleth's shoulder shook.

Ayleth looked up, met her gaze. She spoke through her teeth. "Give back my memories. Now."

"I can't," Hollis said. "Not all at once. It would overwhelm you. It might kill you."

"I don't care." Her hands moved faster than thought. She caught Hollis by the front of her jerkin and, with Laranta's strength coursing through her, sprang to her feet and lifted the other venatrix, all in a single motion. Hollis's feet dangled in the air, and she held onto Ayleth's wrists, helpless in her grasp. "Give them back to me!

Now!" Ayleth roared.

Hollis's jaw worked, and shadow-light flashed in the depths of her pupils. Then she let go of Ayleth's wrists and caught hold of her face with both hands. A burst of magic flashed in Ayleth's head and—

Raw red light in her eyes. Paralysis in her limbs.

A wolf lies beside her, breathing out its last. A huge black wolf, tongue lolling, eyes still gleaming with life. Beyond her lie other bodies—shaggy gray wolf bodies, bleeding and dead.

Her brothers. Her sisters.

She reaches for the black wolf. Only she can't reach. Her arms are numb. Poison binds her within her own body. Her soul cries out, "Mother! Mother!"

A figure steps over the body, silhouetted in firelight. A figure with a hood pulled up over its face and a scorpiona fastened to one arm. It stands over the wolf, straddling that massive, fallen body. It raises a scorpiona, fires—

"No!" she screams, but only in her head. She can't move, she can't speak. She can do nothing.

"There, there, child." The figure crouches beside her, and the voice is Hollis's voice. "There, I will take the pain away . . ."

Hands close around her face. She tries to bite, tries to snarl, tries to howl her rage. She tries to call for her pack, for her family. But the paralysis is too strong, and she cannot resist. She cannot stop the slice of brilliant shadow-light tearing into her mind—

Ayleth landed hard on her back. Her eyelids fluttered as the low ceiling of the undercroft spun before her vision. Laranta moved inside her head, whimpering, *Mistress! Mistress!* but her voice seemed so distant. Ayleth could barely hear it over the echoing death cries of her mother . . . her sisters . . . her brothers . . .

Other memories crowded close. She could feel now how they would overwhelm her, break her mind, if they rushed in all at once, and she shied away from them in terror. But that one memory remained clear—clear, but confused because it was a child's memory, with a child's understanding.

She gasped for breath and pushed up onto her elbows. Hollis sat near, her back against a barrel, her head listing to one side. Shadow-light glimmered around her, the power of her ascendant shade rippling through her soul. "I've given you the last memory before I blocked your mind," she said. "The other memories will return now as well. Slowly."

"My . . . mother." Ayleth shook her head, her face knotting as though in pain. "I don't understand. My brothers and sisters . . . they were wolves?"

Hollis shook her head. "Olecia hid her soul in a wolf host body for seven years. She took you out into the wilds—none of us knew you existed, so we didn't go searching. My guess is that soon after possessing the wolf, she gave birth to a litter. Wolf sons and wolf daughters. Your soul-siblings, as it were. They were inborn, of course. The animal spirits were ousted or suppressed soon after birth, the shade spirits entirely ascendant.

"I knew that Olecia's soul had not been sent to the Haunts. We had hunted her long and hard, but when we finally ran her down, she stabbed herself to the heart. The war was at its crisis then, so we didn't stay to discover her new host. We returned to face the final battle at Dulimurian, taking her body with us and leaving her soul behind.

"After the war, I went searching for Olecia. It took me years, and many times I gave up ever tracking her down.

But at last, seven years later, I found her . . . and you." Hollis's eyes shimmered, this time with a film of tears. "You were a gift, Ayleth. A gift from the Goddess. I knew it at once."

Ayleth sat up. Her limbs shook, and wild rage burned in her heart. She wanted to lunge at Hollis, snap her neck, let her fall broken to the floor at her feet. The images she'd just seen, the memories . . . It felt as though she had only just lived those horrible moments. Her heart broke with sorrow for a family she'd never known she had.

Images crowded into her mind once more. Through her memory flashed a vivid vision of herself—small, wiry, dirty, naked. Running with wild abandon up a forested mountain slope, springing from root to rock to cleft. Wolves ran beside her. Not Laranta, but real, living, breathing wolves. Their spirits gleamed inside them, their eyes flashing with shadow-light.

And Ayleth understood. She had grown up, not among wolves, but among shades. The host bodies they inhabited were nothing more than the outer shell. The beings she had known were not of this world. They were like Laranta—intelligent but other. And they had accepted Ayleth as one of them.

They had . . . loved her . . .

Hollis was speaking again, Ayleth realized. She wrenched her mind painfully back to the present. "I had no idea," her mistress said, "until after I'd taken you. I thought they were animals. Only when I began looking into your mind and memories did I discover what you were to them. And they to you."

The law of the Order was clear. A shade-taken animal was nothing more than a diseased animal and must be put down before it could infect and destroy others. Hollis had acted according to her training, according to her beliefs.

"Why didn't you kill me too?" Ayleth asked bitterly. "Are you going to try to make me believe it was some great act of mercy on your part?"

Hollis closed her eyes. "I didn't kill you because . . . because you are the only one who can save us."

Her words seemed to strike Ayleth's ears and disintegrate before meaning could sink in. Ayleth could only stare at her mistress, her mouth half open.

Hollis sighed. "It's . . . a long story. A lot to explain. And we have so little time. But I will do what I can to tell you, Ayleth. If you will hear me. And trust me."

"Trust you?" Ayleth recoiled. It was all she could do not to lash out in violence. It would be so easy. Hollis was formidable in spirit, but her body was no physical match for Ayleth's even without Laranta's strength coursing through her. "Trust *you*, Hollis? How can I know you won't tell me more lies?"

"You can't know," Hollis admitted. "But I swear to you, I will tell you nothing but the truth. Whether or not you believe it."

Ayleth faced the choices before her, her mouth set in a grim line. She could deny Hollis her chance to say her piece and thereby remain in utter ignorance. Or she could risk the lies in hope of gaining some understanding.

"Tell me then," she said. "But if you try anything—if you touch my mind or manipulate any of my memories again—I'll kill you."

She could see that Hollis believed her. Though she wasn't entirely certain she believed herself.

"Very well," her mistress said. "Listen closely, Ayleth. This is the history of your family—*your* history, to the best of my understanding . . ."

CHAPTER 24

I NEVER TOLD YOU THE SOURCE OF DREAD ODILE'S great power, the power that gave her goddess-like supremacy in this world and led countless shade-taken to worship at her feet.

You know part of the truth. You know that she carried a powerful shade, the *oblivis*-Elemental. What you don't know is that Odile rose to her heights of glory because she controlled the power of not one great shade . . . but two.

Impossible, you say? So it ought to be. And so it would be were it not for the crown.

You know what *eitr* is, of course. You may even have glimpsed it once or twice—a rarity, a metal more precious than gold or silver. Like other precious metals, it can be molded and formed, but it is stronger than iron, truly unbreakable. More than that . . . it is believed to be *alive*. In an inexplicable sense of life that is nearly impossible for our mortal minds to comprehend. And because it is living, it may be possessed of a shade, like all other living things.

This is the secret understood by shade-taken craftsmen of old: witches who once studied the properties of *eitr* and learned to fashion objects, tools, treasures. Treasures in which they entrapped shades and bound their powers.

The last of these *eitr*-shapers was a man called Mauval. You know his name. I have taught you some of his history. Mauval the Great, the tyrant emperor who once ruled over all of Gaulia. As a young man, he was possessed of the same shade that now crouches in Dread Odile's soul. But he sought to increase his power a hundred times over.

To that end, he crafted a band of *eitr*—a crown. And using the *oblivis* which his shade controlled, he reached into the Haunts themselves and snatched another shade. Another Elemental, another manipulator of *oblivis*, the very twin of the shade he already carried. He entrapped it within the *eitr* crown.

When Mauval wore that crown, he joined the power of those twin shades in a force truly godlike. Thus he became Mauval the Great and ruled over all this land for three hundred years—yes, longer even than Odile's reign. He was not stopped until Saint Evander himself, inspired by the Goddess's will, finally broke his hold on the world.

You know the legends of the Saint. Some are true, some are myth, others are something in between. They do not matter now.

All you must know is that after the fall of Mauval, the *eitr* crown—with the shade entrapped in it—was placed in the deepest, darkest vaults, hidden from all save Evander and his most trusted advisers. They thought to destroy it, but ultimately . . . they could not bring themselves to do so.

You see, amid all the horrors perpetrated by Mauval, there was one great good: With the combined power of those two shades he could reach into a shade-taken soul, separate the shade, and oust it from its host. All without harming the host itself.

Think, Ayleth. Think of what a power like this could mean for the Evanderian Order. For the whole world! Shade-taken folk might be rescued without the necessity of death. Even inborn . . . for Mauval's power was great enough even to sever those ties without harming the original host.

You have been a venatrix for so little time. Even so, I know you understand. None of us relish the hard truths of our work. We believe in the salvation of souls, but we mourn for those lives which must end for the sake of eternal redemption. If souls might be saved without lives being lost . . . it would change everything. Forever.

But the power of the *eitr* crown could only be wielded by one who carried the twin shade. When Mauval was defeated, he was given a violent death, and his shade escaped somewhere into a new host. A great hunt went out across the land. Evanderians sought far and wide to find that shade. But more than eighty years passed before it was found and brought back to one of the old castras.

At that time, a worthy Evanderian indoctrinate was chosen to take the shade into his body. For years he studied how to master and control the elements of *oblivis*. When at last the great leaders of our Order deemed him ready, the crown was brought forth so that he might attempt to join the twinned shades and delve into the greater powers.

He was killed in an instant. In the very moment they placed the crown upon his head, he died. And all those within a ten mile radius died with him in a blast of pure, unadulterated *oblivis*.

Many years later, the experiment was tried again. And again. Three times, the Order trained a worthy candidate to wear Mauval's crown. Three times, disaster followed. At last, all hope was lost. The crown was hidden away. The twin shade was caught and contained, made to exist within small animal hosts throughout the years—mice, rabbits, sparrows. Things that could not be turned into effective weapons.

Phasmators continued to study the crown, and it was

at last determined that Mauval had bound it to the blood of his host body. Only he or one of his heirs could hope to wield the crown and survive. But by then it was too late. Whatever family Mauval the Great had was long ago scattered and lost . . . or so it was believed.

There was a woman—Eline, Venatrix d'Arcand by name—who was seized with a conviction she believed had been sent from the Goddess Herself. She devoted her life to finding one of Mauval's heirs. Many laughed at her, mocked her for her foolishness. They no longer laughed, however, when she one day rode back to her local castra with a certain young woman at her side. A young woman named Odile di Mauvalis.

I don't know the details of what happened, of course. But we can guess at most of it. Odile was trained in the Order. She was given the *oblivis* Elemental and learned to master its powers. She proved her devotion to the saint and the Goddess. All the while, the Council watched her, studied her, and prayed for guidance. Eline d'Arcand argued for years in favor of her protégé. Her letters still exist and can be found and read in the castra libraries. In the end . . .

In the end, they placed the crown on Odile's head. And the destruction was greater than ever before. Only, when the clouds of *oblivis* cleared and the ruin was revealed to the world, Odile herself stood tall and whole in the midst. She lived.

But she was no longer the brave and loyal venatrix described in Eline d'Arcand's letters. This woman was reborn in a new and monstrous form. She emerged from that cloud of debris as Dread Odile, a scourge on the nations. She threw down the Goddess's temple, and using the power of the two shades combined, she raised Dulìmurian up from nothing. A city of pure oblidite, black and devastating and beautiful.

You know what happened. I've told you much of the history—how she tyrannized Perrinion for the next two centuries, how she summoned shade-taken to her cause and raised an army that even the might of the Evanderian Order could not hope to defeat. Long and bloody were the years that followed.

Then came the Chosen King.

It was Fendrel who guided his brother into the prophesied role. Inspired by visions and prophecies,

Fendrel rallied the scattered castras of Evander to unite under Guardin's banner. I was with him . . . I fought at his side throughout those years. I believed in the cause; I believed in the Chosen King. Mostly, if I'm honest, I believed in Fendrel. And I believed in the weapon he had found in the secret catacombs of Morlorn—a song spell of tremendous power.

I've told you the tale before. I've told you how two hundred Evanderians played a powerful spell which took their lives but which, in the taking, broke Odile's strength and enabled the Chosen King to cut off her head. But I've never told you what that spell was exactly.

It was called the *Atacara*. The Death Song. It required a company of Evanderians to play, for only then could the music be fully realized. The spell channeled all the magic within each Evanderian soul into a single stream of power, which was then driven directly into the *eitr* crown on Odile's head. We empowered the shade within that crown far beyond her ability to control. She was forced to decide—remove the crown or die.

In the end, she cast the crown from her head and fell to the ground, burned, broken, and senseless. Our brothers and sisters were slain in an instant, the same instant the music ceased. But Odile was stunned. We had our chance.

Fendrel held a few of us back from the sacrifice. It was an honor none of us coveted, but we understood the importance of our role. For the prophecy to be fulfilled, Guardin must cut off Odile's head, dealing a violent death. But we couldn't risk her soul, bound to its shade, escaping to claim a new host. Without the blood of Mauval in her veins, she would never again control the crown . . . but she was a great and lethal force even without the crown. And she had committed terrible atrocities against the Goddess's people. She must be damned to the Haunts.

So, I and my hunt brother, Nane du Vincent, carried Odile's senseless body to the feet of her own idol. There, we and four others of our brethren stood by while Fendrel led his brother to the chopping block. Our orders were clear: four of us were to create a song spell to catch the violently liberated shade. Three of us were to play the expulsion songs and send it hurling to the Haunts. We knew our roles. We were prepared.

Or so we believed.

Just as the Chosen King stepped up to the block, just as he raised his sword and prepared to bring it down on the Witch Queen's neck – just in that final moment, she cried out a curse. She spoke it in a language I did not know, but I felt the meaning . . . and I felt the horror of the binding that curse created.

Fendrel felt it too. I heard him shout, scream.

But then Odile's head rolled. And the curse activated.

I hardly know how to describe what I saw. The entwined spirits inside her body burst free from their host, but instead of focusing all that power, all that energy, on escape, they launched directly into the song spell woven by our colleagues. Those spirits struck the spell, and a reaction rippled through the ether, flowing back into the souls of our brethren. The four were dead before I could even think to react. And Fendrel, Nane, and I were flung from our feet in the force of that ethereal blast.

I nearly fell unconscious. But somehow I managed to cling to the waking world, to lift my head and look.

I saw . . . darkness. Reaching out from the witch's

broken corpse. It flowed with the blackened blood gushing from her death-wound and wrapped tendril fingers around her burned, severed head. I cannot say how it happened . . . but it seemed to me that I had scarcely blinked, scarcely regained my feet, and suddenly she was whole again. Still burned, still battered. Still screaming from the pain of her beheading and clawing at her throat. But whole. And alive.

Guardin was the first to act. The blast through the ether had not affected him, un-taken as he was. He caught up his sword and hacked her head off again. A second blast of power knocked me spinning to the ground.

But Fendrel was prepared. As though he had received some forewarning, he acted. He crawled to Odile's side, and even as those same dark tendrils stretched out to once more reclaim her head, he placed his bleeding hand over the neck wound and cried out a curse—a counter curse to the one Odile had made. He could not undo what she had done, but he could—temporarily at least—render it useless. He placed a block on her neck, preventing the reattachment of her head.

I have never met a man of greater will or greater skill than Fendrel du Glaive. He gave everything to create that curse. Everything. Even then, I did not believe it would hold. But as I watched, the dark magic sought again and failed to reanimate Odile's broken body.

So she lived. Headless. Burned, desecrated. She lived. Inert, but present.

And patient.

Hollis's voice trailed off, leaving Ayleth in a stunned silence. She sat on the undercroft floor beside the paralyzed body of Crisentha di Bathia, and her whole world seemed to spin around her, caught in a maelstrom of madness.

"Do you understand?" Hollis asked at last, breaking the stillness.

With a start, Ayleth looked up sharply at her former mistress. "I . . . I'm not sure. What kind of curse could keep a mortal body alive after a beheading?"

"A dark curse indeed. Magic from an ancient time, forbidden by the Saint. It was called the *Cravan Druch*. In short, Odile cursed herself so that none but her own blood kin could kill her. No matter what was done to her—beheading, burning, dismemberment—she did not die, but would always reanimate."

The idea was so horrible. Too horrible to bear. Ayleth bowed her head, running her hands through her hair, pulling strands loose from her braid. "She must have known about the *Atacara*," she said at last. "She must have known what you had planned for her."

Hollis nodded. Her face was downcast, and there was a heaviness to her voice when she answered. "We had a . . . a Seer. The Order used his powers for strategic planning. He was instrumental in many of our missions, especially as the Chosen King's cause began to gain traction. But . . . he escaped us at last and fled to Dulimurian. It was he who revealed our plan to Dread Odile. He betrayed us."

"A Seer?" Ayleth blinked. Seer shades only ever appeared in inborn hosts. The Order of Saint Evander strictly forbade the admittance of any inborn into their number, and all those discovered were killed, just as Ayleth was due to be killed in a few short hours.

Hollis's gaze flicked to meet Ayleth's, but only for a moment. "He was our prisoner. Our . . . tool. For as long as we needed him, we kept him alive."

"You kept a slave. An inborn slave." The words tasted so bitter, Ayleth could hardly bear to speak them.

"It was war, Ayleth." Hollis said. "We used what we could, did what we must. And we told ourselves that it was good." She shrugged then and dropped her head again. "But we knew. Each of us knew. In the secret parts of our hearts where we did not lie to ourselves. Only we never spoke of it." She closed her eyes, her knuckles tightening as her fingers clutched her own upper arms. "They teach you many things in the castras. How to think with precision. How to read signs and people. How to hunt, how to kill, how to ask only those questions you need to ask.

"What they don't teach you is how to hold on to your honor. What they don't teach you is how swiftly that honor gets chipped away. Until it is nothing but a broken, bloody thing in the center of your soul. And when the deeds are done, and when the war is over, you tell yourself, 'Now it will heal. Now my honor will be restored.' But it never heals. It is never restored. You can put up barriers around what's left, you can guard what remains. You can never have it back."

Ayleth recoiled from Hollis's words, afraid of the truth she sensed. She dared not glance at her own soul, dared not inspect her own honor. She suspected it was already corroded around the edges, beyond all hope of repair.

Instead, she shook her head, focused her mind elsewhere. "And Fendrel?" she asked. "When he cast that counter-curse against Dread Odile's, he . . ."

"He cursed Odile so that while she may only be killed by one of her blood, so she may only be awakened by her kin's blood as well. But in casting that curse, he bound his soul to his shade. He damned himself to the Haunts, and no power of this world or any other can save him."

Ayleth could think of nothing to say in answer to this. Fendrel du Glaive, the hero of Perrinion, the champion of the Chosen King . . . he had turned to dark magic, witch's magic. Yet another illusion crumbled before her mind's eye. All those mighty men, all those shining figures she'd been brought up to revere, were nothing but clay gods in the end. Cracked and so easily shattered.

Hollis ran her hands down her face, pulling at the sagging skin under her eyes. "Fendrel, Guardin, and Nane agreed to display Odile's head in a great parade and to make a show of burning her body here at Dunloch, before the eyes of the king's court." Her voice was strangely calm, as though she were merely detailing the events of a rather dull day. "Of course, no amount of burning could do away with the body, for the curse reformed it within hours of each conflagration. It was Fendrel who invented the plan to hide the corpse and the head in a blood-warded vault so that none but those of the du Glaive line could enter. He and I . . . disagreed. I told him we could not found a kingdom on such a lie, such a dark and dangerous lie.

"But Fendrel was determined. In his mind, the prophecy *was* fulfilled. Odile was stopped, if not dead. And her only known kin—Olecia—was gone. Olecia's soul may have escaped to some other host, but her body was dead and rotted. Without kin's blood, Odile would never again rise.

"But I didn't trust in this little illusion. I couldn't. Somehow I knew that Olecia was still out there. And I knew . . . I knew if I found her . . ."

Another silence followed. A silence which Ayleth's mind filled with slowly growing realization. Blood kin. To kill Odile they needed blood kin. They needed a miracle . . . a weapon . . .

Ayleth's chin dropped to her chest, her head suddenly too heavy to support. How could such a powerful counter curse have been broken? She had not even been in the same room as Odile. Regardless of any curses, any spells, she'd not awakened the witch. This couldn't be her fault.

She frowned, however . . . and remembered lying paralyzed on an altar in an old abandoned shrine house. Remembered two voices, one male, one female, arguing over her body.

"I see no reason to keep her alive. We can gather her blood."

"We have no means to keep it fresh. The blood has to be fresh. We have no bottles of oblidite . . . No . . . she may be our last chance. We cannot risk mishandling this gift."

"We cannot risk keeping her alive either. She can as easily mean our end as our salvation . . ."

She remembered a blast of Anathema magic that sent

her crashing into a wall of the hedgewitch's cottage, and a monstrous figure crawling toward her, speaking through bloody lips. She remembered trembling hands catching her head, holding a knife to her throat, cutting with careful precision.

"Just a little blood. Just a little drop. I don't need more than that. Just enough . . ."

The Warpwitch had taken her blood. And somehow she must have stored it, kept it fresh. Fresh and ready for use the moment they found the Witch Queen's corpse.

Ayleth looked up and found Hollis gazing at her. "They used my blood to awaken her. To reanimate her."

Hollis nodded.

"You must know I had nothing to do with it."

"I know, child."

And yet the guilt remained. Guilt for her very existence. Had she not lived—had Hollis not shown mercy to the feral child, taken her in, and saved her from Evanderian flames—Odile might have slept on forever. Trapped in her deathless horror of existence.

Ayleth closed her eyes. She needed to escape these thoughts; she needed to get away. So she closed her eyes and stood suddenly in the pine forest of her mind.

She recognized it. For the first time, she recognized the mental-scape of her inner world. This was the forest in which she had lived with her wolf mother and brothers and sisters. She'd lost all those memories, but they'd nonetheless wound through the very fabric of her soul.

Laranta approached through the trees, large and black. And now Ayleth understood why it was that her shade took this shape—for it was the image of Olecia's final host, an image Ayleth's unconscious mind associated with protection and love.

Her wolf shade drew near to her now, unsuppressed and powerful. Her red eyes flashed, her teeth gleamed, and she bowed her head to bring it level with Ayleth's. *Mistress?* she said.

Ayleth leaned in and wrapped her arms around Laranta's neck, burying her face in that mental projection of black fur. *"I'm so sorry, Laranta,"* she wept. *"I'm sorry I ever bound you."*

Laranta merely stood. Her heavy head rested on Ayleth's shoulder, offering support, love, comfort, strength. Just as she'd always done.

Ayleth opened her eyes, returning to the undercroft, returning to Hollis. Her former mistress watched her closely, and Ayleth knew Hollis could see the ascendant power of Laranta inside her, no longer restrained by Evanderian bindings.

"I understand," Ayleth said. "I understand everything now. You need me. You need your weapon. You saw that I was Dread Odile's blood, and you recognized your chance. So you took me in, and you fed me the tales of your Saint and your wars. You brought me up to be a good and true Evanderian, and you blocked my memories and suppressed my shade. You took everything I loved from me and I . . . I . . ."

She couldn't speak the words. She couldn't say what she'd longed to say since she was seven years old. She couldn't say *I loved you,* because how could she love the woman who'd killed her family? Who'd taken and shaped her, twisted her into something which perhaps she was never intended to be?

Ayleth turned away from Hollis. She gazed at the inert body of the Crystalwitch, but in her mind's eye she saw that stone slab in the vaults, that creature wearing her face, her brow burned and blackened, her eyes savage and overflowing with *oblivis*.

"Was this your plan then?" Ayleth couldn't bear to look at Hollis as she spoke. "Wait until I was old enough, then bring me down here, somehow get me into the blood-warded vault. Have me stab the corpse where it lay. Then what? Would you have simply let the Order take me? Burn me? Or would you have dealt me the Gentle Death and let my soul be damned?"

No past. No future. Only the hunt.

It all made sense now.

"Please, my girl," Hollis whispered, her words tremulous in the still air. "I wanted to . . ."

"You wanted to end the life of your enemy. I know." Ayleth lifted her chin and pulled back her shoulders. Had she not always longed to devote her life to a noble purpose? Knowing now that she existed purely for the sake of bringing death to a witch . . . how was that any different from the Evanderian calling?

Ultimately, Odile was just another shade-taken. Another unfortunate possessed of a power never intended to be hers. Another mortal-turned-monster who must be put down.

"Very well," Ayleth said, rising from the floor. She adjusted the set of her scorpiona on her arm. "You've done your job well. I will hunt down Dread Odile, and I will end her. And when I am done"—her eyes flashed to meet Hollis's gaze—"when I am done, I'll kill you too."

CHAPTER 25

TERRYN FOUND GERARD IN THE WEST-WING APARTMENTS, seated on the edge of Cerine's bed. The lady was as pale as death following her ordeal. She still wore the filthy rags of her wedding dress, with bloody holes where spines had burst from her back, but the curse was gone, having broken the moment Ylaire's spirit was banished into the Haunts. Its remnant threads would take a little longer to fade, but eventually it would vanish entirely.

Entering the room quietly, Terryn drew the door shut

behind him. Then he cleared his throat to alert Gerard to his presence. He saw his brother's spine stiffen, but the face Gerard turned to him was calm, its jaw firmly set. "What have you found?" he asked, his voice low so as not to disturb the sleeping lady, though by the look of her it would take a great deal to make her stir.

Terryn drew himself up to stiff attention. "No witches remain on the premises save Crisentha di Bathia, who is under our control. We're still trying to account for any violently loosed shades, but I fear there may be several already hiding in new host bodies within the castle itself. The barrier surrounding Dunloch will have prevented them from flying far."

Gerard shuddered, and his jaw tightened. "And the Evanderians? How have they fared?"

"Phasmatrix Domina di Conradin is dead, burned by the Stormwitch's rains. Four others were killed, and still more were wounded or rendered unconscious. Kephan was found with a paralysis poison in his neck, but no one knows who dealt it. He seems otherwise unhurt."

"Good, good." Gerard nodded and turned back to gaze upon Cerine's pale face resting on a snowy pillow.

His hand reached out and hovered over her cheek, but he did not touch her.

Terryn drew a deep breath, then walked around the far side of Cerine's bed to a position allowing him a clear view of Gerard's face. "How long have you known, Gerard?"

Slowly Gerard lifted his head, his eyes moving to gaze into the space over Terryn's shoulder. He knew exactly what it was Terryn asked.

"A few days," he answered softly. "They told me after . . . after Cerine was taken. They showed me the body. Beheaded. Burned. It didn't seem possible that it could still be alive, and yet . . ."

He didn't finish. The words simply trailed away to nothing. Terryn watched the play of expressions moving in his eyes, just behind his stoic mask. "Why didn't you tell me?" he whispered.

Gerard met his gaze then. His expression was stone hard, and he offered no answer.

Terryn cursed. He turned away, ran a hand down his face, pulling at the skin of his scarred cheek. He wanted to walk away. He wanted to leave and never look back, never see Gerard's face again. He wanted to find his horse and ride out from Dunloch, just as he had intended to ride with Ayleth only hours before.

And why should he not? Why should he not find Ayleth even now, and the two of them make their escape? He carried an unsuppressed shade inside him. He was as good as dead, a heretic daring to walk among the devout. Why should he not run away with the inborn witch-girl and never think of the Order again? Never think of Gerard, the false prince, son of the false king . . .

You cannot leave your people now.

The deep, quiet voice spoke through the roaring inside his head.

Terryn shuddered, closed his eyes.

They need you. They need us. The Witch Queen must be stopped. The shade she carries suffers under her dominion. I must save my own, even as you must save yours. Let us work together, mortal man. United we may defeat our mutual foe.

Shaking his head, Terryn pressed the heels of his hands into his eyes. The voice was too strange, the things it communicated too bizarre for him to understand. And he was already so tired, so confused.

In the end, it didn't matter what lies were told; it didn't matter what secrets were kept; it didn't matter if the prophecy of the Goddess was brought to nothing and even Terryn's own faith was reduced to something small, trifling, and foolish; it didn't matter whatever else the world and the fates threw his way. One thing only did he know with absolute clarity:

He would never abandon his brother.

Terryn lowered his hands and pulled himself together, then turned to face Gerard. He pulled his shoulders back and gripped his right wrist with his left hand behind his back. He became a venator once more, addressing his prince. His king. "What are your orders?"

Gerard stood and faced Terryn, though one hand still held onto Cerine's slim fingers. "We'll see what information Venatrix di Theldry can get from our prisoner."

"And then?"

"We'll ride out, of course. Together."

Terryn blinked. Then he shook his head. "No, you can't possibly—"

"Can't I?" Gerard's eyes flashed, and his teeth bared in a grimace. "Am I king or not? No, no . . ." He shook his head, dropped his chin, and heaved a harsh breath. "No, forgive me. I know the answer to that question." He breathed again, exhaling the air from his lungs in a long, slow stream. Then he looked at Terryn. "But let us pretend for a moment that I am king and not the upstart son of a crown-snatching bastard. As such, do I not, for appearance's sake, owe it to my people? To ride out in pursuit of their great enemy and make a glorious end?"

Terryn shook his head. "You shouldn't come. We will take care of this."

"We? Of whom do you speak, Terryn?"

"I speak of Fendrel, Ayleth, Venatrix di Theldry, and myself. The other Evanderians who are fit to ride."

"So you think I would send you and them on a suicide mission while I . . . what? Warm my feet by the hearth fire and await news of your death?"

Terryn could not recall ever seeing his brother's face so grim. "It need not be a suicide mission," he said. "Our ranks are depleted, but so are the Crimson Devils. And Odile . . . if Odile is truly alive . . . she cannot be in fit condition. We may have a chance."

At those words, Gerard shook his head and chuckled,

a cold, hard sound. His hair fell in his eyes, and his teeth flashed in a mirthless smile. "I'm sorry. I don't mean to laugh at you." He pushed the hair out of his face and again met Terryn's gaze. "But make no mistake: This is the end. Don't forget, they have Inren di Karel with them. She can carry them a mile at a time in an instant; she only needs the anchors to do it. For all we know, they've spent the last twenty years planting anchors through the Witchwood in readiness for this very journey. Indeed, they may already have reached their destination."

"What destination, Gerard? What are you talking about?"

"Why, Dulimurian, of course."

The words were as dark and deep as funeral bells tolling in the still air between them. Terryn shuddered as though a phantom had just glided over his grave. "I . . . I don't understand."

"Oh, did you not know that little tidbit either?" Gerard chuckled again. "The *eitr* crown, Terryn. It wasn't destroyed. Nor was it hidden. They left it. My uncle, my father, and whatever other fools they duped into their cause. They left the crown in the ruins of Dulimurian.

The Witchwood has been its guard all these years, but the Witchwood won't stop Odile. Our battle is already lost. Yet we will ride out, even so."

Gerard looked down at Cerine, then bent over her. He ran his hand over the short stubble of her hair, his eyes studying her face as though trying to memorize each feature. "We'll die heroes, not liars," he said, speaking to her and not to Terryn, or so it seemed. "I only wish . . . I wish I dared wait a little longer. I wish I could stay long enough to bid her farewell."

Blood thundered in Terryn's temples. Again he felt his shade stirring inside him, hot in the core of his soul. "So that's our plan, Gerard?" he said. "Ride out together and die?" He swallowed hard, and his left hand squeezed his right wrist painfully tight. He wanted to protest, wanted to insist that Gerard remain behind. How could he, a mortal, with no shade powers, no training in the venatorial arts, hope to combat the likes of Inren and Gillotin and the rest? How could he hope to face Dread Odile, if indeed Dread Odile was returned? It was folly, madness.

And yet, there was such resolve burning in Gerard's soul, bright and visible to Terryn's shadow sight when he looked at this man who was his brother and his king, that despite everything—all the revelations, all the lies—he could not help but believe: Here stood the Golden Prince. The Goddess's promise fulfilled.

Perhaps his ascendant shade was driving him mad. He didn't care. He offered a sharp salute. "If such is your will, it will be my honor to ride at your side. My king."

Gerard grimaced, and pain flashed in his eyes. "Don't, Terryn. Please. Between us, at least, let there be no more falsehood." He let go of Cerine's hand and gestured toward the door. "Go now. Find my uncle. He is at his vigil in the chapel, with my father's remains. He believes his own lies, no matter how the truth blasts him. So tell him . . ." For a moment, words failed him. But Gerard recovered himself quickly and continued in a firm, certain voice: "Tell him he is no longer the king's Black Hood. Tell him his king requires that he turn the hood over to Terryn, Venator du Balafre. Then he must make ready to ride. His king requires his services one last time."

CHAPTER 26

THE DARKNESS OF THE CHAPEL ECHOED WITH THE cries of Dunloch's dead. The Evanderians who had been taken unawares, unable to defend themselves. The untaken men and women, powerless and exposed. The children. All who had fallen prey to the witches.

And behind those echoes, more voices.

The voices of hundreds. Of thousands, even.

Voices he never ceased hearing in the depths of his soul every hour of every day, and especially in the dark of night. The spirits of those who, at his bidding, had died. Died because he believed, believed in a prophecy, in a better world, in a Chosen King. In a Golden Age constructed by his own two bleeding hands.

Fendrel knelt beside the ruination of all his hopes, all his plans, all his dreams. His brother's body lay on the altar before him, blood still flowing from his wounds. The dead king's hands lay folded over the hole in his chest.

This wasn't how it was supposed to end. This wasn't the vision, the glorious new dawn. Fendrel's right arm hung limp and useless from his shoulder while his left hand clung to his brother's lifeless fingers. He hadn't bothered to light any of the sacred candles, and the cavernous space of the arched chapel seemed close and dark and heavy.

His shade stirred in his soul, straining against the suppression spells. It sensed his weak emotional state and sought to take advantage. He had long ago learned to suppress his emotions as a means of suppressing his shade, learned to quell all human frailty in pursuit of his holy cause. But now . . . now . . .

The vision had always been so clear—the high calling, the holy purpose by which he had ordered his life these last twenty-odd years. The Chosen King would end Dread Odile, and the new era would rise. An era of purity and holiness in which the plague of shades on the world would finally be eradicated. He'd sacrificed everything to this vision. Everything and everyone.

He'd been so sure. So very sure.

And yes, he'd lied. But he'd lied only for the good of the nation. Had Perrinion not prospered over the last two decades? Had not the scar through the heart of Gaulia healed? Worship of the Goddess was renewed, peace was restored. Shade-taken were hunted down and mortal souls saved. Did all this not justify a single lie?

And really, the lie was barely a lie! Odile had been as good as dead. Prophecies never came about exactly as expected. Everyone knew that. But this didn't mean they weren't fulfilled.

Fendrel leaned his forehead against the edge of the altar stone. His brother's blood trickled down and matted in his hair and beard. "The Goddess would not mislead me," he whispered, his voice hollow in that dark place.

"She would not let Her servant stray from the path."

This must be a test. One final test to prove his devotion. Would he tremble now and fall at this final blast? Or would he rally and stand tall in the face of his doubts?

He knew what he must do. It was time for the final sacrifice.

Footsteps sounded behind him. Three pairs of footsteps, heavy Evanderian boots ringing on stone. Fendrel shuddered, and for a moment his grip on his brother's hand tightened. He sent a swift prayer for strength to the Goddess, a single breath before a voice behind him spoke.

"Fendrel, Venator Dominus du Glaive."

It was Terryn. Of course it was. Gerard trusted him as he'd been raised to do since infancy. Gerard could not see what Fendrel saw. He lacked the clarity of vision.

Fendrel rose slowly. He gazed down at his brother's face, still twisted in that last expression of shock and pain. He touched two fingers lightly to Guardin's forehead, to the hollow place where his heart should be, and to his lips. A final sign of blessing.

Then he turned and faced Terryn. Two other Evander-ians stood with him—Venator du Ferro and Venatrix di Ranille. All three of their shades were ascendant, but shadow vision easily discerned the binding spells restraining du Ferro's and di Ranille's shades. No such bindings gleamed in Terryn's soul. His shade crouched inside him, unsuppressed, ready to burst into full ascendancy at any moment. A danger to all around him.

The fool.

"I have come from the king," Terryn said, with only an instant's hesitation before stating his sovereign's new title. "He bids you turn your hood over to me. You are no longer the King's Black Hood."

Fendrel looked at his former protégé, his gaze long and hard. He felt his own shade straining again at its suppressions, once more seeking to use his own emotion against him. But he was made of sterner stuff. He had long since learned to suppress emotion for the sake of duty. And his duty now was clear. So clear.

"Venator du Ferro," he said without taking his eyes off Terryn. "Venatrix di Ranille. Do the two of you observe any suppression-song spells within our brother du

Balafre's soul?"

Terryn's pale eyes widened ever so slightly. Heat and shadow-light flared inside him. The two Evanderians exchanged glances. Then they looked at Terryn. They could not have failed to miss the truth of the situation.

"Has our brother turned heretic?" Fendrel continued, taking a step down the aisle, away from the altar and his brother's remains. There was no light other than the shadow-light gleaming in his eyes and the eyes of the other three. The darkness of night was heavy, a curtain around them. "Have you forsworn your oaths, Venator? Do you now spit in the face of your saint?"

"I am the loyal servant of King Gerard du Glaive, first of his name," Terryn replied. But he shifted ever so slightly into a defensive stance. "Turn over your hood, Fendrel. You may yet serve your king and country."

"I intend to," Fendrel spoke through his teeth. His left arm moved—he still couldn't feel his right—and pulled the Vocos pipes from their sheath. He tossed them to Terryn, who caught the instrument on impulse of training. "There," Fendrel said. "Your shade is ascendant, the suppressions broken. Play the spell songs. Bind it back."

Terryn gripped the pipes in his fist. His knuckles slowly whitened. Venator du Ferro and Venatrix di Ranille drew back from Terryn and poised on the balls of their feet. Venatrix di Ranille's hand moved to her quivers.

"Did you hear me, Venator?" Fendrel repeated. "You know the law. You know the will of Saint Evander. Suppress your shade!"

The ether in the space between them churned and sparked as though ready to catch fire, roiling in that tumultuous contest of souls.

Terryn's mouth hardened into a grim line. With a flash of his teeth, he flung the Vocos to one side. It landed, bounced, and rolled into the shadows.

"I thought as much," Fendrel growled. "Evanderians! Bring down this heretic."

Venatrix di Ranille slammed a dart into her scorpiona and took a shot. But Terryn was already in motion. He'd sensed that du Ferro was the less prepared of the two of them and leaped sideways, elbowing into the man and knocking him from his feet. Di Ranille's dart sped useless over his shoulder and clattered into the shadowy pillars supporting the arched chapel roof.

Du Ferro lashed out, the iron spike of his bracer striking at Terryn as he went down. Terryn sprang out of reach and whirled to face his attackers. Brilliant white light flared in his hands, his ascendant shade magic called up at once.

Fendrel didn't wait. He swiped his left hand down across the bleeding wounds on his face. With a muttered word of command, he swung his arm in a sweeping arc. Blood droplets spattered, and curse bolts manifested in the air and sped straight for Terryn, ready to pierce him through.

A blinding flash of light. Fendrel flung his arm up and roared, both his mortal vision and his shadow sight temporarily dazzled. For the space of ten heartbeats he stood helpless in wrath and pain. Then he blinked hard, and his vision slowly returned, just fast enough to see Terryn dart through the chapel door, out into the courtyard.

"Come on!" Fendrel cried and sprang into pursuit. Du Ferro and di Ranille fell into step behind him, and together they charged in pursuit of their prey. They reached the doorway in time for Fendrel to see the flutter of Terryn's cloak as he climbed the porch steps.

Four more Evanderians stood in the cold air of the courtyard outside, their eyes wide and their shades ascendant. "After him!" Fendrel shouted, motioning wildly with his one arm. "Take down Venator du Balafre! He's turned against us!"

At any other time, they might have questioned his command. At any other time, they may have hesitated. But after the night they'd just survived—a night full of witches and horror and death—they looked to their Venator Dominus as they would look to Saint Evander himself. His word was law, and his word galvanized them to action.

Three darts flew after Terryn just as he gained the door of the main keep. Two of them missed, and one caught in the folds of his cloak. He turned, flung out his arm, and a flash of white light burst from his hand. It flew over the heads of the Evanderians, but it was enough to blind them again, to slow them down.

Fendrel hissed a curse and pounded the paving stones

in pursuit.

Fire roared through his veins, searing his body from the inside out. Terryn caught hold of the front stair banister and glimpsed his own hand. Blisters boiled up from under the skin. With every panting breath, he exhaled a stream of smoke, and sweat rolled down his face, soaked his garments.

He couldn't survive this kind of power. If he used it again, it would surely destroy him.

Hearing a shout from behind, he paused on the landing and saw three Evanderians spring through the door below, their scorpioni upraised. He ducked behind a pillar and heard the *tock* of a dart hitting where his head would have been. He reached for his quivers. To his horror, he had no paralysis poisons left. Only the Gentle Death.

He may be exactly what Fendrel accused him of being: a heretic, little better than a witch. But he could not bear to use the Gentle Death on his former brethren.

He staggered, pain scorching through him like a torch

planted in his chest. The Evanderians wouldn't need to use their poisons on him. He'd be dead soon enough. His own shade would overwhelm him with magic. Why had he been so foolish, throwing away that Vocos? He should have done as Fendrel said; he should have used the song spells.

"*Nisirdi!*" he called inside his head. "*Nisirdi, reduce!*"

But he had no control over this being. It responded to his tumultuous emotion, rising in greater and greater power, and did not seem to hear him, no matter how he screamed.

He'd been wrong to trust it. So wrong . . .

A flash of movement. Terryn reached the top of the stair and saw another red hood coming his way, cutting off the path he'd intended to take into the east wing. He turned to run the other way . . . but no. Gerard was in the west wing. He couldn't take this battle anywhere near Gerard and risk him getting caught in the crossfire.

"Du Balafre!" the venatrix bearing down on him cried. "Surrender!"

He saw that she had no darts left for her weapon. Instead, she summoned up her Elemental power, conjuring a ball of fire between her fingers.

With a cry, Terryn darted for a small door in the wall. He opened it just in time to use it as a shield. The fireball burst on the other side of the wood panels, though in truth, it probably couldn't have hurt him as much as the heat already roiling inside him.

The other Evanderians gained the landing and charged up the last flight of stairs. Terryn looked back and thought he saw Fendrel's face, pale and hard, down below. For an instant, their eyes met.

Then Terryn darted through the door and pulled it shut behind him. He stood in a narrow staircase and had a split second to decide—up or down. He chose up. His hands pressed against the close stone walls, leaving melted impressions behind. Every breath was an agony. Though the shadows were heavy, his eyes blazed with shadow-light so bright, it was nearly blinding.

"Ayleth," he gasped. He heard the door behind him open, heard footsteps as the Evanderians gave chase. "Ayleth . . ."

If Fendrel had turned on him, he would go after her next. But where was she? Could he find her, could he warn her? Not if he couldn't shake these pursuers first.

He left the stairwell and emerged into another narrow hall on the fourth story of the keep. Sounds of pursuit drove him like a fox through the forest, darting to elude the dogs. He lost track of the turns he took before he came to another door, another stair, this one leading up in a spiral. Hemmed in on each side, he climbed the treads as fast as he could before bursting out through the door at the top. Frigid winter wind blasted his face but did nothing to cool the heat inside him. He staggered out into the open air beneath a star-strewn sky. His flight had taken him up one of the two castle towers built out over the lake.

And there was no way down save the way he'd come.

"Haunts damn!" he hissed. His tongue burned with each word spoken. He rushed to the crenellations and leaned out, gazing down to the lake far below, its depths gleaming bright with a film of ice. The heat inside him rose faster now, like a volcano, and he knew he had mere moments before the eruption and ultimate destruction.

"Venator du Balafre!"

He turned. Evanderians poured out through the door

onto the tower platform. Three of them already, and more coming behind. He knew their faces. They were his comrades, his brothers and sisters of the Order. He'd trained with du Ferro as a boy, had studied poisons under di Ranille's guidance one spring.

In mere moments, he would die. And in the blast that must come, he could take all of them out with him. Maybe give Ayleth a fighting chance.

He looked into du Ferro's eyes.

The decision lay before him. A single moment poised on the brink of eternity. Was he the heretic, the witch? Would he slay his companions even as they sought to slay him? Would this be his last act in this world before his soul flew free?

Du Ferro raised his scorpiona. He took aim.

And Terryn threw himself over the edge of the crenellation. He heard the snap of the scorpiona firing and felt the prick of a dart in his upper arm just as he soared out into the empty air.

CHAPTER 27

AYLETH STOOD AGAINST THE WALL, ARMS CROSSED and head bent, watching Hollis, who crouched over the still body of Crisentha di Bathia. Her former mistress pressed her forehead to the witch's, holding that broad face between her hands. Penetrating her mind was no easy feat even for a venatrix as experienced as Hollis. The Crimson Devils used mental wards to protect against invasion, and the paralysis poison would make her mind murky.

But Hollis was no novice. Her Apparition shade flared bright inside her, so brilliant that Ayleth could almost see many ghostly wings stretching out from the center of Hollis's soul.

If they were lucky—if the Goddess was still on their side despite everything—Hollis would be able to pull plans from the Crystalwitch's head, to discover what the Crimson Devils intended to do now that they had recovered their queen.

Though Ayleth wasn't in any doubt. They must go in search of the *eitr* crown.

She shuddered. Why, when Hollis mentioned that strange treasure from ages past, had it seemed to strike such a familiar chord in her soul? A chord that quivered with sound that was almost a name. Her lips unconsciously tried to form a word, a strange word that wasn't part of any language she knew: "*Oromor.*"

Why did she know that name? And from where did this vision in her head manifest, hazy and warped like a nightmare . . . a vision of a woman wearing a band of some dark metal, and a voice deeper than nightfall growling in her mind.

At last . . .

"Ayleth."

Ayleth jolted out of her thoughts and looked down at her mistress. Hollis sat up, pulling her hands back from the witch's head as though it burned her palms. She breathed hard through clenched teeth and flicked a glance Ayleth's way. "That's it," she panted. "That's all we need. Please . . . kill her."

Immediately Ayleth knelt beside her mistress and plucked the Gentle Death from among her poisons. It was her last one, but she didn't hesitate. She pricked the dart into the Crystalwitch's neck and watched as the conjoined souls, witch and shade, rose up from the body as it died.

The Haunts yawned to claim its dues.

Ayleth and Hollis both ducked their heads away from the gaping maw of that other world. Ayleth's hand twitched on reflex for her pipes, but Hollis reached out and stilled her hand. This was a witch's soul, bound for a witch's eternal torment.

A dart of guilt passed through Ayleth's soul as she gazed at those two entwined spirits, dragged writhing to that loathsome gate and the crushing chaos beyond. Crisentha was a murderer, a horror, who had slaughtered countless innocent souls. Ayleth thought of the dead men and women she'd seen in the front hall. She thought of all the bodies the Crystalwitch had desecrated over the years, all the souls she had devastated, all the ruin she had left in her wake. This was a strangely quiet end for a monster like her.

But, Ayleth wondered . . . would her own soul follow a similar path one day? Or would someone do her the kindness of burning her alive?

Crossing her arms, she forced these thoughts back and turned her attention to Hollis. Her former mistress was still breathing hard, one hand pressed to her chest. Her shade spirit shimmered with dangerously potent ascendancy, but Hollis did not fight it back. Not yet anyway.

"What did you find?" Ayleth demanded.

Hollis looked up, wincing, her eyes mere slits in her pale face. "They are heading for Dulimurian. They intend to take the Queen's Highway through the Witchwood. They don't have anchors enough for the Phantomwitch to carry them all the way. We might . . ." Her voice broke off for a moment, and she drew a steadying breath. "We might still catch them."

Though the words were spoken with hope, Ayleth felt nothing but horror. The idea of reentering the Witch-wood was almost more than she could bear. And hunting through its depths, trying to catch the most feared and deadly witch of Perrinion's history? She wasn't prepared. She wasn't strong enough. She wasn't . . .

In Ayleth's mind, Laranta moved, her unsuppressed power brimming with eagerness. *Mistress,* she growled. *Mistress, we hunt. We hunt! We hunt!*

A short, sharp, terrible grin flashed across Ayleth's face. Suddenly, she knew exactly what her future held. She didn't need prophecies; she didn't need dreams. She didn't need blood-curses or spells. She was a hunter raised by wolves, and she knew her purpose in this life.

Only now, at long last, she had prey worth pursuing.

"Don't worry," she said. She raised her scorpiona arm and pulled the triggering mechanism into gear. "Dread Odile will never touch her crown."

Hollis nodded, a look of grim hope on her face. She rose, swaying slightly on her feet, but her breathing had eased somewhat. "We must report to the king at once," she said. "There's not a moment to lose."

"What will we do with her?" Ayleth asked, indicating Crisentha's remains.

"Leave it for now," Hollis replied. "She'll do no more harm in this world."

With those words, Hollis made for the undercroft stairs leading up to the door, leaning heavily against the wall as she began to climb. Her invasion of the witch's mind had sapped her strength, and Ayleth knew she even now battled to keep her shade at bay. She would be wise to pause and use the Vocos to suppress the spirit inside her. But she would have need of her powers soon.

Ayleth followed several steps behind her mistress and was still only halfway up the stair when Hollis opened the door. Immediately, Laranta growled in her mind. *Danger, Mistress.*

Ayleth paused, her eyes widening. "*What danger, Laranta*—" she began.

Hollis uttered a short, sharp cry.

Ayleth looked up and saw her mistress silhouetted in the doorway. A fletched dart quivered from her throat.

Hollis whirled around to Ayleth. "Get back!" she cried. Her hands grabbed at the door, trying to close it again, trying to barricade them inside. Before she could pull the door shut, a hand appeared, grabbed hold of her, and yanked her out of Ayleth's sight.

"Hollis!" Ayleth lunged up the steps, propelled by Laranta's strength. She gained the door but was only just quick enough to lurch back before a scattershot of curse-bolts. Black Anathema icicles as long as her arm crashed into the floor and the doorway, breaking through wood and stone alike. They jutted from every surface, barring her exit.

With a roar, Ayleth threw herself at the bolts. As she grabbed and broke them one after another, crushing them in her hands with Feral power, they shattered and dissipated in discordant magic. She pushed through into the passage beyond, braced for another assault.

And stopped abruptly, her hands clenched in fists. Her throat seemed to close up, stopping her breath.

Hollis stood before her. Or rather, she did not stand but hung limp, paralyzed in the grasps of two red-hooded Evanderians. Fendrel stood behind her, bleeding from multiple wounds and surrounded by an aura of ascendant Anathema magic.

He held a black-fletched dart to Hollis's throat, a hair's breadth from her skin.

Laranta snarled savagely and lurched in Ayleth's head, taking her a full step forward. "One step more and she dies!" Fendrel cried. Ayleth wrenched control back from her shade and stopped short. Every muscle in her body jumped with the need for action, and her fingers curled like claws ready to rip and tear.

"I can kill you in a second," she said, looking him in the eyes. "You can't stop me. These tame dogs of yours can't stop me."

The Red Hoods holding her mistress trembled. They saw how far ascendant her shade was. They knew they were no match for her speed or her violence. But they didn't back down.

A grin spread across Fendrel's face but did not reach his eyes. "Can you reach me before I kill her?" he asked.

She couldn't. She was fast. But not that fast.

"Why should I care what you do with her?" Ayleth retorted through her teeth. "She lied to me. She manipulated my head. She killed my family. She is nothing to me."

His grin grew, flashing savage teeth. "Then kill me, girl," he said. His hand never wavered. The Gentle Death poised, ready to strike. One fractional shift of his hand, and Hollis was done for.

Kill, kill! Laranta urged. *He is our enemy! We must kill!*

Every instinct, natural and unnatural, called for her to take action. Now!

And yet . . .

She would never forgive Hollis. Not as long as she lived.

With a vicious curse, Ayleth went down on her knees and held up both hands. "*Down, Laranta,*" she said.

But Mistress—

"*I said DOWN.*"

Her wolf shade snarled, threw back her head, and pawed at the edges of her mind. She was ascendant. Ayleth had no means to control her, to force her to obey. But Laranta backed down, retreating inside until she crouched small. All the ascendant shade power flowed out of Ayleth's limbs.

Fendrel watched. Shadow sight gleamed in his eyes, and he knew exactly what took place within her soul. But he didn't step back from Hollis, didn't remove the dart from its position at her throat.

"All right, girl," he said, "here's how this is going to work. I need you. Perrinion needs you. We need the weapon Hollis has made of you to undo this disaster you have created."

"*I* created?" Ayleth bit out the words, spittle forming on her lips. "You festering bastard, I'll—"

"You'll kill her yet." Fendrel raised his eyebrows and shifted his stance. The black fletching on the dart quivered slightly.

It was agony to swallow back her words. Ayleth clenched her fists, driving her nails into the skin of her palms.

Fendrel's eyes flashed with shadow-light again as he made certain Laranta remained suppressed. Satisfied, he continued. "First, I need to know what information you got from the Crystalwitch."

"That is information for the king."

"And I am the king's Black Hood. You will deliver

what you know, and I shall inform His Majesty."

Somehow, she couldn't believe this was Gerard's will. But Gerard wasn't here. And he couldn't control his uncle anyway. No one could.

"The Crimson Devils plan to take the Queen's Highway through the Witchwood. Their goal is Dulimurian and . . . and the crown."

Fendrel nodded slowly. All color drained from his skin until the shade-blighted blood splattered across his face stood out black and harsh. "Good," he said. "And the Phantomwitch?"

"She doesn't have anchors enough to carry them. They will have to journey on foot. Unless they steal horses, but horses won't get them far through the Witchwood."

"This is true." Fendrel exhaled long and low. Then he whispered, "So there's still a chance." His eyes flashed again, more brilliant than ever, almost exultant. "She's trained you well. I know Hollis. I know how she works, how she thinks. She may have been wrong to let you live, but now that the damage is done, you will serve to correct her error. We can fix this. We can save Perrinion." He lifted his head and called to someone in the passage behind her, "Now. Bring them."

Ayleth didn't look around, didn't shift her gaze from Fendrel's face. Not until another Red Hood appeared in front of her, carrying something heavy in his hands. The stink of iron filled her nostrils. She looked. Her eyes widened.

"No!" she gasped and started to lurch up from her knees. Laranta, sensing her distress, began to swell with power in her soul.

"Stay, girl!" Fendrel snarled. "You'll kill her yet!"

Her heart careening wildly against her breastbone, Ayleth looked up into the Venator Dominus's eyes. She looked at Hollis, so helpless, almost lifeless.

"Submit," Fendrel said. "I don't plan to kill you. You know I can't. We need you now—we need the blood in your veins, or we're all dead. So you're safe for the time being. But we must be safe from you as well."

The Red Hood in front of her moved in again. "Your hands," he said.

He held up the iron mitts. An Evanderian instrument of torture, they were ball-shaped gloves that encompassed hands and snapped around wrists. The iron in such close proximity to her bare skin would cause discomfort and nausea. Far worse, if she uncurled her fists, if she moved her fingers the wrong way even slightly, internal spikes would jab into her skin. Not as deep as the iron spike she'd used on herself a few days ago, but dozens of them at once would riddle her body and soul with iron poison.

Laranta would be trapped, driven by pain too deep down to offer any help. Ayleth herself would be as weak and useless as a kitten.

She stared down at that Evanderian instrument of torture. She still had a choice. She could fight. She could resist. She could let Hollis die, and tear into her enemies, using Laranta's power to rip them to pieces.

Instead, she raised her fists. And the Red Hood snapped the iron mitts into place.

A wave of nausea rolled over her. Though she curled her fists tight, the spikes drove into her skin, and pain flooded through her body as poison flooded her mind. She sank to her knees, and darkness closed in. She tried to keep herself upright, but fell to her side, jarring her hands even more. Perhaps she fainted. But all too soon the darkness passed, returning her to a world of pain. Her awareness clarified, and she moaned, wishing she could return to oblivion.

But then she heard a voice she recognized.

"Where is he, Fendrel? Where is Terryn? What have you done with him?"

Ayleth forced her eyes open a crack. She found she was no longer in the passage by the undercroft. She lay on the floor of the great hall, surrounded by Red Hoods.

"Terryn du Balafre has forsaken his vows." That voice was unmistakably Fendrel's. Ayleth's lip curled, and she turned her head toward the sound. She saw Gerard standing at the base of the stairs, facing his uncle. He wore riding garments, and a sheathed sword hung at his side. His face was wild, terrifying.

"What are you saying?" he demanded, taking an aggressive step toward his uncle, who towered over him, his face shrouded by his black hood. "Where is Terryn? Where is he?" With every word, his voice grew more frantic. Ayleth had never heard him sound like this.

Fendrel reached out a hand and gripped Gerard's shoulder, holding him fast. "Terryn is dead," he said.

The world seemed to break, to shatter into a million

shards of glinting glass before Ayleth's vision. She saw Gerard crumple and sag to the floor; she saw Red Hoods swoop in on either side of him, catching hold of his arms. Somewhere in the distance, she heard Fendrel's voice again, saying, "Bar the king in his rooms. He is not coming on this hunt."

But none of that mattered. Pain rolled over Ayleth's mind once more, drowning her in its unrelenting sea of darkness.

EPILOGUE

THE NIGHT WAS STILL. A WINTRY STILLNESS WITH neither birdsong nor insect hum to break the frozen atmosphere. Even the stream had ceased its babble, its waters edged with a delicate lacing of ice. Not a breath of wind stirred the brittle grass or moved in the branches of the tall, naked oak.

Beneath the oak an old woman sat. She was so motionless, a passerby might think she had been turned to stone. She crouched among the roots of the spreading tree, her shoulders hunched, her hands cupped before her face. For the most part, her gaze fixed upon what lay in her palms, but now and then her eyes would flick upward, her lashes fluttering to break the frost trying to fuse them shut, and look down to where the stream flowed into the Holy Lake. There, only a mile away at most, the tall towers of Dunloch Castle rose to the starry sky.

If one listened closely, one could just hear the old woman's soft panting breaths.

Suddenly, the stillness broke. The old woman, startled out of her immobility, uttered a cry and sat up straight, her hands flying apart as though burned. A stone flew through the air and rolled down to the stream bank. A flare shot out from its center—a flare, not of light, but of darkness so deep, it burned the eyes.

The world tore open. For an instant, the stillness of the winter night filled with a chorus of unearthly screams. The old woman scrambled to her feet and threw herself behind the thick oak trunk. Grasping the bark with white-knuckled fingers, she watched that place where the air ripped and reality rippled. Her eyes glimmered with shadow-light.

Something stumbled through the chaos. For an instant, it looked like nothing more than a shadowy vagueness. The next instant, it coalesced into the form of a young woman—a lady of grace and noble bearing whose golden hair hung loose and ragged around her bare shoulders, and whose gown fluttered in tatters about her legs. She leaped through the opening between worlds and fell on her knees in the tall brown grass, pulling two men after her. She almost lost her hold on them, for the realm she'd just stepped through fought to keep them, to devour them. With a gut-wrenching cry, she hauled them through, one after the other.

The first man was tall and dark-eyed, his shoulders broad but his frame emaciated, as though its once-impressive strength had been sucked away. The second man was even less to look at, a narrow, wretched creature with a sad gray beard made up of ugly fungus-like growths rather than hair.

The young woman recovered first from passing between worlds. She tossed her golden hair and looked back over her shoulder, not at either man, but at the fourth figure they carried between them. A little skeletal thing, more dead than alive, its flesh stripped from the bones, the skin burned and blackened.

The two men staggered and sank to the ground, dropping their burden as they fell. The poor creature collapsed in the tall grass, arms outstretched, head bent at a strange angle, and did not move.

The young woman looked around at the cold, winter-bound landscape, her eyes flashing with shadow-light. She spied the old crone pressed against the tree trunk and raised a hand in greeting.

The shivering woman peeled herself away from the oak and took a step toward them, stooping to pick up the anchor stone on her way. "Did you find her, Inren?" she called out, her voice thin and sharp with hope. "Did you find the queen?"

Without answering, Inren turned instead to the men, who were still bent over on their hands and knees, shaking with dread. She couldn't very well blame them. A flight through the hellish Haunts was no easy matter even for her, and she was used to it. Her comrades had made the journey with her only a few times before, and each time they had emerged quivering like jellies in a bowl.

"Gillotin. Zarc. Get up," she snarled. "We have a long journey before us yet."

The bearded Zarc cast her a withering glare but otherwise didn't move. Dark-eyed Gillotin, however, pulled himself together. He reached for the broken thing lying beside him in the dirt, catching one skinny arm and pulling it carefully to him, like a gentle mother trying to rouse a sleeping infant.

The thing moaned. The sound sent shivers shooting down Inren's spine. But the old woman gasped and clasped her hands together. She went down on her knees, then on her face, prostrating herself before the corpse-like being.

"My goddess! My goddess!" she cried, tears choking her voice.

At the sound of that voice, the broken, burned thing stirred. Its head lolled on its weakened neck. A pair of blazing yellowed eyes peered out from among strands of black hair and fixed on the old woman. "Zilla," she croaked. "Zilla, my dear—"

Her voice broke off in a fit of coughing so violent, her brittle body appeared ready to break into a thousand

SYLVIA MERCEDES

pieces. But Inren saw a hundred thousand spell threads woven together, holding all those mortal pieces in place, refusing to let the body die and the spirit free.

Inren compressed her lips into a tight line. This wasn't what she'd hoped for when she set out to reclaim her goddess. In her mind, in her memory, Odile was glorious, beautiful, powerful, unstoppable. This thing, this broken thing . . . it wasn't Odile. It couldn't be.

A creature so wrecked, so frail, could never wear the *eitr* crown and survive.

"Get up, Zilla," she growled, kicking her sister witch in the haunch. "We don't have time for this. Where's my anchor?"

"Here." The old woman sat upright, holding out her fisted hand, and dropped the gleaming stone into Inren's outstretched palm. A hundred strands of tentacle-like threads reached out from its center, all plunging into Inren's soul. She had formed the threads herself, carefully calling each one to life, carefully fastening each bond. When activated, those spells were powerful enough to draw her back into this world from the Haunts, allowing her to travel in and out of this reality in the blink of an eye.

But an activated anchor would also leave a distinct trail of magic. A trail even the most inexperienced of shade hunters might follow.

Inren grimaced. It took hours, sometimes days, to create a strong anchor stone. Her supply was low, and she would not have time to make more in the hours to come. But she knew enemies would be upon them soon. Evanderians might even now pour through the gates of Dunloch, riding hard through·the night.

So she caught hold of all those spell threads and wound them tightly around her fingers. When she had them all firmly in her grasp, she gave a sudden wrench. The threads broke—the spell shattered. The anchor lost its luster and became nothing more than dead lump of oblidite in her palm. The broken ends of spells wafted from its center, swiftly rotting.

Inren tossed it over her shoulder and turned to her companions. "We have to get moving," she said.

"What's the hurry?" Zarc demanded. His pale face had regained some of its color, and he got to his feet. "The king is dead."

"Fendrel du Glaive is still alive," Inren snapped. The others cringed at that name. They all knew who their true enemy was. Not the king. Never the king. "He will rally his hunters and be on our trail by dawn. We must get our queen to her crown."

"We are more than a match for a handful of Evanderians," Zilla said, setting her jaw. "We may not be as powerful as we once were, but we are not weak." She looked around then, blinking with sudden realization. "Where is Ylaire? Where are Scias and Crisentha?"

"They are gone," Gillotin answered. He stood up, adjusting his careful grip on the queen, handling her as he might handle fractured glass. "Ylaire is dead. The others . . . I don't know."

A spasm of pain shot through Inren's soul. And with it— Oh! with it came a deadly stirring deep down inside her. That other spirit crouched in the depths of this host body. Fayline, momentarily suppressed but still present in spirit. She would use Inren's emotions against her in a bid to rise to ascendancy.

She had to fight. She must stay focused.

"If Scias and Crisentha live, they may slow our

enemies," she said. "But we can count on nothing more. We must move. Zarc, take our queen. Zilla, help him."

The two witches jumped to obey, easing the frail creature from Gillotin's arms. Though neither the Windwitch nor the Stormwitch was strong, twenty years of death had left Odile's body wasted to a shadow. Between them they carried her without difficulty.

"There are horses in the next town," Zilla said. "We can take them easily enough."

"Good." Inren turned to the Corpsewitch. "Gillotin, I want you to stay behind. They will certainly send out scouts and find my broken anchor. Wait until Fendrel arrives and do whatever you can to harry him and his followers. Kill them if you can."

The Corpsewitch answered with a smile, drawing a knife and sliding the blade across his scarred palm. Fresh blood flowed along its edge, and the red glare of Anathema magic flared in the darkness. "I'll kill du Glaive," he said. "And the granddaughter. She'll not live to see another sunset."

"No."

Inren's heart stopped. She felt a jolt of surprise pass

through her comrades like lightning jumping from one soul to the next. Every pair of eyes swiveled to Odile.

Their queen, their goddess, lifted her burned, hideous head. White-ringed eyes glittered as she fixed her gaze on Gillotin. "Do not kill my granddaughter." Her severed vocal cords, only recently re-knit, throbbed and shuddered, producing a rasping, awful sound. "I charge you by all the loyalty you once bore me: Bring the girl to me. Alive."

Gillotin opened his mouth. Inren felt all the protests he wanted to speak, for they were the same as those clamoring in her own head, desperate to be spoken aloud. Odile held his gaze. Her neck trembled with the strength required just to keep her head upright. At last, Gillotin bowed and placed both hands over his heart in a gesture of absolute servitude.

"Your wish is my command, Adored One."

ABOUT THE AUTHOR

Sylvia Mercedes makes her home in the idyllic North Carolina countryside with her handsome husband, sweet baby-lady, and Gummy Bear, the Toothless Wonder Cat. When she's not writing she's . . . okay, let's be honest. When she's not writing, she's running around after her little girl, cleaning up glitter, trying to plan healthy-ish meals, and wondering where she left her phone. In between, she reads a steady diet of fantasy novels. But mostly she's writing.

After a short career in Traditional Publishing (under a different name), Sylvia decided to take the plunge into the Indie Publishing World and is enjoying every minute of it. The Venatrix Chronicles is her first series as an independent author, but she's got many more planned!

Don't miss the continuation of Ayleth's adventures in
Book 6 of The Venatrix Chronicles!

Captured by those who should be her friends,
Hunted by those who claim to be her family,
Ayleth must decide once and for all where her true loyalties lie.

QUEEN OF POISON

Meanwhile be sure to read Song of Shadows:

Visit www.SylviaMercedesBooks.com
to get your free copy.

Made in the USA
Monee, IL
01 April 2021